PRAISE FOR THE HILLS KIDS

"The Hills Kids is such a hilarious and exciting extravaganza. I couldn't take my eyes off it until the very last page!"

LEIA, 11

"The book inspires me to go on adventures and it turns on the creative part of my brain. I also find that I love drawing the things that happen."

MIA, 11

"It was the most amazing book I've ever read. I loved how funny Ollie was and I loved Broos's accent. When is the next book coming out?"

LEVI, 8

"The Hills Kids in three words: funny, funny and hilarious. I really loved this book because of the great characters and because it's set before most technology was developed and is very different to my every day life."

MILA, 10

"We loved reading The Hills Kids as a family and looked forward to reading it each night. We fell in love with the characters and their adventures."

ELIE, MUM

"The Hills Kids was a really funny story with great illustrations. When I started reading it, I couldn't put it down until I reached the end."

DJANGO, 12

"It's a great book. I love it! It's got lots of action, which I really like."

ARI, 11

"I loved this book. I found myself transported back to my youth and a time where every day revealed a new adventure. The loveable gang have a bond that only true friends can share. It's a winner!"

MARK, BRUNSWICK HEADS LIBRARY MANAGER

"The Hills Kids is a joyful, uplifting, evocative book set in the days before computers and tablets and other devices. The kids spend their days getting up to mischief outdoors, creating and exploring with a sense of wonder. It's an absolute pleasure to read this book to my 10 year old daughter every night as we giggle at the group's antics."

AMANDA, MUM & BOOKSTAGRAMMER
@LITTLEBIGSTORYREVIEW

THE HILLS KIDS

BOOK ONE

GARETH VANDERHOPE

Cover and internal illustrations by Gareth Vanderhope.

ISBN 978-0-6485949-0-1 (paperback); ISBN 978-0-6485949-1-8 (hardback)

A catalogue record for this work is available from the National Library of Australia

For children aged 8 to 12
Juvenile fiction/Middle-grade fiction
Adventure fiction/Humorous fiction
This book uses Australian/UK spelling

Published by Swooping Books, NSW, Australia
www.garethvanderhope.com/swooping-books

Swooping Books acknowledges the Traditional Custodians of Country throughout Australia and recognises their continuing connection to land, waters and culture. We pay our respects to their Elders past, present and emerging.

For Lily and Mia and all kids who love adventures . . .

CONTENTS

Author Note

The characters in this book pull off some crazy stunts and get up to all sorts of mischief. Before embarking on your adventures or picking produce, ask permission from a parent, guardian or responsible adult. Please don't attempt the stunts, as injury may result.

By the way, this book uses Australian terms and spelling. Some dialogue uses modified grammar and spelling to reflect character accents and natural language style. The accents depicted are specific to the characters and cannot be generalised to all people within those cultures.

PART ONE

ONE

THE BILLYCART BLOWOUT

On a misty winter's morning in the Dandenong Ranges, a place also known as the hills, a bunch of kids scream in the distance, and a weird whirring noise grows louder by the second.

Then all at once, a black piglet squeals past—*Wheeeeeeee!*—followed by Russell, a lanky teenager, rolling down the steep mountain road in his hotted-up homemade billycart.

Perched on an open wooden trailer attached to the billycart is Archie, a spiky-haired younger boy, laughing and screaming as they whoosh past lush ferns and ginormous eucalyptus trees. "Watch out for the pothole!" he yells, pointing ahead.

"Hold on tight, Archie. It's gonna be a bumpy ride," shouts Russell.

The front wheels thump into the pothole, and the trailer flings up with a *Katwang-WHOOP*.

"Whoooaaaaa," screams Archie, catapulting into the air. "Whoopee," he cheers, landing back with a *DONK*. "This is the best billycart in the world!"

Indeed, an extraordinary billycart it is. Custom-built by Russell over several months, the marvellous machine includes an impressive list of features: Speedy rubber tyres, fat at the back and skinny at the front. Spoked wheels, lubricated by slippery hair grease. A racy steering wheel cover made from his dad's leather tie. Lever-operated brakes, ingeniously crafted using flip-flop thongs for brake pads. And a deluxe wooden trailer specially designed for his little mate Archie to ride on down the treacherous road.

"Faster, Russell, faster!" shouts Archie as they flash past a hand-painted sign nailed to a power pole that says:

CHILDREN! DRIVE SLOWLY!

Russell swivels around and waves in a downward motion. "Get down low if ya wanna go faster!"

The boys lean forward, allowing the wind to rush over their heads. Immediately, with improved aerodynamics, the billycart speeds up, and the whirring tyres morph into a feverish hum.

Two other kids fly past the sign.

Pippa, Archie's best friend and fellow adventurer number one, whizzes down the hill on a cruiser skateboard, her long plaits flailing about as she zigzags along. "Wait for me!" she calls, skidding one foot on the ground to control her speed.

Ollie, Archie's other best friend and fellow adventurer number two, is squashed inside an antique metal buggy, his round glasses all frosted up from the chilly air and his boofy red parka inflated by the wind thrust. "Yeeeeeeeee," he squeals, rolling down the road like a maniac.

Kimba, Archie's mischievous scruffy black dog and fellow adventurer number three, scampers behind the rolling rabble, barking madly, *ruff ruff ruff ruff!*

Meanwhile at the bottom of the hill, Fergus, a kooky artist, inventor and family friend of the kids, crunches through the gears of his ex-army jeep while driving up the road in search of his lost piglet.

Wheeeeeeeee! The piglet streaks in front of the billycart.

In an emergency manoeuvre, Russell yanks the brake lever. The flip-flop thong clamps against the wheel, which screeches and smokes as the billycart swerves around the scared piglet. "Yeeeee-haaaa. Whaddaya think of that move? Steers like a dream, eh? Woohoo!"

Archie shows his approval with two thumbs-up.

Unaware of the approaching billycart, Fergus turns up the classical music blaring from his radio and accelerates towards a hairpin bend, singing passionately, "Bom boppa bomm bomm, bom boppa bomm bomm, bom boppa bomm bomm, bom boppa bommm."

Travelling at a rubber-burning, heart-thumping pace, Archie and Russell approach the same bend.

"Car! Car! scream Pippa and Ollie, whose higher position on the road gives them a clear view of the oncoming vehicle.

Russell gazes up, eyes bulging. "Whooaaaa!" He steers hard left to avoid a deadly collision with the jeep. But the trailer jack-knifes violently and rips apart from the billycart.

Russell and the billycart fly down the sheer embankment, leaving Archie stranded in the trailer, mouth wide open, sliding along the wet bitumen, unable to steer or brake, heading straight for Fergus's jeep!

"Jump, Archie, JUMP!" shriek Pippa and Ollie.

The army-green beast roars around the blind bend.

Faced with certain death, superpower energy shoots into Archie's legs, and he leaps for his life, sailing over billowing ferns and between two trees.

CRACK-k-k-k. The trailer smashes into the jeep's bullbar, splintering into a zillion pieces.

As Archie tumbles down the bank, Fergus hits the brakes, fishtails across the road and slams into a boggy ditch.

Pippa and Ollie jump off their contraptions and peer down the slope, fearing the worst.

"Oh no," gasps Pippa.

"What a catastrophe," exclaims Ollie.

At the bottom of the gully, surrounded by tree ferns and mist, rests the battered billycart, squished nose-deep in mud, the back wheels spinning wonkily in the air.

Nearby, Archie and Russell are slumped on the ground, covered in grazes, dirt and spiky burrs. After a moment of stillness, they stir, sit up, brush themselves off and gawk at one another like stunned groper fish. Then, as if hearing a funny joke, Russell grins at Archie, Archie grins at Russell, and they explode into raucous laughter.

Not only are the boys happy for surviving the dangerous stunt, but they're also thrilled to have another legendary tale to tell.

Ruff, ruff, rooowww, barks Kimba, leaping onto Archie's lap in a licking frenzy.

"Oi! Stop it, you lick monster. Eeew, yuk, no! STOP!"

Fergus calls down from the road, "Glad to see you're in one piece, fellas. Hey, has anyone seen my piglet?"

TWO

THE PONGO-BONGO BIKE

"Oh my gosh, are you guys okay?" calls Pippa, sliding down the bank on her bottom.

Russell cracks a toothy smile and nudges Archie in the ribs. "Not a scratch. Right, buddy?"

"Yep, not a single scratch," replies Archie, raising a grazed elbow poking through his ripped knitted jumper. "We were lucky all right."

"That wasn't lucky, that was insane," babbles Ollie. "You were sliding along the road like a sheep without an udder."

Pippa lifts an eyebrow. "Errr, I think you mean he was sliding along like a ship without a rudder."

"No, I mean like a shaved sheep down a shearing chute. *Hee-hee!* Then you flew down the bank like a superhero frog. It was zangdogobulous!"

Russell wanders off to inspect the mangled billycart. He pauses midway, eyes agog in fake surprise. "Is it a bird? Is it a plane? No, it's Archie, the wonder frog."

Archie giggles, enjoying the moment of froggy fame. High above, a mountain ash tree sways in the wind, the leaves roaring like distant waves at a beach. As Archie rests back on a patch of buttercups, a long ribbon of bark flaps against the smooth cream trunk. The hypnotic tap, tap, tapping makes his eyelids grow heavy, and he drifts into a daydream.

"I've got to admit, you did look like a leaping frog," says Pippa with a giggle.

Archie's eyelids flicker.

"Are you asleep?" she asks.

"Mongoose . . ." he murmurs in a drowsy voice.

Ollie peers over his glasses. "Did you say pongoose?"

After a moment of deathly silence, a drop of bright red blood trickles down Archie's forehead.

Concerned his friend has passed out from a bump on the head, Ollie bites his nails and bumbles around in a panic. "Pongoose? Wongoose? What are you talking about? Knock-knock, is anyone home?"

Archie doesn't respond, because deep within his mind, he's peddling down a forest track on a gleaming silver BMX bike. Trees, bushes and leaves whizz by in a blur. He ducks under a wonga vine, bunny hops over a fallen branch, powers through a cool fern gully and sloshes across a shallow stream . . .

"Help! Help! Somebody call an ambulance!" shouts Ollie, glancing around. "Where's that crazy man Fergus gone? He'll have a phone."

In the hope that flower power may help, Pippa sprinkles buttercup petals over Archie's face. "Wake up, buttercup. Wake up, buttercup! It's working. Something's happening! Can you hear me? Wake up, wake up!"

A pollen cloud wafts up Archie's nose, which twitches a few times. Then he bursts into an almighty sneeze, "Ah, ahhh-choooooooo!" Green snot erupts from his nostrils in two long wobbly strands. "Errr, has anyone got a tissue?"

Russell chuckles in the background while attempting to straighten the billycart axle.

Disturbed by the pendulous snot display, Ollie reaches inside his parka and passes Archie a clean hanky. "I thought we'd lost you, booger."

"Settle down, Ollie. I was only daydreaming."

"What about the blood on your head? Are you sure you're okay?" says Pippa.

"Oh, that's nothing." Archie casually blows his nose. "It must've come from the cut on my arm." He wipes the blood off his forehead. "See. I'm as good as gold."

Satisfied her friend is okay, Pippa launches into a handstand. "Hey, what were you saying about a mongoose? I've heard if you see one, it brings good luck. Did you daydream about a mongoose?"

Archie contorts his face into a googly-eyed monster and says in a gruff voice, "Yes. A big hairy mongoose."

Ollie's eyes dart around nervously. "I thought they were little and cute."

"No, I mean a Mongoose bike. It's a BMX."

"Hey, that reminds me," says Russell with a larrikin glint in his eye. "Are you still getting around on that fancy *Pongo-Bongo* bike?"

Archie peers to the ground. "Oh, please don't mention that bike, Russ."

Pippa flips up out of a bridge pose. "What bike? You didn't tell me you had a bike."

"Yes, do tell us about this Pongo-Bongo bike of yours," says Ollie, surprised he knows nothing of Archie's secret.

"Come on, tell them the story. It's a classic," encourages Russell.

"All right, I'll tell you the story. But nobody laugh, okay?"

The friends shake their heads, lips squeezed tight, smiling like innocent angels.

"So, it's Christmas morning," begins Archie. "I wake up real early and creep into the lounge room, hoping to find a brand-new BMX waiting for me, just like I'd asked for. But instead, I find a little kids' bike with a rainbow Pongo-Bongo sticker on the frame, hard plastic tyres, a glossy yellow seat, training wheels, a white basket on the front and glittery purple streamers spewing out the handlebars. It's parked right there next to the fireplace, wrapped in gold tinsel with a card that says, 'Merry Christmas, Archie. Love, Mum.' I couldn't believe it. What on earth was she thinking!"

Russell and Ollie remain tight-lipped, their cheeks puffed out like bullfrogs, until the pressure is so great they explode into spit-riddled laughter.

Although Archie can see the funny side of the story, he feels embarrassed, angry, and tormented all at once. Embarrassed for owning a bike way too young for his age. Tormented for missing out on a BMX for Christmas. And angry for being laughed at by his friends. Unable to find an antidote to his emotions, his face glows red, and he lashes out, "Stop it, you guys. You said you wouldn't laugh. It's not funny!"

"You're right. It's not funny—it's hilarious!" adds Russell, cracking himself up.

Pippa stares hard at Russell. "You should be ashamed of yourself, teasing Archie. There's nothing wrong with handlebar streamers."

With eyebrows raised and a goofy smile, Ollie nods in agreement.

"And he can always take off the training wheels," continues Pippa. "Besides, I've seen you doing your paper round on a bike like that, Russ."

Keen for a good debate, Russell puffs out his chest and responds, "Yeah, one time I had a puncture on my racer, so I borrowed me little sister's bike. It's got a comfy banana seat, swanky cherry-pink streamers, a handy basket on the front—perfect for paper deliveries. Not something I'd want for Christmas though." His eyes go all dreamy. "A Kawasaki Ninja 900 sports bike, now that's another story."

"It's okay, Pippa. I get what Russ is saying. The Pongo-Bongo is nothing like my dream bike. I wanted a BMX for Christmas—*a Supergoose Mark 2*. I've been reading all about them in a BMX magazine at the library. They're brilliant for doing cool tricks and riding down forest tracks. I've started saving so I can buy one myself."

Russell slaps Archie on the shoulder. "Dream on, Archie-boy. The Supergoose 2 is a sweet ride for sure, but they cost an arm and a leg. How ya gonna find the cash for one of those?"

"Well, I'll earn pocket money selling chicken eggs and doing odd jobs. I'm gonna sell chestnuts on the side of the road too."

"Yeah, been there, done that," says Russell cynically. "I used to sell chestnuts when I was a little tacker like you. I'd say I made about thirty bucks on a good year. Not enough for a new bike though, matey."

"But, Russ, things have changed. It's big business selling chestnuts now. I could've made a fortune last year. But I was visiting my dad down the coast for the Easter holidays, so I missed out. I made heaps the year before. I still have twenty-five dollars stashed in my money box. And I know where to find the best chestnut trees in the whole of the Dandenongs, trees that grow the most humungous shiny brown nuts, like golden nuggets."

Dollar signs swirl in Ollie's wide glassy eyes. "Did you say golden nuggets?"

"More like fools' gold," says Russell, slicking back his jet-black hair with a glob of hair grease from the billycart axle.

Ollie extends his arms forward and chants in a monotone zombie's voice, "Golden nuggets. Golden nuggets. I must have the golden nuggets."

Electrified by thoughts of treasure and wild adventures, Pippa performs a front walkover and leaps to Archie's side. "Hey, can I come chestnutting with you? I'm saving for something special too."

"Sure, you and the zombie can come. But chestnut season isn't until next autumn. That's almost a year away."

Russell wrenches the billycart from the mud. As he plonks it onto firm ground, a spring flies out from under a wheel. *BOING-Twang-g-g-g*. "Looks like the suspension's had it. Better get this wreck back to the workshop." He hoists the billycart over one shoulder. "Good luck chasin' the 'Goose, Archie. Catch ya later, dreamers."

Archie's stomach groans, *grrrrrruuuooorrp*. "I'm starving. Who's hungry?"

THREE

SOUR THINGS ARE ESSENTIAL

Wheeeeeeeeeeee! The piglet bursts from the forest and bolts past the kids, followed by Fergus waving a green fishing net and a floppy bunch of celery. "Come back, piggy, piggy. Oink, oink, oink. I've got a special treat for you!"

Gruff ruff, barks Kimba, busting to join the pig chase.

Archie restrains him by the collar. "No. Bad dog. Leave the piggy alone."

"What's Fergus up to with that piglet anyway?" says Pippa.

"Mum says he's breeding them as models to paint for a big art exhibition," says Archie. "He's calling it *Hogs of the Hills*."

Wheeee! Wheeee! The hysterical piglet gallops up the hill.

"Somebody stop that pig!" yells Fergus, thundering by in his blue gumboots.

The kids leap and lunge for the piglet. It darts through their legs, and they fall over themselves in fits of laughter, slipping and sliding in the mud.

Ollie scrambles to his feet. "You know that's no ordinary piglet. It's a rare heritage hog—*a large black*. It's a signature dish up at the country club. I tasted a sample the other day after golf with my parents. Mmmm, so juicy, so tender."

"Aww, she's so cute. How could you even think of eating her?" says Pippa, giggling as the piglet ducks and weaves around Fergus's swishing net.

Another gurgly sound reverberates from Archie's tummy. "I tell you what, I feel like something tangy."

"Me too," says Pippa. "I'd love to suck on a juicy cumquat. My Oma has a tree in a big pot. It's always covered in fruit when I visit her. They're sooooo sour. Sometimes I even eat them whole, skin and all. And I love squeezing the juice on her poffertjes."

"Poffer-what?" asks Archie.

"Little Dutch pancakes. They're delicious with honey and cumquat juice."

Ollie fake-spits in rapid-fire action. "Forget cumquats. Too many pips. How about green plums? They pack a powerful zing-a-ling. There's enough acid in those babies to power a light globe, maybe even a Smurf village. Mmm, crunchy tangy plums. Me want some now."

"Yeah, plums would be great," says Archie. "But I don't think we'll find any in winter, not even green ones. And I've never seen a cumquat tree around here. I know where to find lemons though. Big juicy ones too."

Pippa's face lights up. "Yes, sour lemons. That'll do the trick. Where's the tree?"

"It's not far from my place, near the top of the hill. But there's a teensy-weensy problem."

"Problem? What problem?" questions Ollie. "I thought your neighbours didn't mind us picking their fruit. Besides, if we don't pick the lemons, those rascal possums will eat them. That'd be a gastronomical tragedy."

"Yeah, why should the possums have all the lemony fun," says Pippa.

"It's not the neighbours who mind us picking the fruit," explains Archie, eyes widening, "it's a vicious dog called Okka that does."

Ollie's cheeks droop in dismay. "Vicious . . . dog? I don't like the sound of that."

"How do you know Okka's so mean?" says Pippa.

"Because he nearly killed me. It happened a few weeks ago when Mum was making gado-gado for dinner. You know, it's basically a plate of veggies with delicious peanut sauce on top. But here's the thing. You've gotta put something sour in the sauce, like lemon juice, or else it tastes like peanut butter sludge from an old gumboot."

Kak-arrkk, gags Ollie, screwing up his face.

"But Mum forgot to buy a lemon," continues Archie. "I wasn't going to eat veggies with gumboot sludge, so I offered to get a lemon from the neighbour's garden. That's when I first met Okka. The mad dog spotted me near the tree and chased me all the way home in the dark, barking and growling. I thought I was a goner."

"Did you get a lemon for the sauce?" asks Ollie, concerned that Archie had to eat gumboot sludge.

"Yeah, I nearly lost a chunk from my leg, but I made it back with a lemon. It was the best peanut sauce I've ever tasted."

Ollie nibbles his thumbnail. "I tell you what, how about we pick wild strawberries down the lane instead? I've never seen vicious dogs there, just delicious strawberries. So juicy, so fruity-fresh. What do you say?"

"Nah. Even if we're lucky enough to find some, they're hardly sour at all," says Archie. "I really want a juicy tangy lemon, straight from the tree."

Pippa eyeballs Ollie. “Come on, you said you wanted green plums. Imagine the zing you’ll get chomping into a lemon. Aren’t your taste buds saying (she leans closer and says in a gruff voice), ‘Give me a lemon. I want a lemon’?”

“Okay, okay, you’re right. I *do* feel like a tanga-langa treat. Something that’ll blast my taste buds to the moon.” A rubbery strand of saliva dribbles down Ollie’s chin. In true goofball style, he slurps it back up. *Shhluuurrop*.

A short while later, as the kids sneak through the long grass below Okka’s house, Kimba spots a white poodle ambling up the road. After greeting her with a polite sniff, they scamper off and disappear under a tangle of wild red roses.

Archie calls in a whisper, “Kimba, come back. Kimba!” But the scruffball has vanished. “Oh well, he’ll come back when he’s ready. He always does.”

A frosty breeze rushes through the grass, numbing Pippa’s ears and nose. She slides on a purple woollen beanie and parts the head-high sedge grass. At the top of a weedy hill stands an impressive lemon tree covered in eye-popping yellow fruit. “Wow, fab lemons. So how can we pick them without Okka attacking us?”

“Our only chance is to sneak up there when he’s asleep or not around. We’ll have to be really quiet when we pick them coz he’s got supersonic hearing.” Archie curls his fingers into pretend binoculars and peers into the distance. Behind the lemon tree, obscured by a holly bush, is a pale blue house with a white veranda. “It’s too far away. I can’t tell if Okka’s there.”

Ollie rummages through an outside parka pocket. “Wait a minute. I’ve got a solution.”

"How many pockets have you got in that super-duper parka of yours?" says Pippa.

"Hmm, let me think . . . Ten inside pockets. Twelve outside pockets, including three on each sleeve. Four secret pockets and"—he opens a gaping hole in the parka's ripped lining—"I call this bad boy *the Abyss*. It comes in handy for those odd-shaped items."

"Like a kitchen sink, I suppose," says Pippa, amused by her friend's pocket obsession.

Unperturbed by the comment, Ollie digs around a left inside pocket. Then he searches in another on the right. "Here we go. This should solve our little problemo." *Swish!* He slides out a kaleidoscope, and without skipping a beat, points it to the sky while twisting the end. "Ooh, pretty patterns . . . Nope, not what I was looking for."

The search continues.

"Ah ha!"

He whips out a metal slinky from one pocket.

A rusty potato peeler from another.

A rainbow pocket umbrella.

And a wooden clothes peg.

"Hang on, getting warmer. This might be it." With the flair of a magician, he pulls out a ballerina doing a pirouette.

Archie scrunches his eyebrows in confusion. "Err, how's that going to help us get the lemons?"

"Sorry, not what I was after. I like to be prepared for every situation. You never know, she might come in handy someday." Ollie slips the figurine into a pocket and plunges his arm elbow-deep into the Abyss. "Voila!" Proud as a pork sausage, he presents an exquisite pair of antique brass binoculars coated in shimmering blue and green mother-of-pearl.

"You're a genius," says Archie.

Pippa runs her fingers along the binoculars' glossy surface. "They're gorgeous. Where did you get them?"

"Well, my great-grandmother was an opera singer. I expect my great-grandfather used them to view her performances in the big halls. I discovered them inside a leather suitcase hidden at the back of a high cupboard. It's a treasure chest up there, I tell you."

"Can I have a go?" says Archie.

"Certainly. They've got a wide field of view, a generous 3x magnification, an extendable handle for extra comfort—perfect for spotting rabid dogs."

Archie focuses on the veranda where Okka usually sleeps. "I can't see him. He's probably inside or around the back. You take a look, Pippa."

She flicks down the handle and peers through. "All I can see are muddy boots. Hang on. There's something else . . . Huh!"

"What is it?"

"There's a cockatoo in a cage."

"Poor cocky," sighs Archie. "It should be free in the forest with its friends." He glances up at a flock of wild sulphur-crested cockatoos screeching above the trees.

The caged cocky flutters its wings, flares out a yellow crest and squawks, *arrrk, arrrrk*.

Pippa's heart sinks. "We should sneak onto the veranda and set it free."

"It's not as simple as that. You can't just release a captive bird," says Ollie, who fancies himself an expert in keeping pets. "It probably wouldn't survive a single day in the wild."

"You're right," says Archie. "Anyway, we don't have much time. We've gotta get the lemons while we can. This could be our only chance to avoid Okka."

FOUR

OKKA THE SHOCKER

Snap! Pippa rips a lemon from the tree. The branch flings backwards, showering icy water droplets over everyone.

"Freeze," whispers Archie, preparing to run for his life.

While the kids listen for signs of Okka, a calling currawong flies past, *clee-a clee-a clee-o, clee-a clee-a clee-o*.

Archie's shoulders relax. "It's okay. We're in the clear."

"Perhaps *twist* the lemon off next time," says Ollie quietly, brushing the droplets off his face and parka. "A little care and precision wouldn't go astray, don't you think?"

Pippa shoots him a narrow-eyed glare.

In the belief they are free from danger, the friends continue their sour-thing mission. But, little do they know, Okka, a black-and-white Australian cattle dog, is asleep under the veranda, dreaming about a squashed frog on the road—his favourite morning snack.

Back at the tree, gazing up, Archie's mind boggles because near the top are the largest, most dazzling lemons he's ever seen. Understandably, a temptation like this is hard to resist. So he climbs the trunk, dodging the long thorns protruding from the branches. With no bag handy, he curls the front of his jumper into a pouch and fills it with five ripe beauties.

Ollie peers up, eyes pleading as he whispers, "That'll do. Hurry up. Let's go before Okka comes."

"Okay, okay, just one more," says Archie, reaching for a grapefruit-sized lemon above his head. He twists it around, but it doesn't budge. He pulls hard—*Snap!* As the bulbous fruit breaks free, his elbow thrusts backwards, striking a thorn. "Ouch!" Stabbing pain zaps all the way to his fingers, which spring open, releasing the pouch. "No!" he cries, watching the lemons tumble from his jumper and crash to the dirt, *Boof-Boof, Ba-Boof-Boof-Boof.*

Okka wakes in a fit of anger, made worse by the smell of children. And with teeth gnashing, he dives onto the gravel driveway, scattering stones as he bolts for the lemon tree, barking ferociously.

Archie's eyes bulge like golf balls. "Ruuuuunnnnn!"

"Arrrrrrgggghhh," screams Ollie, storming down the hill, lemons flinging from his parka.

Unable to resist the prize fruit, Archie shoves three into his trouser pockets, then leaps from the tree and blazes down the slope behind Pippa. Unfortunately, his pockets have huge holes in them, so the lemons slip down his pants and roll underfoot. "Whooooaaaaa." Arms and legs fly and the ground turns to sky as he flings horizontally in the air . . .

BOOMFFF!

He slams flat on his back, staring up at the clouds, winded and gasping for air.

Pippa spins around and thrusts out one hand to help. "Get up, Archie! Quick, he's coming!"

Approaching fast, Okka's paws pound on the grass, and his savage barking morphs into a spine-chilling roar.

Gasping, unable to breathe, unable to move, Archie reaches for Pippa's hand. As she wrenches him off the grass, air rushes into his lungs, and they run screaming down the hill.

Okka thunders towards the kids, ears pinned back, jaws wide open, preparing to attack.

Then suddenly a wild tornado of black fur, green burrs, rose petals and snapping teeth explodes from the bushes, *GrrrrRoo-RooRooRooo! Gruff Ruff Ruff Ruff Ruff!*

"It's Kimba!" cheers Pippa.

Okka skids to a halt, eyes white with fright.

Unknown to the kids, Okka has a secret fear of small yappy-snappy dogs. It started many years ago, when, on a routine sniff and widdle around the neighbourhood, a hotheaded Scottish terrier, named Bunny, leapt out from behind a bush and bit his tail. Ever since that day, Okka has bolted at the sight of anything small, black and furry.

Yelp! Urrh urrh urrh, cries Okka, scampering back to the veranda with his tail between his legs.

Still shaking from the adrenaline rush, Archie shoves a bunch of lemons up his jumper, and he and Pippa join Ollie, a blubbering mess, hiding behind a boulder across the road.

Seconds later, Kimba leaps into Archie's arms and lunges at his face in a sloppy tongue-licking frenzy.

"Good dog for scaring that mean Okka away. I knew you'd come back. Okay, okay, settle down. That's enough licking. Hop off. We've got lemons to count."

The friends sit in a circle under a tree fern and take long, deep breaths to settle their pounding hearts.

Relaxed and ready for fruity fun, Pippa points to Archie's bulging tummy. "Looks like you're having triplets."

Three lemons roll out from under Archie's jumper. "You were right. How many have you got?"

Pippa grabs two from her jacket pockets. "And now for my secret stash." She removes another two from under her beanie and smiles proudly.

"Not bad," says Ollie, clapping politely. "Pretty impressive. Especially the lemon under the hat trick. But check out *my* fruity booty." He whips out four lemons from his parka. "Wait, not finished." He reaches down his brown corduroy pants, digs out three more and rolls them over to Pippa.

She screws up her face and kicks them back in disgust. "Errr, I think they're yours."

Ollie wiggles the fruit near Pippa's nose. "What? What's wrong with these? They smell like lemons with a hint of undies. Quite a delicacy really."

"Eeew, yuck. Get them away!"

Archie's stomach gurgles and groans. "That's enough, you loopy-loops. Let's eat some. I'm starving." Carefully avoiding Ollie's lemons, he selects one from the pile and bites off a thick chunk of skin. A zesty citrus aroma fills the air. *Mmmmm, reminds me of Nanna's lemon slice.* Soon an unpleasant bitterness grows in his mouth. So, using his lips as an air-powered cannon, he spits out the skin. It whizzes past Pippa's ear and slaps onto Ollie's forehead. Archie shrinks his head into his shoulders. "Oops, sorry."

Ollie's left eye twitches as he calmly peels the skin off his face and wipes off a small wet patch. "Ah, yes, well, I suppose that's one way to prepare a lemon. I myself prefer a more elegant solution." Quick as a flash, he draws a special edition Swiss Army Knife from a parka pocket and twirls it around his fingers in a fast whooshing motion. Then, using his fingernails to prise out the tools, he flips out a screwdriver, a bottle opener, scissors and a small blade. "This'll do the trick." He plunges the knife into the lemon and slices it into quarters.

"Now for the moment of strewth!" Equipped with a smile-shaped wedge, he clamps it between his teeth and bites down hard. *Zzzinnnnngggg*. A tormenting tartness tingles his tongue and his head goes fuzzy-wuzzy. "Ahhrerrrreeeee! So tangy, so tangy, so tangy!" he howls, munching the fruit in painful glee, squirting juice like a spitting camel.

"Ooh, I can't wait," says Pippa. Her tummy bubbles and her mouth waters as she peels a flawless *undie-free* lemon. "Okay, here goes . . ." She plunges her teeth into the flesh and sucks the juice. "Eeeeeeeeeeee!" The tanginess builds to a crescendo, exceeding her coping capacity, resulting in a sequence of blubbering, mouth-smacking, tongue-waggling contortions, "Blubablubablubabluba, hooowwwweeeeeee!"

A perfectly peeled, bite-sized lemon sits in Archie's hand. "This, my friends, is what I call a tang grenade." And proceeding on a taste-bud demolition mission, he stuffs the fruit into his mouth and squirms on the grass, eyes streaming tears, grimacing and howling from the supercharged juice. "Ayayay-ayayay, so sour! Ayayayayayayaya, so sour!"

Once everyone has satisfied their sour craving, Ollie's stomach rumbles, and he announces, "I need a sweet treat to cleanse the palate and tame my tummy. Lemons are *not* a filling fruit."

"I agree," says Pippa. "I'm still really hungry. Hey, got any treats at your place, Archie?"

"Nah, just some stale old bread. Wait a minute . . ." He peers up the road with a dreamy look in his eyes. "Follow me, you two. I've got a plan."

FIVE

MRS MARPIN

The friends skip down a gravel driveway and poke their noses through the bars of a tall locked gate. Mossy steps descend into a garden of nodding winter roses, billowing ferns and bright pink azalea flowers, leading to the entrance of a damp hills house. This is Mrs Marpin's place.

At the ripe age of 84, Mrs Marpin lives with her beloved Labrador dogs, named Roger and Lady. Archie and his sister Josephine are fond of Mrs Marpin because she often ties a bag of home-baked goodies to the fence adjoining their backyards. He loves discovering the mouth-watering treasure when feeding the chickens in the morning and is tantalised by the seemingly endless supply of lollies she hands out at every opportunity. Although lately, due to the coldness of winter, the neighbour has taken to sleeping for most of the day, so there hasn't been much lolly action.

Ollie pushes off from the gate, frowning in disappointment. "Nobody's home. I officially announce this quest for a lolly, a big fat folly."

"Wait. Don't give up so soon," begs Archie. "Mrs Marpin's there all right. She's probably just asleep."

"You've got lollies on the brain," says Pippa, pointing to the house. "Look, the curtains are closed, the door's shut, there's no smoke coming from the chimney. It doesn't seem at all like she's home. And even if she is, how will she know we're here?" Pippa rattles the towering gate. "We can't even knock on the front door."

"The girl has a point," says Ollie. "And if we climb over, we might give her a heart attack. It's a conundrum, a real pickle of a situation."

Unconcerned by the lolly barriers, Archie grins knowingly, for he's been in this situation before. "It's okay. We don't need to knock. Just follow me." He draws a deep breath and calls out in a buoyant singsong voice:

"Mrs Ma-a-a-a-r-r-r-pin. Mrs Ma-a-a-a-a-r-r-r-r-pin."

Pippa and Ollie join in, creating a chorus that echoes down the valley:

"Mrs Ma-a-a-a-r-r-r-r-pin. Mrs Ma-a-a-a-a-r-r-r-r-pin." And on and on they call, until after ten or so minutes, Archie pauses. "Shhh, I hear something."

Woof woof woof, tippity-tappity, tippity-tappity echoes the sound of Lady and Roger barking and shuffling their paws on the slippery floorboards inside the house.

Amid the kerfuffle, a latch clicks, a screen door creaks open, and out rush the dogs, whipping their tails back and forth like fly swatters.

Mrs Marpin steps onto the porch. "Settle down, Lady. Settle down, Roger." She pops on a wide-brimmed hat trimmed with a violet scarf and buttons up a snuggly cream overcoat. "Come along," she says, and with the dogs by her side, totters up the slippery steps.

"I can't see a lolly bag or anything sweet. She's sugarless," whispers Ollie.

"Don't worry," assures Archie. "She always has lollies."

While they peer through the bars, waiting in earnest, a tiny fairy-wren lands on a fern frond. It dives into a pedestal birdbath and thrashes around, washing its vivid blue plumage. After shaking dry, it calls in a happy chirrup and flits away as the dogs approach.

Finally Mrs Marpin arrives at the gate, her hat glowing in the crisp winter sun. Without saying a word, her kind grey eyes twinkle as she removes a white paper bag from an overcoat pocket. And much to the children's delight, she passes out a selection of shiny wrapped caramels: glimmering gold, sapphire blue, plum purple, ruby red, tangerine orange and emerald green.

Eyes popping with excitement and mouths watering, Ollie, Archie and Pippa slide their fingers through the wire and gather handfuls of the treats.

When the bag is empty, Mrs Marpin smiles—the kind of smile that comes from bringing happiness to others. "Now, you enjoy those. But don't eat them all at once."

"No, we won't. We promise."

"Good. Now, come along, Lady. Come along, Roger."

With fists full of lollies, the kids poke their noses through the gate and call out, "Thank you, thank you, Mrs Marpin. See you again soon!"

Satisfied her job is done, the sweet neighbour totters back down the steps, Lady and Roger by her side, wiggling their bottoms and wagging their tails.

As the friends wander up the steep road, clutching bundles of caramels, Kimba jumps and whimpers at Archie's side, begging for a treat.

"Here you go, boy. Catch."

Kimba leaps high and snaps the lolly in his jaws, proceeding to chomp on the chewy goo as he trots up the hill. However, being poorly evolved for eating lollies, the caramel sticks to the roof of his mouth, and his front teeth jut out at a rather odd angle.

"*Hehehe,*" giggles Pippa. "Check out Kimba. He reminds me of a Tasmanian devil."

"You're such a funny dog," says Archie, tickling Kimba's chin while extracting the lolly from his mouth.

Ollie waggles his pointer finger. "Naughty, naughty, you shouldn't feed caramels to dogs. Bad for their teeth and gums, you know. He'll get gingivitis."

"Get a grip, Ollie. It's just one lolly," says Archie, clueless as to the meaning of gingivitis.

Unimpressed by the excuse, Ollie tilts back his head, stretches out a long strand of sticky caramel from between his front teeth, and without a hint of irony, sucks it back into his mouth, *sluuurrrrrrp*. "Don't say I didn't warn you, Archie."

At the peak of the hill, the kids take turns gazing through Ollie's binoculars at the valley below. Known as The Patch, the distant farming village appears as a mosaic of greens, blues and yellows, illuminated by sunbeams bursting between two billowing clouds.

"Hey, that's my house, the one with the red roof," says Pippa, nudging Ollie to take a look.

"Sorry, a little busy at the momento," he replies, totally engrossed in an unwrapping ritual. Even though each lolly has the same caramel flavour, Ollie imagines this one will taste like peppermint, owing to its emerald-green wrapper. *Chomp.* "Mmmm, minty." While rolling the treat around his mouth and clanking it against his teeth, he relaxes back on the grass and piles the other lollies onto his belly.

"Let me see," says Archie, taking a turn. "You're right. That is your house. These binoculars will be great for spotting chestnut trees in autumn."

Pippa selects a gold lolly from her stash, marvelling at its gleaming wrapper. "Do you really think we can make a fortune selling chestnuts?"

"I don't think we can, I know we can. By next autumn, I'll be riding my new bike for sure." Archie lies on the grass and counts his lollies. Up above, two curious kookaburras fly onto a gum tree branch and laugh, *kookoo-kookoo-ca-ca-ca-ca-kookoo-*kookoo*-ca-ca-ca-ca-ca.*

The friends chant in unison, "When the kookaburras call, the rain will fall."

An ominous thunder rumble peels across the swollen grey sky, and a raindrop splats on Archie's nose. "Yep, I reckon the clouds are about to blow. We better go soon."

"Just a bit longer," says Pippa, unwrapping her caramel. "I love it up here." As the lolly approaches her lips, a swooping kookaburra snatches it from her fingers and flies into the forest. She screams and jerks backwards, bumping into Ollie, who bumps into Archie, who bumps into Kimba, sending their lollies scattering across the grass.

Having witnessed the swooping kookaburra from afar, two boys on dragster bikes approach and powerslide to a halt, spraying gravel onto the grass and all over Kimba.

Unhappy about the stones in his fur and sensing danger, Kimba bares his razor-sharp teeth and growls at the boys.

"Oooh, so scary," smirks Leo, the local bully, hopping off his bike. "Whaddaya call that pathetic mangy creature? A mop with four legs?"

Archie jumps to his feet. "He's not mangy. He's just got burrs from running through the bushes."

"Yeah, leave Kimba alone, you bully," snaps Pippa, standing beside Archie, arms crossed.

Surprised by the brazen insult, Leo does a double-take.

In an attempt to make peace, Ollie steps forward, smiling sheepishly. "Umm, I think there's been a little misunderstanding. What she said was, 'Leave Kimba alone, he's woolly'."

Before Leo can respond, Neville, the other local bully—a tall, gawky lad who doesn't say much—notices the lollies scattered on the grass and alerts his curly-haired friend via a sneaky elbow nudge.

"Look out! Swooping kookaburra!" shouts Leo, pointing to an empty tree branch overhead.

Ollie, Archie and Pippa fall for the trick and duck for cover under their arms.

In that instant, Leo and Neville dive onto the grass and stuff their jean pockets with the lollies, snaffling every last one they can find.

"Go, go, go!" shouts Leo.

The bullies leap onto their bikes and speed away, doing wheelies as they shout, "Suckers! Ha-haha, hoo-hoo!"

"Huh!" gasps Pippa, scanning the grass. "They've taken our lollies." She waves her fists and yells in a fury, "I hope you get rotten teeth, you bullyboys!" All red-faced, she turns to Archie. "They can't get away with this. Let's chase after them."

"Nah, we'll never catch those mongrels without bikes."

Devastated by the turn of events, Ollie flops onto his hands and knees and scrabbles through the grass in search of stray caramels. "Found one! It's strawberry flavoured!" He raises the ruby-red treat victoriously above his head.

Whoosh-SNAP.

A kookaburra swoops down and plucks the lolly from his hand. Shocked, devastated, hungry, Ollie remains frozen, mouth wide open, fingers pointing aimlessly to the clouds.

Perched on a high branch, the kookaburra bangs the lolly against the tree trunk—*Whack, Whack, Whack*—ensuring the caramel is well and truly dead.

Archie drapes his arm over Ollie's shoulders. "Don't worry, buddy, kookaburras can't get rotten teeth, coz they don't have any. At least *you* won't get gingivitis now, whatever that is."

The kids' faces flash white as spectacular lightning arcs across the sky. A chest-thumping thunderclap follows, and blustery wind whips their hair backwards.

"Quick, we better find cover! I think we're in for a big one!" shouts Archie.

SIX

THE WIBBLY WOBBLY WOODPILE

Later that night, a tremendous storm rages.

Archie's mum, Florence, bellows from the kitchen, "Archie! You need to collect more wood before the fire goes out."

The thought of venturing into the foresty garden during a thunderstorm sends shudders down Archie's spine. And so, he ignores the request. Instead, teeth chattering, he grabs a metal poker and prods a damp log in the fireplace. Three slater bugs scurry out from under a clump of steaming moss and disappear down a wood crack. *At least the bugs are warm.* Archie rubs his numb big toe, poking through his purple odd sock, and snuggles up to Kimba, curled in a ball, shivering.

Above their heads, torrential rain roars on the corrugated iron roof, rising and falling in metallic waves. Beads of water trickle through cracks in the ceiling and drip into a half-filled aluminium pot on the floor. Blustery wind whistles through the windows, rattling the thin glass panes, and a small tree branch strikes the roof.

BANG.

Yelp! cries Kimba, jumping in fright.

Archie cuddles him and gazes up, wondering if a tree might crash through the roof at any moment. "It's okay, boy. We're safe here."

In reality, they are far from safe, because surrounding the house stands a forest of mountain ash trees—*Eucalyptus regnans*—the tallest flowering tree in the world, with a nasty reputation for crushing roofs.

"Arrrrchhieee! I told you we need more wood for the fire," screams Florence, bursting into the room. She switches on the television, twists the aerial to improve the fuzzy reception, and plonks on the couch to watch the news.

"All right, Mum, I'll go in a minute. I'm just trying to get it going again." Archie crouches over the fireplace and blows on the blackened logs. No flames appear, not even a warm glow; the wood just hisses, smokes and steams a little more.

Kimba sneezes from the ash dust and stares up with big sad chocolate-brown eyes.

"Don't worry, buddy. We'll be warm and cosy when I get more wood," reassures Archie, stroking his fur.

Truth be told, Archie, Florence, and his big sister Josephine are hopeless at building fires, especially when using wet wood in the damp, poorly designed fireplace. Even so, the optimistic boy hopes that tonight will be the night when he masters the art of fire-making.

A thunderclap BOOMS overhead, shaking the foundations of the house. The light bulbs flicker, the television zaps, and the power cuts out, plunging everyone into darkness.

Josephine bursts from her bedroom, screaming, "We've lost power!"

They all race around in a panic, bumping into furniture and each other while searching for torches, candles and matches. To avoid being trampled, Kimba scampers into Archie's room and hides under the bed.

"Here's a torch," says Florence, clicking it on. A dim orange light appears, then fades away. She whacks it on the side. "Oh, the batteries are flat!"

Sporadic flashes of lightning punctuate the darkness as Archie rummages through a drawer crammed with junk: scrap paper, playing cards, tangled string, staples, glue, rubber bands, incense, a headless doll. He fumbles over several long, round waxy objects. "I found candles!" Right at the back, his fingernails scrape down the rough edge of a small squashed box. "And matches too!"

With a candle tucked under his chin, Archie swipes a match against the box's striking surface. A spark flies but fizzles out. "Urgh, come on, light you silly thing." He swipes another . . . and another . . . and another.

They're all duds. Now only one remains.

Josephine lunges for the match. "Give me a go!"

"No. I can do it." Archie turns away and swipes in a firm downward stroke, igniting a fizzing flare that swiftly settles to a healthy flame.

"Quick, light the candle," urges Josephine.

"Can't you see I'm trying? The wick's buried in wax. It won't light." A wind gust blows down the chimney. The flame flickers. "No, no, don't go out!" In desperation, Archie tips it upside down. The flame grows brighter, leaping and lurching up at his fingers. "Ouch, aargh!"

"What are you doing, you maniac!" shouts Josephine.

Florence clasps her cheeks and shrieks, "You're going to burn the house down!"

Thinking fast, Archie rotates the candle horizontally and directs the flame underneath the covered wick. "Come on, melt." Hot wax drips onto his fingers. "Arrggh, hot, hot, hot." Just as the match withers to nothing, the wick appears, and a yellow light grows from the candle. "Yes!"

Thunder rumbles all around and rain swells on the roof as Josephine and Florence huddle close to Archie, their glowing faces mesmerised by the flickering flame.

"Well done," says Josephine, lighting another candle. "How about we play Monopoly tonight?"

Florence embraces the kids, squeezing them so tightly their cheeks squish together. "Why don't we start by reading a few chapters from *The Magic Pudding*. We haven't read from the classics for a while."

"Brilliant!" says Archie, beaming. "I'll get some wood so we can sit by a nice cosy fire."

"Good boy. And get sticks too. We'll need to get the fire going again. Oh, and watch out for red-back spiders."

"Yes, I will, Mum. I always do." After fastening his coat and hood, Archie fixes the candle in a glass lantern and opens the door—*PERWOOFFFFFFF.*

An explosion of wind and rain flips off the hood, blasts his hair skyward, pops open the lantern and extinguishes the flame. "Cripes!" he gasps, shivering in the blinding dark.

High above and all around, shadowy gum trees swing wildly in the violent storm, branches creaking, leaves roaring. Amid the pelting rain, sticks plummet from the sky and smack onto the sodden ground.

While peering into the pitch-black foresty garden, searching for the path to the woodpile, lightning squiggles across the sky, turning night into day for a brief moment. "There it is!" And with the direction now fixed in his mind, Archie grabs a blunt axe and sloshes up the track.

Squalling rain lashes his face, obscuring the way even more

than the blackness of the night. To stay on course, he scrapes the axe-head along a low stone wall. But a few paces on, the wall peters out, replaced by garden beds. So Archie feels for the gravel path, using his feet as eyes to navigate up three slippery steps. Bushes and ferns hiss from the sides, whipping and lurching at his arms and legs. As the track levels out, more mud than gravel, his boots slip and slide over a well-trodden tree root, and the familiar aroma of a flowering wattle bush blasts up his nose. *Nearly there.*

Around the next bend, on course for the woodpile, a lightning bolt zaps from the sky, arcing in a cataclysmic dagger that explodes into a towering mountain ash tree. The garden flashes white as sparks spray out from the trunk, whooshing in a fountain, followed by a falling branch, cracking and groaning.

Crack-kak-K-K-K-keeeeoooorrrraaaaAAAAARRRRRRR

Nowhere to hide, no time to run, Archie curls into a ball on the path, hoping, praying, as a mammoth tree limb, the size of a mega dinosaur, plummets to earth.

BOOM

CRUNCH

WALLOP.

The ground shudders. Huge leafy branches whip the track, thrashing up and down before settling to a deathly stillness.

A few steps away from the disaster zone, a pile of wet bark stirs—and out pops Archie. Shaken but unharmed, he surveys the scene. Since a monstrous jumble of branches now blocks the path to the woodpile, turning back seems like the only option. But then he pictures Kimba shivering beside the cold fireplace, gazing up with those big sad eyes. And he imagines reading stories and playing Monopoly with his mum and Josephine beside a cosy fire all night long. *I have to get the wood. This is an emergency!*

And so, while rolling thunder peels across the sky, he clambers onto the fallen branch. The fresh scent of eucalyptus provides comfort as he pushes through a curtain of drippy leaves and fights through tangled twigs. Further along, rain belting all around, the thickened limb provides a handy slide that takes him back to the track, straight into a puddle. Ankle-deep in water, Archie flounders in the shadows, searching for landmarks. *Where am I?*

Another dazzling lightning display zigzags across the sky, illuminating a leaky iron tank turned on its side, filled with damp fungus-covered logs.

Seizing the moment, Archie dashes up the path, past a massive hollowed-out tree trunk, and arrives at the wood stack in complete darkness. Greeted by the cacophonous clamour of rain on metal and the musty smell of decaying logs, he gazes into the cavernous blackness. *How can I watch out for red-backs if I can't see a thing?*

Although Archie is fearful of red-back spiders, he's never seen any in the woodpile and is determined to get the wood. So, teeth gritted, he plunges both hands into the shadows and feels along the logs, tracing fingertips over rubbery fungus, soggy bark and moss.

Upset by the intrusion, a cockroach scuttles onto Archie's hand, gripping on with its sticky itty-bitty feet. "Urghh!" He flicks it off, then rips out four logs from the stack and tosses them onto the ground.

Eeeek, eeeek! squeals a frightened animal as it scurries for cover behind the woodpile.

Archie jumps. *Don't panic. Probably just a possum. I just need a few more logs*. After a nervous breath, he reaches into the tank once more, and feeling blindly, clutches onto a perfect-sized log at the top of the stack.

ZAPPATTA-BOOM.

A cracking double lightning bolt illuminates a humungous huntsman spider perched on the log in Archie's hands, and it's staring straight back at him with its eight beady eyes. "Aaa-aaaaaaah!"

Archie lurches backwards onto the slippery logs and runs along them on the spot, arms swinging wildly to keep balance, legs zipping out of control. "Whoooaaaa." Finally, his feet slip out from under his body, the logs tumble away, and he flies into a muddy puddle.

Cold sludge oozes into his boots. Then a violent wind squall swooshes past, leaving an eerie silence in its wake: no wind, no rain, no thunder, just water droplets falling from the leaves, *drip drop, drippity drop drip.*

Drenched, shivering, bewildered, the frozen kid gazes to the heavens and cries out, "Somebody help me!"

As if answering his call, millions of white angels float down from the clouds, dancing and glistening in the the swirling electric sky.

"Snow. It's snowing!" he whispers, opening his mouth wide. The delicate ice crystals tickle his tongue and settle on his face and eyelashes. For now, all that exists is the magic of snow. That is, until the cruel wind whips up again and the snowflakes transform into whopping great hailstones pelting down in a rage, pummelling his head and shoulders. "Ooh, ouch, arrgh!"

Desperate for shelter, Archie grabs the logs and hurries to the tree hollow near the tank. As he prepares to leap inside, a bushy-tailed fox rushes out.

They freeze.

The stunned fox stares at Archie, its wild emerald-green eyes lit up by distant lightning. Archie stares back, wincing from the pinging hailstones. For a moment, the two are united by their quest to find refuge from the hail.

A thunderclap explodes nearby. The startled fox darts away, finding shelter under the fallen branch.

Archie crawls into the tree hollow and snuggles against the soft dry bark. Outside, bucketloads of hail pound the earth, forming mounds of ice at the foot of the tree. Safe and snug inside the hollow, he rubs his numb fingers and imagines sleeping there for the night, curled up like a possum. The fantasy is short-lived, however, as a savage wind whips through the entrance—a bitter reminder of winter's scorn. Shuddering in the icy cold, with hailstones bouncing off his rubber boots, Archie clutches the bundle of wet logs and thinks, *I can't wait for springtime.*

PART TWO

SEVEN

THE TRICKY CHICKENS

"Arrrchieee! Get uuuuupp!" screams Florence from the kitchen.

Archie wakes and sits bolt upright, his hair standing on end like he's seen a ghost. At the foot of the bed, Kimba digs into a blanket and curls into a compact ball of black fluff.

"Archie! Get up! I need you to feed the chooks, and pick up sticks, and pull out blackberries, and dry the dishes, and clean the gutters on the roof."

"Urrrgh," he moans, escaping into a dark hideaway under the doona. As an odd job payment plan has yet to be agreed upon, Archie ignores his mother's demands and clicks on a torch. The cosy light shines on a book about Harry Houdini, the great escape artist and magician. Following a few page flicks, he pauses on a riveting black-and-white photograph of Houdini dangling from his ankles, his entire body submerged inside a water-filled glass tank.

A wet black nose pokes under the doona, followed by Kimba's slimy tongue licking the picture.

"Oi, stop it, Kimba. Houdini didn't lick his way out, you silly dog." He slaps the book closed.

BANG. A door slams in the background. "Arrrchieeee! I told you to get up!"

"All right, all right, I'm coming." He flops out of bed, and with Kimba trailing by his heels, stumbles into the lounge room, past Josephine practising the piano, and enters the tiny wood-lined kitchen.

"About time you got up," says Florence, shoving a bucket of food scraps into one of his hands and an egg basket into the other. "Josephine's done her jobs. Now it's your turn. You need to feed the chooks and collect the eggs. They'll be starving hungry by now."

"Speaking of eggs, can I keep some to sell at the Kallista Market? I need the money for my new bike."

Florence dunks a dirty pot into the dishwater. "What on earth do you need a new bike for?"

Archie's brain pops and fizzes—so bemused by her lack of understanding, he goes crosseyed.

"He's not riding that bike, Mum," says Josephine, standing in the doorway, hands on hips. "I've seen him trying to do jumps and tricks. The bike's useless. He's already broken some spokes. And what's with the streamers? Give him a break, for goodness sakes."

"Oh, I don't know what all the fuss is about. They're lovely streamers."

Kimba cocks his head to one side and hangs out his tongue.

Archie stares at his mum with puppy-dog eyes, smiling sweetly. "Please, please, pretty please."

Florence glances around, and struck by her son's angelic face, remembers him as a cute little boy with long locks of blonde hair. "Ooh, my munchkin, yes, you can sell the eggs we don't use." She turns to the sink and places the clean pot on a skyscraping stack of drying dishes. "I'll ring up later and book you a market stall. Of course, you'll have to pay me back for the booking fee and any other production costs. The next market's in three weeks, so you better get busy collecting those eggs. And while you're at it, I need you to pick up sticks, and pull out blackberries, and clean the gutters on the roof. Oh, and don't forget to—"

CLONK. The screen door slams in the background.

Florence whooshes around, spraying bubbles across the floor. "Archie? Archie! Where have you gone!"

The boy and dog scoot across the veranda and head for the chicken coop along the sun-dappled path. A welcoming spring breeze, neither warm nor cold, carries the sweet custardy aroma of purple freesias and creamy-white jonquils growing wild in the garden. *It's going to be a great day,* thinks Archie, imagining all the eggs he'll find in the nesting boxes and all the money he'll earn at the local community market.

While bounding up the path, Archie swings the chook bucket forwards and backwards. With each swing, the bucket swoops higher and higher. Sloppy porridge, soggy tea leaves, old cabbage and potato skins slosh up the edges. Then in one swift move, he swings the bucket all the way around in a perfect loop without spilling a single drop. *"Hee-hee!"*

He prepares for another loop-the-loop but aborts the trick when a mysterious object comes into view. Next to the chook pen, tied to the wire fence, is a bulging white bag. "This could be our lucky day, Kimba. Let's see what Mrs Marpin's left for us this time."

Over at the fence, Archie unties the bag and sniffs inside. *Mmmm, homemade pumpkin scones with blackberry jam and whipped cream.* After shoving one into his mouth, he tosses a chunk to Kimba, who catches it mid-air, slonking it down in three mouth chomps.

Archie licks his lips and fingers. *Yum. I could eat the lot, but we better save some for Mum and Josephine*. He returns the bag to the fence for his sister to find later. Then he picks up Kimba and secures him under one arm. "Time to feed the chooks, fella."

Although Archie is standing next to the chook pen, he doesn't go inside. Instead, he scatters the food scraps on the ground, gazes up a giant Californian redwood tree and calls, "Chook, chook, chook, chook, chook."

An instant later, flapping wings fill the sky as seven chickens burst from the canopy in a cacophonous calamity. Swirling, whirling, squawking and twirling, they land in a cloud of feathers, leaves and dust.

Archie's chickens began flying up the tree last summer, when, on a moonlit night, a conniving fox broke into the pen and devoured four fat hens. The surviving chickens, plus four replacement hens, were so distressed about the lax security arrangements they decided that sleeping in the redwood tree was the safest option. That's why the clever birds fly up to the high branches to roost for the night, popping down at sunrise to lay their eggs.

While the chickens scratch and peck through the food scraps, Archie climbs inside the chicken coop to collect the eggs. *I wonder how many we have today*. He peers into the hay-lined nesting boxes. *What? No eggs? That's strange*. He searches everywhere but finds nothing, not a single egg. *Where on earth are they laying them?*

With nature calling, Archie heads to the toilet located outside the back door. While standing at the loo, something peculiar catches his eye. There, snuggled up behind the outlet pipe, are three creamy-white eggs. *Ha-haaa! So this is their new hiding spot*. Excited and relieved, he snaffles them off the floor.

Over the following five mornings, Archie springs from bed to check for hidden toilet treasure. On each occasion, he finds three freshly laid eggs, still warm to the touch. On the sixth day, a Friday, he peers behind the outlet pipe and gasps, "Huh! No eggs! Oh no, not again." To the boy's horror, the floor is bare, apart from a daddy-longlegs spider in the corner.

Troubled by the turn of events, Archie follows two white chickens in the hope they may reveal a clue. "Where have you hidden your eggs, you cheeky chooks?"

Bokurrrk! Bokurrrrrk! they answer as Kimba bursts through the open screen door.

"No, Kimba!"

The hens flutter to safety up the redwood tree. Seconds later, the mischievous mutt returns, eyes sparkling and tail wagging, for he loves nothing more than razzing the chickens.

Archie crouches and ruffles Kimba's fur. "Naughty dog. You shouldn't chase the chooks. I tell you what, how about we put those hunting instincts to good use? You can help me find the missing eggs. What do you say, boy?"

Kimba jumps onto Archie's lap and sniffs the egg basket.

"Good dog. Eggs. Find the chicken eggs."

Tail whipping, Kimba extends his tongue to full length and licks Archie's fingers.

"No, silly, not my fingers. The eggs. Find the eggs."

As if understanding the command, Kimba pricks up his ears, tenses his body and sniffs the air excitedly.

"That's it. Can you smell them? Show me where they are."

Kimba growls, licks his lips, straightens his tail and leaps to the ground in pursuit of another chicken, barking and skidding in leaves along the way.

"Never mind, I'll find them myself," mutters Archie. *Where's a good spot to lay eggs, I wonder?* He charges over to the tree hollow and peeks inside. *No eggs in here.* He searches in the woodpile, inside the shed, around the back of the chook pen amongst the ivy, in the leaf strainer of the water tank and even on the roof of the house. Alas, he returns eggless and sits hunched over on a rickety garden chair.

Florence calls from the kitchen window. "Arrrchieee! You need to have breakfast and get ready for school or you'll miss the bus."

"All right, Mum, I'm coming." He trudges back to the house. Along the way, a speckly black-and-white hen meanders past, clucking anxiously, *bok bok, bok bok bok bok.* "Good little chook-chook. Show me the way to your eggs. I'll feed you lots of grubs if you do."

The hen totters under a lime-green metal pyramid frame and sits beside a dying pot plant with drooping leaves and yellow spots.

What's she doing under Mum's garden pyramid? he wonders, recalling Florence saying that pyramids have special powers and can heal sick plants.

Kimba returns in a spritely trot, tongue dangling to one side, and upon spotting the hen, springs to action once again.

Archie whisks him under one arm. "No, Kimba, you bad dog. There's no time for chasing chooks. I have to organise a clubhouse meeting with Ollie and Pippa. We've got a mystery to solve—the mystery of the missing eggs!"

EIGHT

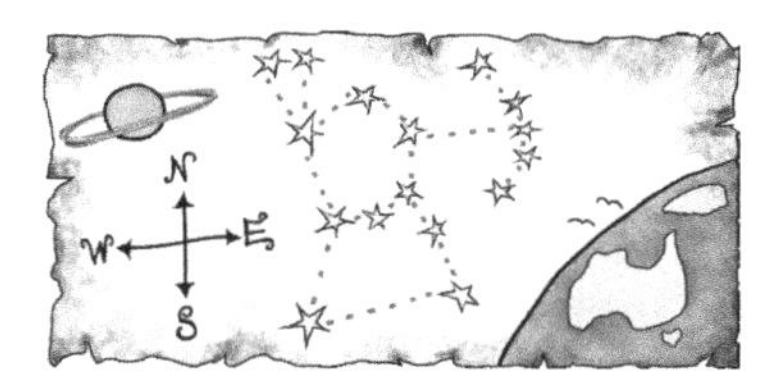

THE TREASURE MAP

After school, Pippa and Archie crawl inside their hideaway—The Lilly Pilly Clubhouse. Located near a vacant bush block at the bottom of Archie's garden, the clubhouse is made from a sheet of corrugated iron propped up against a lilly pilly tree.

Archie lays a hand-drawn map on the dirt floor beside Kimba's swishing tail. "This is the big tree where the chooks sleep. And here's the pen where they're supposed to lay their eggs." He points to a drawing of seven chickens behind bars. "For ages, I've been getting three eggs a day from the nesting boxes. Then a week ago, the chooks started hiding them over here, behind the loo. Everything was going great until they switched spots again. Now I haven't the foggiest idea where the eggs are."

Pippa twirls a plait around her finger. "Hang on. You've got seven hens, right?"

"Yeah."

"So why only three eggs in the nesting boxes?"

"I'm not sure. We were getting seven eggs a day until last summer when a fox ate four of our best-laying hens. Mum bought four new Egyptian Fayoumi chickens from this chook farmer out the back of Monbulk. But no matter how much I feed them or how comfortable I make the nesting boxes, they don't lay any eggs."

"Weird," says Pippa. "Hey, what's this green triangle on the map?"

"Uh, that's Mum's pot plant pyramid."

"You've got a pyramid?"

"Yeah, a lime-green one made from welded metal poles. It's a sculpture that Fergus built for Mum. Apparently, it's got superpowers and heals sick pot plants."

Pippa raises one eyebrow. "Does it actually work?"

"Nah, the plants just shrivel up and die. But Fergus has been selling them like hotcakes at the Kallista Market. He can't make enough of them."

"Ding dong!" announces Ollie, popping his head below the corrugated iron roof.

"About time you got here. You're late. We have to help Archie find his chicken eggs. He's selling them to raise money for his new bike."

"In that case, what are we waiting for? This is an urgent matter indeed," says Ollie, scurrying into the clubhouse.

Archie squashes next to Kimba to make more room. "Okay, so listen up. I have to tell you about a weird clue. This morning I saw a chicken sitting under Mum's pyramid. I reckon it's got something to do with the missing eggs."

"Hmmm, you could be right," says Pippa. "Pyramids *are* magical and mysterious. I've been learning all about them at school this week."

"Tell me about them. What have you learnt?"

"Well, in Egypt, over four and a half thousand years ago, a pharaoh named Khufu built three pyramids. The biggest one's called the Great Pyramid of Giza. He built it as a huge tomb to be buried in after he died. The ancient Egyptians believed that to reach the afterlife, they had to travel through a mysterious underworld. They were buried with food, clothes and treasure to provide everything they needed for their long journey. Unfortunately, robbers stole Khufu's body and all the treasure a long time ago. We don't even know what they found."

"That's because *there was* no treasure," declares Ollie. "And Khufu was never found, because he wasn't buried there. If you study the facts more closely, you'll see that aliens built the pyramids. No doubt about it."

Pippa tuts and rolls her eyes. "If you say so, Ollie. Anyway, according to my teacher, each side of the Giza pyramid aligns to a different direction—north, south, east and west. A sealed entrance was placed on the north side."

"They would've needed one of these to work out the exact directions," says Ollie, slinging a brass compass onto the map. "It belonged to my great-grandfather. Look, it's moving north! Works every time, *hee-hee*. And did you know, according to the latest edition of *UFO Today*, the compass was invented two thousand years *after* the Giza pyramids were built. So the Egyptians either used advanced alien technology or a time traveller brought them a compass. Take your pick."

"Maybe it was Doctor Who," says Pippa sarcastically. "Can I please finish my story?"

Ollie palms his hair to one side and sits up straight on his best behaviour. "Sorry, sorry."

"Thank you. So, as I was saying, the peak of each pyramid points to a different star in the Orion constellation. They're the brightest stars in the night sky."

"I have it on good authority the aliens came from the Orion constellation," states Ollie. "After their intergalactic spaceship crashed on Earth, they built the pyramids as megalithic power stations to recharge their hyperspace fuel rods. How else were they going to fly home?"

"Yeah, yeah, and I suppose kangaroos make a boing-boing sound when they hop?" says Pippa.

"Yes, they do. Right, Archie?"

"Of course. And frogs go doink, doink, doink."

"Hey, you goofballs, this information might be important, so listen up for a second."

The boys zip their lips as Pippa continues.

"In Greek mythology, Orion was the name of a gigantic huntsman. It's amazing. When you draw a line between the Orion stars in the night sky, it makes the shape of a huntsman holding a shield and a club."

Ollie's hand shoots up. "Excuse me. What does this have to do with Archie's missing eggs? Getting a little side-tracked, don't you think?"

"Urgh! We're examining the evidence. It's what all good detectives do."

"I've got an idea," says Archie. "How about we align the pyramid on our map to north, south, east and west, just like the Great Pyramid of Giza?"

"Great idea. It might give us a clue," says Pippa.

"Okay, since the chickens enter on this side of Mum's pyramid, this will be the north-facing side." Archie rotates the map until the entrance faces the same direction as the compass arrow. "There we go. Perfect."

"I'll be the judge of that, my friend," says Ollie, polishing his glasses. "We've got to ensure there's no parallax error." With his line of sight directly over the compass, he rotates the map a fraction of a millimetre to the right. "Perfectamango. Now it's facing north."

The friends stare at the drawing in silence, hoping a miracle will point them in the direction of the missing eggs.

Nothing happens.

"Wait a second. I've got something that might help," says Pippa, rummaging through her school bag. "Here it is." She pulls out a library book about the Egyptian pyramids and finds a double-page photograph of the Orion constellation. "How about we slip this under the map so we can trace the position of the stars?"

"It's worth a try," says Archie. He lifts the paper while Pippa slides the book underneath. Once Ollie fine-tunes the alignment, Archie selects a yellow pencil and traces the Orion stars onto the map.

"Oh my gosh!" says Pippa. "Do you see what I see?"

Archie beams. "Yes! I can't believe it. Each Orion star is lined up to a different landmark: the chicken coop, the toilet, the woodpile, the pot plant pyramid."

"It's a sign!" says Ollie, gawking at the sky. "The aliens are returning. There's no other explanation."

Pippa draws a black line between each of the stars, creating a dot-to-dot picture of Orion the hunter.

"Wow, check out the huntsman's club," says Archie. "It's pointing to the chicken tree. That's the only spot I haven't searched for the missing eggs. Maybe they're hidden in nests up in the high branches!" Using a thick red marker, he draws an X over the tree.

"Hang on, it's not finished yet," says Ollie. He sprinkles dirt all over the map, smudges it around and blows off the excess dust. "That's better. Now it's a real treasure map."

NINE

THE LILLY PILLY TREEHOUSE

CLANK. A golf ball-sized rock strikes the Lilly Pilly Clubhouse roof. Ollie, Archie and Pippa jump in surprise and stare goggle-eyed at two pairs of legs and muddy boots standing at the clubhouse entrance.

To everyone's dismay, Leo pokes his head under the corrugated iron. "What have we got 'ere? Some kind of treasure map, eh? Oh, I see, X marks the spot. Buried a stash of lollies, have we? It just so happens we could do with a refill. Stocks are low. Right, Nev?"

A pink gum bubble appears under the clubhouse roof, growing bigger and bigger and bigger. *POP*. Neville peels the sticky goo off his lips and nose, replacing it with a smug smirk. "Yeah, half a tube of sherbet, one aniseed ball, four pieces of bubble gum inside a packet of footy cards, and then we're out."

As Neville blows another bubble, creating a distraction, Leo reaches in and snatches the map off Pippa's pyramid book.

Kimba growls, snapping his jaws in quick succession.

"Control that pussycat of yours or he's gonna scare a mouse," says Leo, sniggering.

"*Hor-horr*, good one," chuckles Neville, all the while keeping a safe distance from Kimba.

Archie springs out from under the corrugated iron and fronts up to Leo. "Give back our map. It's not yours."

"Yeah, give it back," asserts Pippa, joining Archie's side. "There's no lolly treasure. Anyway, you don't know how to read that map, you dingbat."

"What did you say?" snarls Leo.

Ollie scrambles out from the clubhouse on hands and knees and springs to his feet, his left eye twitching as he says in a nervous but soothing voice, "Now, now, gentlemen. There's been a simple misunderstanding. What she said was, 'You don't know how to read that map. You better ring Matt'."

Neville gawks at Leo in befuddlement. "Who's Matt?"

"Never mind, numbskull."

Still awaiting a reply to his peacemaking effort, beads of sweat soak Ollie's underarms.

"I suppose ya think ya smart, ya little twerp," responds Leo. "Do you think I'm stupid or somethink? And anyways, I reckon that book's got everythink I need to read ya treasure map. Or should I say *lolly* map?"

Pippa grinds her teeth and crosses her arms. "It's some-*thing* and every-*thing*, not *think*. And you'll have to get past us if you want that book." She links arms with Ollie, who links arms with Archie, who clutches Kimba tightly.

Leo grabs a long stick and swishes it back and forth while stepping forward. "Let's get 'em, Nev!"

WHOOSH. Out of nowhere, a wobbly wooden spear flies overhead and bounces off a nearby tree trunk.

Frozen in surprise, Leo and Neville gaze at the vacant bush block from where the spear came. Bracken ferns, wonga vines and sword grass thrash about as if a beast is about to emerge.

Then suddenly Russell and his best mate Dion burst through the bushes, dressed in camouflage clothing, swishing machetes through the thick scrub. They climb a broken wire fence, with Russell balancing a freshly cut messmate tree trunk on one shoulder and Dion clasping a bundle of spears handcrafted from blackwood saplings. The lads have been doing bushcraft activities, a favourite hobby of theirs.

"Oi, bozos! LEAVE THEM KIDS ALONE!" bellows Russell, approaching fast.

As they arrive at the clubhouse, Dion selects a spear from his bundle, and eyes fixed on Leo, casually sharpens it with the machete blade.

Leo drops the map, his whole body trembling, and he and Neville flee down the hill, screaming, "Whoooaaaaaaa."

Russell winks at Archie. "Right then, we need to talk about security arrangements for youse lot. Who's gonna help me build a new clubhouse up this lilly pilly tree?"

The friends squeal, jumping for joy at the marvellous idea.

"Let's call it The Lilly Pilly Treehouse," suggests Archie.

"Yes, I love it," says Pippa. "With a removable ladder to keep out the baddies."

Ollie raises his pointer finger. "And an intercom system. We can run string down the trunk, connect a can to each end and talk to each other from a distance. And we'll need a secret password, like *honk-monkey*. No, no, that's too weak. How about *bottom honker forty-two?* Wrong password, no rope ladder."

Russell drops the messmate trunk onto the dirt and draws a deep breath through his nostrils. "Mmm, I love the smell of messmate in the morning."

"But it's the afternoon, Russ," corrects Archie.

"All right, keep ya shirt on. It might be the arvo to you, but I only woke up two hours ago."

Dion throws his sharpened spear at a gum tree and frowns as it bounces off the trunk. “Doh!” Despite having no formal training in the art of spear making, he’s desperate to craft one that will stick into a tree.

Meanwhile, Ollie, keen for a bit of bushcraft himself, flips out a miniature saw on his Swiss Army Knife and hacks away at the messmate log.

Russell whips out a long shiny carpenters saw from his backpack and swishes it through the air. “Right-eo, Olleo, let the professional take over.” The younger kids stare wide-eyed, stepping back while the passionate teen and budding Samurai leaps onto a rock, shouting, “Hi-Yah! Yayayaya-yeeeeee!” In the silence that follows, a wedge-tailed eagle screeches high above. Russell gazes to the sky, then lowers the saw and jumps back down, smiling. “Enough muckin’ about, let’s cut some stuff.”

The friends straddle one end of the messmate log while Russell saws furiously, slicing it into six equal lengths. “Okey-dokey, crew, these are the support poles. We’re gonna need more wood, nails, screws and anything else you can find that might be useful.”

“There’s heaps of stuff in the garden shed,” says Archie. “Follow me.”

Inside the ramshackle shed, Pippa holds up an overflowing pile of seagrass matting. “Hey, look what I’ve found. We can use it on the floor. And check out this window frame. It even opens and shuts.”

“Great,” says Archie, dragging out some wooden planks and a tangle of rope. “These should come in handy too. Maybe we can make a rope ladder.”

Ollie opens a metal trunk. "Ah-haaaa! Just what we need—house paint and brushes. Ooh, ooh, ooh, and two empty baked bean cans." As he puffs into a tin to remove a cobweb, strange hollow sounds boom back, which inspires him to make more weird noises: "Wowowowow. Chicka. Chicka. Wakka. Wakka."

Next, to everyone's surprise, he launches into a baked bean can beatboxing extravaganza!

"Chicka bombom, chicka bombom
WAA!
Chicka bombom, chicka bombom
YO BOY!
Tikka tikka tikka tikka
Plum pudding, plum pudding,
Widdleewup widdleewup
YO YO YO.
I'm da man, in da can.
Oh, Frodo, where did you go-go?
Chikka chikka wakka wakka—"

"Hey, beat boy," says Pippa, waggling a ball of string. "Will this do for the intercom?"

Lost in beatboxing la-la land, spinning round and round, he responds in a deep, slow voice, "This is planet Earth. Is anyone out there?"

"Errrr, I'll take that as a yes."

Ollie loses balance and crashes into a mysterious covered object. "Hey, what's under this black plastic?"

"Please don't touch that!" says Archie, shaking his head and tensing his shoulders.

Unable to stop himself, Ollie removes the cover, revealing Archie's Pongo-Bongo bike, floodlit by sunlight streaming in through the window. Everyone shields their eyes as dazzling rainbows emanate from the iridescent Pongo-Bongo sticker.

"Whoaaa, nice set of wheels," exclaims Ollie. "So you got it for Christmas last year, you say? Hmmm, interesting choice. What did you say your mum was studying?"

"Renaissance history," says Archie in a monotone voice.

"Makes sense," continues Ollie. "She must have confused you with a court jester. Probably the odd socks and love of magic that did it. Well, it may not be a Supergoose like you wanted, but it has mudguards and a handy basket. Just think of all the things you could carry: chestnuts, blood plums, banana passionfruit. And no mud splats on your bottom!"

Pippa ruffles the sparkly streamers and glances at Archie's purple and orange odd socks. "Perhaps Ollie's right. It certainly matches your colourful socks, Archie."

"Yeah, fat lot of good that'll do me. I should've sold it before I bent the spokes doing stunt jumps. Some little kid would've loved it."

Pippa and Archie resume their search for treehouse items, rummaging through another box of junk.

Ding! Ding!

They look up to find Ollie sitting on the undersized bicycle, dressed in a spotty red-and-green party hat, ringing the bell. *Ding-aling-aling-aling*. "Hey, your Pongo-Bongo bike might be no good for stunts, but we could turn it into a pedal-powered blender. Just think, banana smoothies made with our own feet! Mmmmm."

"I think we found our court jester," says Pippa, raising her eyebrows and shaking her head.

"Yep. He's a joker all right."

Back at the lilly pilly tree, Russell bolts the last messmate pole to the trunk. “Right, that’s the foundations done. We’ve just gotta build the frame, lay the flooring, whack on a roof, and give it a lick of paint.”

The friends drop their building materials in a heap. Then with a *Whiz Bam Whackedy Woo-dah Slam* and a *Ping Pong Slippedy Sloppedy Dong,* the Lilly Pilly Treehouse is built.

Russell stands below the masterpiece, grinning. “Not bad if I don’t say so meself. That should keep you crazy possums out of trouble.”

WHOOSH. Dion hurls a spear at an unsuspecting oak tree, and it sticks into the trunk with a *THWOMP*. “Woohooo! Ooh, ooh, ooh!” He jumps for joy, thrusting both fists in the air. “Did anybody see that? Anyone?”

“Wouldn’t have missed it for quids,” says Russell, showing his respect with a cracking high-five and thudding chest bump.

While the older boys bask in bushcraft glory, Archie, Pippa and Ollie clamber up the wobbly makeshift rope ladder.

“Phew-weeee, strong paint fumes,” says Archie as he crawls into the treehouse.

Ollie pinches his nose and says in a funny chipmunk voice, “Smells like sweaty socks in an igloo.”

Pippa ties back the curtains, pushes open the window and inhales the fresh mountain air. “Ahhh, that’s better.”

“Hey, let’s test the intercom,” suggests Ollie. He grabs the empty baked bean cans and flicks out a puncturing tool on his Swiss Army Knife. “We just need to make a hole in the bottom of each tin. This should do the trick.” *Ping! Ping!* “There we go. Now thread the string through the holes like this . . . tie a quadruple knot . . . and berzinko! All systems are go, go, go. You two wait here while I run the string down the trunk.”

Crouched below the treehouse, Ollie pulls the string tight and speaks into his baked bean can. “Hello, hello, this is Beany-Boy at the tree base. Is anyone out there? Over.”

Like magic, the words vibrate up the string, into the can, through Archie’s ear canal and into his brain, which zaps a smile to his face. “This is Flying Fox in the treehouse. I read you loud and clear. I need a security clearance. What’s the password? Over.”

“Bottom honker forty-two. Over,” responds Ollie with glee.

“That’s a snippety snap. You’ve got clearance to continue, Beany-Boy.”

“Okey-dokey, what’s our mission, Flying Fox? Over.”

“Climb the chicken tree and retrieve the eggs. Over.”

“That’s a big ten-four-eo,” confirms Ollie. “I read you cloud and dear.”

Pippa grabs the can from Archie. “Breaker, breaker. Hey, Beany-Boy. This is Sugar Glider in the treehouse. That’s *loud* and *clear*, didn’t you know? Meet you and Flying Fox at the chicken tree tomorrow after the school bell goes ding-a-ling.”

Ollie belches into the can, *burrrrrrp*. “I read you *clown* and *spear*. Beany-Boy, over and snout. Oink.”

TEN

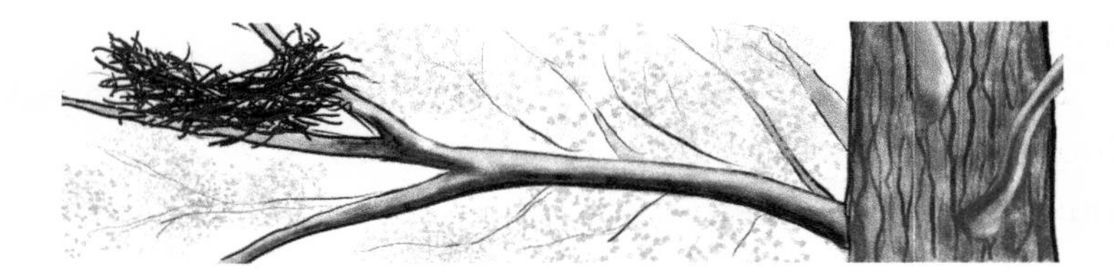

THE TREMENDOUS CHICKEN TREE

"Wow, that's high," says Pippa, gazing up the tall, broad trunk of the Californian redwood tree—the tremendous chicken tree.

"At least the branches are spaced nicely. It'll be like stepping up a giant ladder," says Archie.

Ollie points way above his head to the first branch. "Umm, one question. How do you suppose we get up there in the first place? A little high, don't you think?"

"Ah, that's a cinch," says Pippa. "All we have to do is run up the trunk, leap onto the branch and swing our legs over."

"Exactly. Easy-peasy," says Archie.

Ollie drags his palms down the smooth creviced bark and places one finger on his chin. "Hmm, easy for a flying fox or possum, perhaps. But without a strong tail or claws, we've got Buckley's chance of making it."

"We don't need a tail or claws," says Archie, walking backwards. "All we need is a long run-up so we can get enough speed. I've climbed heaps of trees like this one." About twenty paces from the trunk, he grabs a stick and scrapes a line in the dirt. "This can be the starting line."

"Okay," calls Pippa. "Ready, setty, go!"

The instant Archie takes off, he slips on a leaf and skids in the mud. Recovering quickly, he powers towards the tree and scuttles up the trunk. But his worn shoes have no grip, so he slides back down, arms and stomach scraping along the bark as he falls to the ground.

"Told you so," says Ollie, lending a hand. "On a positive note, that was the best tree-sliding, stomach-scraping, bottom-bruising extravaganza I've seen in months."

"Urgh," grunts Archie, poking his finger through a holey sole. "I've had it with these stupid shoes. They're useless!" He rips them off, swings them by the laces in a double loop-the-loop and hurls them onto the compost heap. Now free from the burden of slippery shoes, new confidence surges as Archie treads across the dirt and leaves back to the starting line for a second attempt.

Ollie blows a shrill umpire's whistle, *Trrreep-Trrreep*. "Your toes are over the line."

"Are you kidding me?"

"Rules are rules, my friend."

"Okay, okay," grumbles Archie. He inches back his toes and curls them into the earth in preparation for a fast start.

Trrreep. "Take your shark, get a pet, blow!"

Archie sprints across the yard, scampers up the trunk with his grippy gecko toes, and leaps into the air before grabbing the first branch with both hands.

"Keep going! You can do it!" shouts Pippa.

For every second that Archie dangles from the tree, aching pains grow in his arms, and his fingers burn as they cling tenuously to the bark. "I just need to reach the . . ." He kicks wildly, searching for a foothold in the trunk. All he finds is air. So using every skerrick of strength, he pulls up, shaking while rising, and swings both legs over the branch in relief.

"Amateur," mutters Ollie, rolling his eyes.

"Yay, great job, Archie. My turn now," says Pippa, skipping to the starting line.

Trrreep-Trrreep. This time Ollie whisks out a yellow paint-sample card from his parka and waves it above his head.

Pippa thrusts up her arms in protest. "Really? A warning? But my feet are behind the line. See."

"The bows of your shoes are too long. A tripping hazard, didn't you know?"

"You're so pernickety," she complains, fixing her laces.

Trrreep. "Take your position. Ready, confetti, crow!"

Sleek as a snow leopard, Pippa bolts across the yard, scoots up the trunk and reaches for Archie's outstretched arms. *Slap*. Their hands lock together.

"Whooaa," gasps Archie, losing balance, almost toppling head over heels.

Pippa curls up her knees and hooks them over the branch. "Let go, Archie, or I'll pull you down."

"Are you sure? I don't want you to fall."

"Yes, I do this all the time on the monkey bars."

"Okay, I'm here if you need me." The thought of letting go sends shivers down Archie's spine, for he's never swung from a tree by his knees and fears for Pippa's safety. But, worries aside, he backs her confidence and lets go . . . "Huh!"

In that heart-leaping moment, Pippa dangles down with the grace and skill that only comes through hours of practice on the monkey bars. Her plaits swish over her flushed cheeks as she swings back and forth, and back and forth. Then, using the momentum of a forward swing, she curls upwards and sits on the branch triumphant.

"Wow, that was unreal. You could be an Olympic gymnast," praises Archie.

Ollie calls out, "Not bad for a beginner. Didn't point your toes though. Lose a point for that."

Pippa pokes out her tongue. "All right, smarty-pants, show us what *you've* got."

"Just saying," says Ollie, redrawing the starting line. He pulls up his long white socks, ties his shoelaces into a triple knot, straightens his glasses, and gallops towards the tree.

DONK.

Having misjudged the angles, the goofball bounces off the trunk and lands on his bottom. "Ouch! That's it. I'm going home. I've had enough of this monkey business."

"Wait! Don't go. We need you," calls Archie, jumping back down. "How will we carry the eggs without your super-duper parka? I really need them to raise money for my new BMX. Once I have a good bike, we can race Puffing Billy to Emerald Lake. You want to race Puffing Billy, don't you?"

Ollie nods at quadruple speed.

"Of course you do. We all do. So how about Pippa and I help you climb to the first branch? Whaddaya say?"

A dreamy closed-mouth grin appears on Ollie's face as he imagines climbing down the branches in his egg-filled parka and riding through the forest in pursuit of Puffing Billy—a grand old steam train popular with kids and tourists. "Well, I suppose I could give it another go. But we better find eggs up there, because my services don't come *cheap, cheap, cheap!*"

Pippa calls down from the first branch, "You'd better take your mark. Time is money."

"Come on. You can do it, big fella," spurs Archie, standing beside the trunk.

In preparation for take-off, Ollie blows on his hands, jogs

briskly on the spot, shakes out each leg, touches his toes, and nods to Pippa.

"On your mark, get spaghetti, go!"

Off he sets, in the springy, loping style of a pole-vaulter. And in the ridiculous, bumbling style of a clown, he runs a few steps up the trunk, clambers awkwardly onto Archie's shoulders and reaches for Pippa's hands.

"Gotcha," she says, gripping his wrists.

"One, two, three, PULL!" shouts Archie.

Pippa pulls, Archie pushes, and Ollie stomps all over Archie's head. Finally, after one almighty push-and-a-pull, Ollie flops his legs over the branch and hugs the trunk.

"Whoopee," cheers Pippa. "You made it!"

ELEVEN

ALL THE WAY TO THE TOP

As the friends prepare for their epic climb up the tremendous chicken tree, Ollie peers down at seven hens loitering around the tree base. "What are those chooks up to?"

Suddenly two hens launch off the ground, followed by another and another and another, stirring up a mini tornado as they flutter to the high branches.

Yellow light from the afternoon sun floods Archie's face. "They must be roosting for the night."

An hourly chime sounds from Ollie's digital watch. "It's five o'clock. *We'll* be roosting for the night if we don't get moving."

"You're right. We better start climbing," says Archie. He grabs the branch above his head—*SNAP*.

The brittle limb breaks midway and plunges to the ground, cracking on a rock below. "Far out, brussel sprout. That was a dead one. Be careful, you two."

Pippa tugs on another branch, checking that it's alive. "This one feels solid."

"Wait," says Ollie. "Don't forget to check for slippery moss. Moss can be lethal stuff when you're seventy metres up a tree."

Archie leans closer to the others. "And remember, we're in the chicken tree, and where there's chickens there's—"

"POOO!" screams Pippa, pointing to the sky. "Watch out!"

A sloppy blob of chicken poo plummets towards their heads, narrowly missing Ollie's left ear before splatting on the branch beside Pippa. "Eeew, yuck!"

Worried about a second poo attack, Ollie hunts through his parka for a defence system.

"Incoming!" shrieks Archie as a barrage of six white blobs fall from above, on target for a head-splattering, nose-whacking stink up.

Nanoseconds before impact, amid panicky screams and squeals, Ollie whips out the rainbow pocket umbrella from his parka and clicks it open—*THWOOF*.

The poo strikes with a *Dwoppa Ploppa Thwatta Dacka Splatter*.

"Oh my gosh, that was close. Your rainbow force field saved us," praises Pippa.

"Didn't I say we needed you?" says Archie.

Smiling proudly, Ollie whips out a pocket-sized packet of tissues and wipes the umbrella. "Be prepared for anything at all times, that's my motto."

While Ollie returns the clean umbrella to his parka, Archie peers skyward. "I bet those chickens have more surprises for us. We're sitting ducks here. Let's get moving."

The kids continue climbing the branches, carefully avoiding dead or weak ones. Before long, the ground fades to a distant memory, and the magical world of the redwood emerges—tree boughs spanning out like giant octopus arms, shimmering green carpets of needly leaves, and whispering wind whirling all around.

"This is the most beautiful place in the world," says Pippa, gazing out over the sparkling branches.

Excited to see and rushing to climb up to her level, Ollie slips on a patch of moss. "Whoops. It's stunning all right. But looks can be deceiving. One false move and you're as dead as a door snail."

"As dead as a *doornail,*" corrects Pippa.

"Nope, can't kill a nail. But a *snail* jammed in a door, that's another story."

"Hey, I see a chicken," whispers Archie. "I'll climb up and see if she's hiding any eggs."

Ollie straddles a branch equipped with bendy twigs for levers and knobbly bumps for buttons, which to a fertile mind is, in fact, an intergalactic spaceship. "You go ahead. I'm going to fly this baby through an asteroid belt and head down a wormhole to visit myself in a parallel universe."

Further up the tree, Archie creeps closer to the hen perched in an oval hollow. "Don't be scared. Good little chicken, chick-chick-chick. You hiding any eggs up here?" He slowly extends an arm to search under her belly. The frightened bird squawks hysterically and flutters to another branch.

Archie glances at the tree hollow, expecting to see at least one gleaming white egg. But all he finds are three downy feathers and a few dry leaves. "What? That can't be right." Disappointed, he calls to the others, "False alarm. There's no eggs here. Let's keep climbing."

The friends step higher and higher up the tremendous chicken tree, inspecting one perch after another, discovering that each one is eggless.

"Look! There's a nest!" says Pippa, pointing to a bundle of dry twigs wedged in the outer fork of a long tree bough.

To see better, Archie skedaddles up to the branch. "You're right. It's definitely a nest. The perfect size for a chicken. I'm gonna check it out."

Before Pippa and Ollie have time to respond, Archie wraps his arms, legs and feet around the bough and caterpillars across to the nest.

Pippa calls out, "It's too dangerous. Come back!"

"You're a fooligan. A fooligan!" bellows Ollie.

Halfway along the narrowing branch, Archie whispers, "I've gotta get the eggs. I'm nearly there. I can make it."

But then a wild wind hits, roaring through the canopy, swaying the branch to the left and back to the right, and up, down and all around in a giddy rocking motion.

Swamped by nausea and the world spinning, Archie grips the branch for dear life. Unable to move, unable to speak, his cheek presses against the soft moss. A small piece dislodges and spirals down, drifting on the wind currents, sparkling in the sunlight before vanishing into the abyss below.

Once the wind passes and calm returns, the egg-obsessed kid regains his confidence and continues caterpillaring along until reaching the nest. "It's massive. I reckon it's made by a chicken for sure." As he wriggles closer, the branch creaks and bows, forming a treacherous mossy slide.

"Eeeeeeeeek," screams Pippa, aware that one false move and he'll plunge fifty metres to the ground. "Leave the eggs! It's not worth the risk!"

Ollie covers his eyes. "I can't look. He's gone completely bonkers."

Remaining coolheaded, Archie secures himself on a side branch and calls out, "I'm okay. Nearly there." Desperate to discover what's in the nest, he stretches tall and peeks inside. And there he finds, snuggled in a soft bed of leaves and grass, five speckly blue eggs. "I've found eggs. Definitely not from a chicken though. I think they're—"

Clack-Clack!

A swooping magpie pecks Archie's scalp, drawing blood. "Ouch!"

The bird circles around for a second attack and swoops down, hovering in the air, beating its wings around Archie's face and head. Claws flash. Feathers thrash. Fierce squawks and beak clacks distort in his ears.

Rah RAH

Clack-Clack!

Swish-Clack-Whoosh.

"Help, I'm being swooped! Arrggghhh!"

"Hang on, Archie! We'll distract it while you climb back," shouts Pippa.

"Keep your head down or you'll lose an eye!" adds Ollie, who, thinking quickly, rips off his parka and waves it around as if trying to insight a bull in a bullfight.

On cue, the magpie glimpses the bright red fabric and sets a new course.

"Over here, maggy, maggy, maggy," calls Ollie, whose eyes bulge when he realises his stunt has worked a little too well. "Uh-oh. We're in trouble. Maggy attack at twelve o'clock." He clambers for the umbrella. "Quick, hide my parka while I open the force field."

In a chaotic flurry, Pippa shoves the parka under her jacket and Ollie clicks the umbrella's latch. "Doh! It's jammed. Come on, open, you rascal!"

At the same time, Archie scrambles along the branch above, anxious to reach the trunk.

Rah! Rah! Rah! screeches the magpie, a virtual heat-seeking, beak-snapping missile.

"Hold on tight. We're gonna take a hit," hollers Ollie, ducking in anticipation of a magpie peck.

Pippa plucks a bobby pin from her hair and presses it into the umbrella's latch—*Ping-THWOOOFF.* The force field bursts open, and they hide underneath, eyes squeezed shut, bracing for impact.

BOMP!

The magpie bounces off the springy rainbow fabric and swoops back around to dive bomb Archie, still halfway along the wobbly tree limb, caterpillaring at top speed.

Rah-Rah! Clack-Clack-Clack!

"Argh, get away!" he shrieks, waving one arm wildly.

However, being a male magpie with eggs to defend, nothing deters him, nothing except—

Kah! Kaah! KAH! KAAH! A mighty crow flashes through the tree canopy, swooshing its broad shiny wings.

The birds collide mid-air, locking talons as they plunge in a topsy-turvy free fall—screeching, pecking and thrashing their tangled wings.

Archie scrambles to the trunk and clings on tight. "Phew, that was freaky. I nearly lost an eye."

The crow rockets up through the leaves and branches, chasing the magpie into the open sky. They arc in opposite directions. The fight is over.

Moments later, the magpie's partner returns to the nest and fixes a few loose twigs with strands of grass. Then she sits on the eggs and sings a beautiful flutey song.

"Mmm, magpie eggs for breakfast. Yummy," jokes Ollie.

"Well, I did say we'd find eggs," says Archie.

"Yes, but I don't think free-range magpie eggs will sell all that well at the Kallista market, my friend."

Archie slumps his shoulders. "Where are those chickens hiding their eggs?"

"Chin up. Look on the bright side," says Pippa. "At least the magpie eggs are safe from all that drama. Speaking of drama. Hold on, everyone!"

The kids wrap their arms and legs around the trunk as another wind gust roars through the branches.

High above, the needly leaves whir up and down in musical tones. Ollie peers up. "I suppose we might as well see what's at the top. You never know, there might be a goose sitting on a nest of golden eggs."

Up, up, they go, climbing branch after branch to the top of the tree, where they cling to the bendy tip, swaying around and around and around. In the valley below, a sea of greens, reds and yellows cross-fades to a smoky blue haze over the distant Warburton Mountains.

"This is amazing. What a view," gasps Pippa.

"This is insane. I'm going to spew," moans Ollie.

Archie sings out, "Cooooo-wee!"

The crow returns, gliding on air currents above the valley, its broad wings glowing orange from the setting sun.

Archie turns to Pippa. "Do you think it's Banjo?"

"Anything's possible."

"Umm, if I'm not mistaken, that's a crow, not a twangy banjo," states Ollie.

"No, Ollie, ya goof," says Archie. "Banjo's a grown man. He's a friend of ours you haven't met yet. He always says: 'When you see a crow, you know it's Banjo, come to help out'."

"Well, the crow sure helped us today," says Pippa. "Hey, Archie, perhaps Banjo can help us find the missing eggs."

"Of course. We should've thought of that before. He knows everything about animals. Mum said he's staying with Fergus for a while. How about you two sleep at my house tonight? We can walk to Fergus's in the morning to visit Banjo."

Pippa and Ollie grin from ear to ear, for they love nothing more than sleepovers and adventures.

High in the sky, circling above their heads, the crow calls, *arrh, arrrrh, arrrrrrh.*

TWELVE

FAIRYLAND

The following morning, on their way to see Banjo, the friends skip down the hill, laughing and dreaming as they pass bright orange montbretia flowers growing wild along the roadside.

"Hey, let's make flower rockets," says Archie. He clasps a bunch of the sword-shaped leaves and tugs hard, unearthing a cluster of bulbs attached at the bottom. "Check this out." Holding the leafy end, he swings the plant back and forth and whisks it into the air. As the bulbous head rockets skyward, the strappy leaves and fiery orange flowers whip behind.

At the peak of its climb, the bulbs turn, and the montbretia plummets back down—swiftly, smoothly and ever so delightfully, crashing to the ground with a *thwack*.

"How about we take a shortcut through Fairyland?" says Archie, rushing to rip out another plant rocket.

Pippa stumbles backwards, nearly falling onto her bottom as she uproots some weighty bulbs. "Yes, I love Fairyland in the springtime." She blasts the montbretia high above the power lines. Everyone watches intently as the returning bulbs smash onto the road, scattering helter-skelter.

"No, no, no, that's not how you do it," says Ollie. "This is how it's done." Using both hands, he hurls a clump of ten or more plants to the treetops, and with little consideration for their flight path, responds to Archie's earlier suggestion. "Good idea. If we cut through Fairyland, we can check out the banana passionfruit along the way."

Meanwhile, Ollie's skyrocketing flowers, having reached their peak, split apart and shower down over the kids' heads.

"Eeeeeeek! Scatter bombs!" screams Pippa.

"Whooaahharrggghh!" holler Ollie and Archie.

Ruff ruff ruff ruff, barks Kimba.

Everyone skedaddles down a gravel lane, leaving the bulbs crashing to the road behind them.

"You're crazy," says Pippa, flicking a montbretia leaf across Ollie's leg.

He squashes a bulb between two fingers and flicks it over one shoulder. "They're noxious weeds, you know. Best to pull them out by the bunch."

A short while later, the light fades to a dappled pink as they wander through a corridor of cherry blossom. The delicate petals hide the sky and hum with bees collecting pollen. Along the lane edges, tiny red berries poke out from under a carpet of dark green creeping leaves.

"Wild strawberries!" exclaims Pippa. She dives onto her hands and knees and pops a berry into her mouth. "Yummm. Look. There's heaps more."

Ollie scrabbles madly through the leaves. "Bingo! I found a whopper." After presenting the pea-sized strawberry to the others, he squishes it on his tongue. "Mmmm, tastes like water with a hint of citrus, a note of blackberry, a touch of dirt and a mild sweetness. Not bad, not bad at all." He searches for more. "Ooh, I've found another whopper. There's hundreds of them!"

While Ollie gorges on the berries, Archie observes, out of curiosity, an overhanging branch, noting hundreds of tiny dew-kissed leaves emerging from their winter slumber. "Hey, the trees are sprouting. Won't be long till chestnut season."

"Well it better be a bumper crop," says Pippa, "because if your eggs don't turn up, selling chestnuts is your last hope of getting a new bike. You realise that, don't you?"

"Yeah, I know." Thoughts drifting, Archie imagines finding the eggs in the forest and filling a pack with golden chestnuts.

"Yes, well, we could all do with a bumper crop," adds Ollie. "What are you saving up for, Pippa?"

She curls both hands into a tube and peers to the sky. "I'm saving for a telescope so I can study the stars and the moon. What about you?"

"I'm saving for a computer so I can program it to play a little tune."

"You're so funny," giggles Pippa. And without warning, she dashes down the lane. "Race you to Fairyland!"

Strawberry juice spurts from Ollie's mouth as he makes chase. "Come back! You cheated!"

Kimba bolts in the opposite direction, having spotted his favourite playmate, the white poodle.

Still dreaming about chestnuts, Archie finds himself alone, standing among the strawberries in the dappled cherry blossom shade. "Hey, wait for me!"

At the end of the lane, where the sky beams blue, the friends run onto a sunlit grassy hill punctuated by bright yellow dandelion flowers and white puffball seedheads (known to the kids as fairies). On the high side, sloping flowerbeds dazzle with daisies, marigolds, geraniums and lavender—and a banana passionfruit vine creeps over a tall wire fence. On the meadow's lower far edge, hugged by wispy rising mist, stands a tranquil forest of mountain ash trees, lush ferns and undiscovered mysteries. This is the place they call Fairyland.

"Yippee," squeals Pippa, diving belly-first onto a bed of golden marigold flowers.

"Thunderbobble," booms Ollie, landing in a clump of red geraniums.

"Make room for me!" calls Archie, flopping onto a patch of white daisies.

The friends roll over—sweaty, red-faced and puffing. They gaze up at the banana passionfruit vine covered in pink star-shaped flowers and long green fruit dangling down like fat sausages among the leaves.

"Mmm, won't be long till they're ripe," says Ollie.

Pippa glances around. "Where's Kimba?"

"He's run off chasing that white poodle again," says Archie. "He knows his way around here. He'll find his way home."

A bubble rises in Ollie's tummy, owing to an excessive intake of wild strawberries. "Hey, Archie, I've got a secret to tell you." He leans closer and rips out a meaty burp, *Burrrrrop.*

"Oi!" complains Archie, squirming.

Pippa sits up in disgust, holding her nose while fanning away the fermented strawberry smell. "Let's go, you goofballs. I want to pick some fairies and make a wish."

As Ollie tumbles onto the grass, a tiny field mouse scoots between his feet. The surprised lad dances on the spot in a squealing panic—*"Hoohoheeheho!"*—fearing it might scuttle up his wide cuffed pants.

"Aww, the poor thing's scared," says Pippa.

"Ollie or the mouse?" giggles Archie.

The animal scurries down the meadow, zigzagging around dandelion flowers and fairy puffballs until finally it escapes into the forest.

Pippa picks a blazing-yellow dandelion flower and drifts it up and over her head. “This is the sun rising and setting.” She picks a puffball by the stem and raises it to her lips. “This is the moon rising.” She blows hard, launching a constellation of fairy seeds into the sky. “And these are the shooting stars.” She closes her eyes and makes a secret wish.

Eager for a turn, Archie plucks a fairy and holds it close to his face. The fluffy white sphere wiggles in the breeze, tickling his nose. Then in one big puff, he blows it to smithereens. While the seeds float all around, he closes his eyes and whispers to himself, *Please keep Kimba safe*.

Inspired by the theatrical performances and keen to show off, Ollie grabs a fistful of the puffballs and blows like a crazed buffoon. Zillions of fluffy seeds explode into the air and drift into Pippa’s hair. “Wooowooo. A snowstorm!”

“Quick, Ollie, you’ve got to make a secret wish before the fairies fly away,” insists Pippa.

“Yes, yes, I’m doing it now.” A peaceful grin appears as he makes a wish.

For a moment, Fairyland is silent.

And then, far off in the distance, deep within the forest, comes a series of exotic birdcalls:

Queeee-yah, queeeee-yah
(a wailing yellow-tailed black cockatoo)
Warble-ow-warble-ee-warble
(a flutey magpie)
Kookoo-kookoo-ca-ca-ca-ca
(a laughing kookaburra)

Clee-a clee-a clee-o
(a lonely currawong)
Screech-screech
(a zippy crimson rosella)
Weeeeeee-whip! Choo-Choo
(two whipbirds)
Doodle-oot-doo, doodle-oot-doo wee-woo
(a tooting butcherbird).

Then comes a metallic hammering noise:

Ping
Ping
Ping
Ping

"Ahh, yes, that would be the metal pole-pinging warbler. An extremely rare bird. Haven't seen one in donkey's ears," comments Ollie.

"Years," corrects Pippa, shaking her head.

A chainsaw sound bellows from the forest, *Rouwwrrrowww.*

"And I suppose that's the mating call of the endangered blue-billed chainsaw warbler?" adds Pippa sarcastically.

"No," says Ollie, "I'd say that's the mating call of a spotted chainsaw wren. Strange. Not normally found this far south."

Archie tunes in to another birdsong, searching his mind for answers . . .

Cheep-chupwup-wup, cheep-chupwup-cheep.

"Yes, I've got it! You know Old Bill who runs the animal sanctuary, up the mountain, near the forest?"

Pippa and Ollie nod.

"When I was visiting him with Mum, he went into the garden and whistled that same chirpy tune. Then a lyrebird came out of the bushes and walked right up to him for a pat. It was amazing."

"Oh my gosh, you're right," says Pippa. "It must be a lyrebird. They can copy any birdcall. But I never knew they made chainsaw sounds. Weird."

"How about we sneak into the forest for a look," suggests Ollie. "Maybe it's doing the famous lyrebird dance."

"Oh, yes. I've always wanted to see a lyrebird dancing," says Pippa.

Archie heads for the forest. "Come on. We can follow the sounds."

THIRTEEN

BURPA-TWERPA

The friends slide down a bank and descend into the cool, moist gully. At the lowest point, where only glints of sunlight reach the ground, a shallow trickling stream twists its way through tall tree ferns and rocks coated in velvety moss. Under the canopy of unfurling fronds, they skip over the water and hop from rock to rock across a mud patch, where they stop and listen for the lyrebird calls.

Weeeeee-whip! Cheep-chupwup-wup, cheep-chupwup-cheep.

Pippa points at a screen of fern fronds and whispers, "Shhh, this way."

They continue in a slow crawl, pressing their hands and knees gently on the fungusy forest floor to avoid stick cracks or leaf crunches that will scare the lyrebird away.

Goosebumps sprinkle over Pippa's arms from the cold gully air. She pauses behind the ferns and parts two fronds, revealing a scratched earth clearing and a dirt mound.

Everyone freezes in excitement and awe as the brown male lyrebird, about the size of a rooster, springs onto the mound and prances about, stomping, twirling, hopping and wiggling. Keen to impress a nearby female, the dainty fellow raises two long stripy feathers over his head and fans out a bedazzling lacy white tail that vibrates, flicks, and shimmers as he sings.

Kookoo-kookoo-ca-ca-ca-ca
Clee-a clee-a clee-o
Weeeee-whip! Choo Choo
Doodle-oot-do doodle-oot-doo
Queeee-yah, queeeee-yah
Cheep-chupwup-wup, cheep-chupwup-cheep
Tsuu, Tsuu, Tsuu, Tsuu
Rouwww, Rouwww
Ping Ping Ping Ping . . .

A strawberry bubble floats up from Ollie's tummy, and he discharges an earth-shuddering burp, *BOOOORRUURRRRPP.*

Spooked by the noise, the lyrebirds dash down a fallen tree trunk, calling in alarm as they flee. *Whisssk! Whisssk! Whisssk!*

Pippa thrusts her hands to her hips. "Oh, Ollie! You scared them, you burpa-twerpa."

"No time to talk. Chase those birds!" Without thinking, the excitable lad runs along the trunk. But the surface is so wet and slimy he slips over and rockets down the smooth trunk on his belly. "Whooooaaaa." With no way to brake, he flings off the end and crashes into a metal pole—*CLANG.*

Hearts thumping for fear of their friend's safety, Archie and Pippa slide down the log on their bottoms.

"Are you okay? Are you hurt?" says Pippa, crouched by Ollie's side. She inspects a red lump on his forehead.

"Yes, I'm fine. It's just a flesh wound. I must say, that's a funny place for a pole. Look, there's a whole row of them."

"I wonder what they're for," says Archie. He thumps one with his palm. "Gee, they're pretty solid too."

Pippa jumps onto a freshly cut tree stump and trickles sawdust through her fingers. "This is terrible. Who would cut down trees at Fairyland?"

While everyone searches for clues, a crow swoops down from the sky and lands on a pole, observing the kids for a moment before flapping away.

"Banjo," says Archie under his breath. "Let's keep moving. We have to talk to Banjo about the missing eggs. He might know what's going on at Fairyland too."

FOURTEEN

THE SECRET TUNNEL

Back at the Fairyland shortcut, Ollie, Pippa and Archie gaze up at a mass of mountain wiregrass, resembling a supersized ball of green wool, covering the forest and blocking the way to Fergus's place.

Ollie whacks the grass several times with a stick. "We'll never get through this mess without a machete or a bulldozer."

"There must be a way around, or we can try climbing over," says Archie, leaping onto the mound. To his surprise, the wiregrass snares him with its sticky foliage. "Ermm, can someone help me get down, please?"

"Never fear, Ollie is here!" *Swish.* He accidentally pulls Archie's pants down.

"Oi!" yells Archie, scrambling to pull them back up.

While Ollie drags him down by the ankles, Pippa pokes her head into a small opening at the base of the mound. "Hey, I've found a secret path." She gazes down a grass tunnel that vanishes deep into the forest. The perfectly round walls glow bottle-green near the entrance, fading to black as it snakes off into the distance.

Archie gazes inside. “Wow, this is amazing.”

Ollie pops his head in and grins. “Hoopidy-doopidy, this is what I call a shortcut.”

“Could be a wallaby track,” says Archie. “With any luck, it might take us down the hill, near Fergus’s place. The grass is pretty dense though. We won’t be able to see our way if it gets any thicker.”

“And we’ll need better light to watch out for snakes. Urrgh, I hate snakes,” shudders Pippa.

Ollie reaches into a deep parka pocket and whisks out an animal head torch buried in a spaghetti mess of straps. “Voila!” After sorting out the tangly-wangly elastic, he slides it over his head. “Better test the batteries.” *Click*. Two bright lights shine from the eyes of a cute koala. “What do you think? It’s even got an emergency beacon.”

Archie pats him on the back. “Brilliant. You and your parka never cease to amaze me. Lead the way, Mr Koala. You can be our headlights when we need them.”

The friends vanish down the wiregrass tube, crawling on hands and knees. The further they go, the thicker the grass walls become, so thick the wind and birds soften to a muted song. Although the air is still, it billows with the smells of adventure—sweet, minty, earthy.

“So why’s Banjo staying at Fergus’s place?” asks Ollie, ducking under a twisty vine.

“I’m not really sure,” says Archie. “I know he travelled here all the way from the top of Australia, from the Kimberley, where there’s crocodiles and wild camels. That’s where he grew up, eating bush tucker and learning all about the land and animals. Mum said he’s got a wandering spirit and goes wherever help’s needed.”

“Oh, I get it now,” says Ollie, veering around a tree root.

"He must've known you needed him to find the chook eggs. Makes sense, I suppose."

"Well, he does love chickens," says Pippa.

"Especially in Mum's chicken soup," jokes Archie, giggling.

Now deep within the wiregrass tunnel, almost in complete darkness, Ollie pauses at a fork in the track. He clicks on the koala head torch and flashes the light down both tunnels. "It seems we have a choice to make. Pity those wallabies didn't leave a sign of some kind. Never mind. I've got a backup strategy." In a spritely singsong voice, he recites a catchy poem, pointing left and right as he goes:

"Creamy beany in my soup,
Stir it well, it turns to gloop.
Eat it with a silver spoon,
Then you'll blast off to the moon!"

"The rhyme never lies. We're heading right, comrades."

"Wait a sec. There is a sign." Pippa points to a pile of green dung at the left tunnel entrance.

"Could be from a wallaby or an echidna," says Archie.

Ollie pokes the dung with a twig, attempting to roll a single blob down the hill. However, being flat on all sides, similar to a dice, it doesn't roll an inch. "Ahhh, just as I thought. Scientifically speaking, if the dung is green and doesn't roll, it's from a wombat. You see, wombats have square bottoms designed to create square dung that won't roll down their burrows. Ingenious, don't you think?"

"Yeah, but where do you learn this stuff?" asks Archie, amazed by Ollie's expertise in dung trivia.

"Books, my friend, books. I've got a whole series on animal dung. You can borrow them if you like."

"Errr, thanks. Maybe some other time. I'm busy reading about Houdini at the moment."

"No worries. The offer's always open. Right then, left it is. The wombats will be asleep in their burrows, so we should have a clear run down to the road."

Led by the glowing eyes of Ollie's koala torch, the friends take the left tunnel. As it descends the hill, the grass walls cocoon around them. By wriggling along on their tummies, they squeeze through into a wider section, where the path travels between a miniature forest of red-and-white spotted toadstools and translucent pink mushrooms sprouting from logs. Further along, the tunnel continues down the hill, steeper than before. At one point, a massive tree trunk, hollowed right through, creates another tunnel. Ollie enters first, followed by the others. He shines the light around. Everyone gasps, their attention seized by the wonder of hardened tree sap stalactiting down the walls in sparkling ruby-red shards.

They snap off a few pieces and continue on, exiting the hollow and descending a steep rocky section before arriving at a dirt mound outside a large hole in the ground.

Ollie directs the beaming koala eyes down the hole. "Last stop, everyone. We've reached wombat headquarters." He leans over the opening. "It's a long tunnel, that's for sure. Probably three metres deep. Who knows how far it goes? Those wombats are better diggers than a bulldozer."

Archie crawls around the burrow to see if the grass tunnel continues. But the path, rarely used by the wombats, is overgrown by spiralling blackberry canes, the thorns creating an impenetrable barrier. "There's no way we're getting through here. Hey, why don't we use the wombat burrow as a shortcut instead? We've got your torch to see. And if it leads to the road, it'll save us backtracking up through Fairyland."

Ollie shakes his head in horror. "Oh, no, no. I've heard that an angry wombat can crush a person's skull. And they don't like intruders. My cousin crawled down a wombat burrow once and nearly didn't make it out alive. The furry maniac pinned him against the dirt wall with its bottom for a whole hour. They're boofy bullies, those wombats."

"S'pose you're right," says Archie. "I remember when I was little, Josephine read me a book about a wombat that bashed down a door to eat a bunch of carrots. With heads like that, I wouldn't want to meet one down a burrow."

In the brief pause that follows, little thudding sounds echo from the hole.

Ollie's left eye twitches, and he slowly crawls backwards.

Pippa pokes her head through the top of the wiregrass. "Hey, guys, I can see the road at the bottom of the hill. And there's a massive fallen tree that'll take us all the way down."

"Uh-oh. We've got company," says Ollie, his lips quivering as two glowing eyes appear in the burrow, followed by a series of grunts and growls.

Easily mistaken for a cuddly teddy bear, the male wombat—a pudgy barrel of brown fur, with stubby legs, a round head, cute small eyes, a black button nose and little pointy ears—charges at the intruding kids, screaming in a frenzy, *HAAAA-AAARRRRH!*

Nowhere to run, nowhere to hide, Ollie whips out a jagged shard of tree sap and brandishes it about. But as it swishes from side to side, the brittle material crumbles to pieces, leaving a useless blob. "Errr. Not a problem. Don't panic!" I'm switching to the emergency beacon!"

As he fumbles for the switch on his koala torch, Pippa swings herself up onto the fallen tree and reaches down for the others. "Quick! Climb up here!"

Suddenly the emergency beacon engages, and the Koala's eyes flash electric red, enraging the wombat even more than before. Now a strobing ball of anger, the screeching wombat headbutts the boys' bottoms as they crawl for their lives.

"Arrrrrggghhh! Killer wombat!" they scream, circling round and round the burrow in a crazy crawlathon.

"Turn off the beacon! Turn it off!" shrieks Archie.

While continuing his frantic crawl, Ollie slaps at his head with one hand, hoping to find the right button. Then, just as the raging ball of fur is about to bowl him over, he swivels around on both knees and powers on the supercharged, one thousand lumens high beam light.

Startled by the blazing koala eyes, the wombat thunders back into its burrow.

Meanwhile, the boys scramble up through the tunnel roof, and together with Pippa, skedaddle down the fallen tree in single file, squealing and shouting. At the bottom of the hill, they jump onto the gravel road, relieved to be back on familiar ground, thrilled the shortcut was a success.

As they continue up the road, retelling the story of the crazed wombat, Archie points into the distance. "Hey, there's Fergus's jeep. We're nearly there."

FIFTEEN

FERGUS'S PLACE

"Woohoo!" The excited kids bound past Fergus's army jeep and skip through his eye-popping garden entrance—the mouth of a giant lizard. The impressive sculpture, carved by Fergus from a ginormous fallen tree, stands as a reminder to everyone who visits: be prepared for crazy fun!

"Let's check out the rocket," says Archie, darting up a path. He whizzes around a boulder stack, piled as high as a house, and dashes past red waratah flowers and grass trees topped with long needly leaves and spectacular flower spikes shooting high into the sky.

Pippa runs her fingers across a clay lyrebird sculpture nestled amongst ferns and mossy rocks. She glances up and giggles in wonder at a family of shop mannequins doing the splits and handstands on top of the boulder stacks.

Lost in a maze of funhouse mirrors, Ollie faces off with a bizarre alien creature. More goofy than scary, it has a cone-shaped head that stretches up like thick slime. And its mouth is enormous, so big you'd think it might pop. The neck is short, but the belly is round and bloated, attached to little stumpy legs that can't stop wiggling and jiggling. "Hey, look at me! I'm an alien! So funny, *hehe-heee.* This place is insane!" In search of more fun, Ollie scoots around the bend and bumps into a skeleton wearing a black bowler hat and bow tie. "Oh. Hello, Mr Nobody. *Hehehehe.*"

"Up here!" shouts Archie, waving frantically from the open window of a towering silver rocket. "Check out the new flying fox." He points to a bicycle handlebar and pulley attached to a zipline that extends from the rocket all the way across the garden. "Climb up. There's a ladder inside the rocket."

Archie fastens a helmet, grips the flying fox handle and leaps off the wooden launch pad.

Whizzzzzzzzzzzzzzzzzzzzzzzzz

"Wahoooo!" he cheers, legs dangling as he speeds past a chicken coop, four heritage pigs and a fishpond.

Whizzzzzzzzzzzzzzzzzzzzzip-BOOMFF.

The flying fox crashes against two bouncy tyres at the end of the cable. Archie jumps into a sandpit and races back to the launch pad, dragging the handle via a long rope, shouting gleefully, "It's awesome!"

Next, Pippa whizzes down.

Whizzzzzzzzzzzzzzzzzzzzzzzzz

Waratahs and banksias whoosh by in a blur. "Wheeeeeeee!" She zips over the pigpen, raising her feet to avoid a mud bath and a trough of food slops.

Whizzzzzzzzzzzzzzzzzzzzzip-BOOMFF.

"Whoopee, it's so much fun!"

Ollie tightens his helmet straps while Pippa rushes back to the rocket. Then, in a moment of insanity, he sprints across the launch pad and lunges for the bicycle handlebar. Unfortunately, owing to a patch of mildew on the decking, he slips at the last moment and grabs the handle at a rather awkward angle.

"Arrrhoooaaahh!" The garden spins in a topsy-turvy muddle as he whooshes out of control past the grass-tree spikes and the chicken coop.

Z
Z
Z
E
E
E
e
e
e
z
z
z
Z
Z
Z
Z
e
e
e
E
Z
Z
Z
Z

"Whoooarrgghh, Mayday, Mayday!" Unable to hold on, he flies through the air, arms and legs spread wide, and splash lands in the squishy food slops. "Woohoo, let's go again!" he yells. "Oh, hello, piggy. What-you-doing? No, no, don't lick my face! *Hehehe-hahaha*."

After everyone's had several turns of the zipline, they race onto a footbridge and peer down at the pond. The water's glassy surface reflects their inquisitive faces and the clouds above. Disturbed by the children's gaze, an orange fish swishes around a frog fountain and a yellow fish darts under a lily pad, stirring up a school of tadpoles that skitter to safety under floating duckweed. On the far side, near a cluster of reeds and pink lily flowers, a turtle pokes its head above the water, takes a breath and submerges under a blob of sparkling jelly-coated frogs' eggs.

"Hmm, I wonder what this does," says Ollie, who, acting before thinking, turns a chrome metal dial attached to the bridge. Bubbles rise from the pond. Seconds later, water gently cascades from the frog's mouth—a jolly green fellow dressed in a suit and top hat. "Funny frog, *heee-heee*." Curious about the frog's spurting potential, he turns the dial around and around and around and around, stopping only when the bridge begins to shudder and groan. "Uh-oh."

SWISSSSSSSSSHHHHHHH.

All chaos breaks loose as water explodes from the frog's mouth. It shoots up to the treetops, higher than the rocket in a spectacular display. Rainbows glisten in the sky as water rains down on Pippa and Archie, soaking their hair and clothes.

"Turn the fountain off, Ollie. Turn it off!" they shout, laughing and squealing as chills ripple down their spines.

"Oh, all right, spoil the fun." Ollie swivels the chrome dial back the other way.

Once calm returns, the sound of a strumming guitar drifts over to the pond.

Pippa points to Fergus's wacky house. "Hey, there's Banjo!"

SIXTEEN

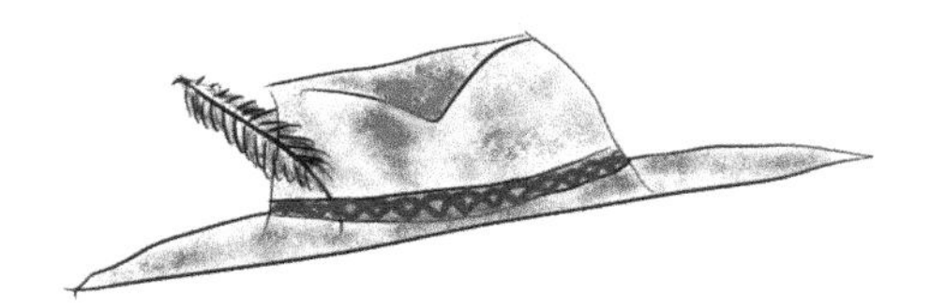

BANJO

"Banjo, Banjo!" call Archie and Pippa, bounding up the stairs to a curved wooden deck.

Seated in a wicker armchair, Banjo leans forward, tilts back his leather bushman's hat and greets them with a beaming smile. "Hey, kids! What you been up to?"

Archie wrings out his soaked T-shirt.

Ollie scrapes pig slops off his cheek.

And Pippa wraps her wet, seed-coated hair into a topknot.

"Little bit of mischief by the look o' things," says Banjo, gazing up and down at the ragamuffin kids.

Glancing up innocently, Archie replies, "Oh, no, we haven't been up to any kind of mischief. But we have been trying to solve mysteries."

"By the way, this is our good friend Ollie," says Pippa. "He doesn't always have an egg on his head, but he is an egghead."

"That's a nasty bump you got, young fella. You run into a wombat or somethin'? Tough heads those wombats."

"No, we escaped the wombat. But I did bang into a pole-pinging warbler."

"*Hee-hee,*" laughs Banjo. "Never heard of that bird. But I got just the thing for that egg on ya head." He stands up, tucks his shirt into his trousers and moseys down to the garden. Crouched below a flowering bottlebrush tree, Banjo searches through the weeds. "Ah, this is what I'm lookin' for." His fingers brush over the ribbed green leaves of a native plantain. Taking care to preserve the root, he picks a rosette and presses it between his palms until a squishy paste forms. "Here you go, fella, rub this on. Good bush medicine, this one. It'll help that egg heal up quicker."

Ollie presses the herb against the lump. Bright green juice dribbles down his face. "Actually, feels quite soothing."

"Hey, Banjo," says Archie, "we need your advice about another egg problem. Can you help us?"

Cock-a-doodle-doo, interrupts a rooster perched on the silver rocket.

Banjo rubs his chin while observing the impressive bird. "Aaaaaah, eggs ya say? I better sit down for this. Sounds like serious business."

Archie nods. "Yes, it's very serious. A real-life mystery."

"Go on then, tell me about this mystery of yours," says Banjo, sinking into the armchair.

"Well, it all started a week ago when my chooks stopped laying eggs in the nesting boxes. Luckily I discovered their hiding spot behind the toilet. Everything was going great for a while. Then the eggs went missing again. I looked everywhere for them. We even climbed the chicken tree. But they've completely vanished! The thing is, I've gotta find those eggs coz I need to sell them for my new Supergoose bike."

"And don't forget about Fairyland," says Pippa. "Someone's been cutting down trees and hammering in metal posts. There was a whole row of them in the forest."

"And we keep seeing crows," adds Archie. "They've been following us as if they're trying to tell us something."

Banjo jolts excitedly in his seat. "Kaarnka! That's how you say *crow* in my language, the Walmajarri way."

"Kaarnka, kaarnka, kaarnka," repeat the kids.

"Alright, alright. Gather round, little kaarnka. I got a story to tell ya."

The friends settle at Banjo's feet and gaze up, eyes beaming as he begins the tale.

"A long time ago, when I was a young fella, about your age, I spotted a bushy tree covered in grevillea flowers—big orange ones. Aww, and they taste so good when you lick the nectar. My tummy rumbled for that sweet sugar. Mmmm, good tucker, I thought. So I stomp across logs and dry leaves to get to those flowers. Then, *whoosh!* A big black crow come out of the sky and land on a dead branch above my head. It calls, *Kah! Karrh! Kah Karrh!* I thought it was saying, 'Watch out! Watch out!' So I stop, look around, but see nothin'. Ahhh, tricky crow, I think. But then, just as I'm gonna take a step towards those tasty orange flowers, I see movement in the leaves. There's a deadly snake, a death adder, curled up right in front of me! Would've been little bit short life if I trod on that snake, *hee-hee*."

Eyes wide like moons, Banjo leans closer. "The crow it warn me alright. That's because we're connected by the Dreamtime. We're family. And just like family, we look after each other. So, kids, whenever you see a friendly crow nearby, you know it's me, come to help out!"

Mesmerised by Banjo's story and tantalised by his connection to crows and the Dreamtime, the kids sit up straight, eager for more.

"And what about the sweet nectar? Did you get some?" asks Ollie, busting to hear the end of the story.

“Of course! I just stood as still as a rock till that deadly snake went around me. Then I scurried up that tree, quick as a possum. Mmmm, best nectar I ever tasted.”

“So what about the crow we saw? Was it warning us about something?” says Archie.

“He tryin’ to tell you somethin’ alright.”

“Huh!” gasps Pippa. “Is it Fairyland? Is something bad going to happen to Fairyland?”

Banjo gazes intensely at a billowing mass of dark grey clouds on the horizon and scrunches up his eyebrows. “Big storm comin’, I reckon.”

The kids’ mouths drop wide open, thinking this is a bad sign for Fairyland.

“Cheer up,” says Banjo, smiling brightly. “I’m just sayin’ it might rain later.”

Pippa sighs in relief. “Oh, Banjo, you’re such a trickster. But what about Fairyland and the crow?”

“Ah, that crow, he’s not worried about Fairyland for now. He’s just crowin’ to say, ‘go see Banjo coz he’s got a surprise for ya’.”

“What have you got? What’s the surprise?” asks Archie.

“Hold your horses. I want to play you somethin’ first.” Banjo picks up his steel-string guitar, places it flat on his lap and plucks the strings:

Da do dee-dee
Da dee do-do,
Da do dee-dee
Da do dee-do.
Da dee da-do
Da do de-do,
Da dee da-do
Da da dee-dee . . .

As the kids bounce around to the plucky-clucky chicken music, Fergus bounds from his art studio and waltzes over in canvas runners, hand-painted with gold stars, rainbow swirls and smiley faces. "Bok bok bok bokuurrrk!" he squawks, wiggling his bushy eyebrows while skipping up the stairs. "Hey, kids. Bokurrk!"

Archie, Pippa and Ollie roll over laughing as Fergus struts around on the deck, arms flapping, lips contorting into odd shapes, crowing at the top of his voice, "Roo-ra-roo-ra-rooo!"

When the tune ends, Fergus skips back to the studio, singing, crowing and kicking up gravel along the way. "Da doo de-doo da dee da-doo. ROO-RA-ROO-RAROOOO!"

Banjo rests his guitar beside the chair. "Come closer, kids. We gotta have a yarn-up about those chickens and them missin' eggs." Eyes fixed on Archie, he says in a kind, firm voice, "Now listen up, fella. You're not gonna get a Supergoose by stealin' from a chicken. You gotta leave them hens some eggs. Coz if ya take 'em all, they gonna keep hiding 'em."

"But I don't understand. Why are they hiding them?"

"Well, those chickens are a little bit clucky, I reckon," says Banjo.

"Ahhh, so the clucking is a secret chicken code. If we break the code, we'll find the missing eggs," babbles Ollie.

Pippa and Archie glance at each other, sharing an "Oh, Ollie" moment.

"*Hee-hee,*" chuckles Banjo. "No, Ollie, those chickens are clucky coz they wanna have baby chicks. That's why they hiding their eggs."

"That makes sense," says Archie. "But why are the chickens sitting under Mum's pot plant pyramid?"

"Ah, well, you better ask Fergus about that. That's his secret business. Now, hang on a minute, I got somethin' for those clucky chickens." From behind the armchair, Banjo pulls out a large cardboard box and places it on his knee. "Take a peek, go on."

Slowly, Archie lifts the lid, just wide enough for a red crest to pop out. Then, opening it a little wider, a stunning black rooster pokes its head through the gap and glances around, clucking nervously, *bok bok, bok bok bok.*

"Wow, he's beautiful," says Pippa, admiring the rooster's glossy black and shimmery green plumage.

"Looks feisty," notes Ollie, opting to keep a safe distance.

Banjo fastens the lid and passes the box to Archie. "Take this fella home, and I think ya gonna find what ya lookin' for."

"Thanks, Banjo, you're the best."

In the background, Fergus calls excitedly from the studio. "Hey, kids! I want to show you something."

SEVENTEEN

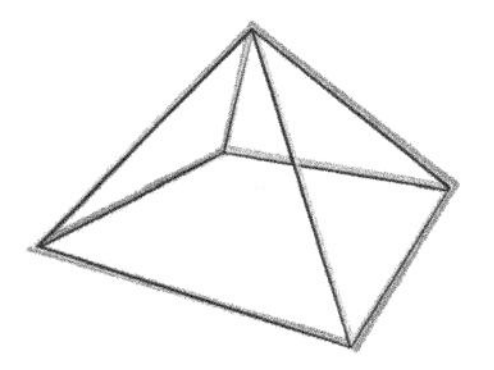

THE PYRAMIDUBATOR

Twang-whoop! Fergus releases a slingshot, catapulting a paint-filled balloon across the studio. *SPLAT.* Black paint explodes all over a white canvas perched on an easel.

"Hee-heee! What do you think of my pig painting, kids? I'm doing a whole series for my *Hogs of the Hills* exhibition. There's quite a buzz about it already. And I've heard along the grapevine that Sir Mick Jagger might be coming. We go back a long way, Mick and I. That's him up on the wall. It's a little-known fact that he's a fan of heritage hogs. There's even an extinct swamp pig named after him, *Jaggermeryx naida,* more commonly known as *Jagger's water nymph.* A long-legged swamp dweller, it had big flappy lips, just like Jagger. Handy things when you want to suck up swamp plants or belt out a tune."

"Who's Mick Jagger?" whispers Ollie in Pippa's ear.

"A famous rock star," she whispers back. "Hey, can anyone see a pig in that painting?"

"I see flappy lips," says Archie quietly. "Apart from that, it reminds me of a muddy puddle in a snowstorm. I think Fergus has gone crackers."

"Must be the paint fumes," mutters Ollie under his breath.

Eager for a compliment, Fergus pokes out his tongue and does a funny jig. As he kicks and leaps about, his fuzzy hair and beard bob up and down. "So, what do you think?"

"Umm, errr, great pig," they answer in unison, trying not to hurt his feelings.

"Of course, it needs a few finishing touches, a few highlights to bring out the personality of the pig," says Fergus, gazing at the painting. "Here, let me show you." He pulls on the tail of a wooden crocodile and opens a walk-in cupboard from which he wheels out a shiny silver vacuum cleaner. "Got this for a bargain at an auction of ex-Russian rocket equipment." Working swiftly, he unfastens the hose from where the air sucks in and attaches it to where the air blows out. "By swapping the hose around, you'll see we get something far more useful than a vacuum cleaner." The kooky character pops on some clear protective goggles. "Stand back, kids." His foot presses down on a glowing red button. The vacuum's turbine motor winds up, building in volume and pitch until reaching a deafening supersonic multi-tonal whine. Blue lights flash. Then the hose twists and flips as air blasts from the chrome nozzle, blowing the kids' hair backwards.

"A supersonic airbrush!" shouts Fergus above the noise. With the hose aimed at the canvas, he raises a palette of paints into the air stream. Globs of purple, red, silver, yellow and black fly across the room, striking the painting with a *Splattery Dappery Thwacka Whacka Womp!* Exhilarated by the creative chaos, he skips closer and hops about while directing the hose up, down and around, blowing the paint all over the canvas. "*Wheee-heee, hee-hee!*"

Once finished, the kids gasp, amazed by what they see—an impressive heritage pig featuring cute floppy ears, a curly tail and luscious flappy red lips, bearing a remarkable resemblance to Sir Mick Jagger.

"Hey, who wants to see my new invention?" says Fergus, keen to show off another of his creations.

"Me, me, me," answer the kids, raising their hands, stretching tall in excitement.

"Excellent! Come this way!" The zany character hops and skips down a curved corridor, tinkling the end of a paintbrush along a glass-bottle wall before stopping at a fake tree. Covered in shiny fabric leaves and silver globes, the tree extends right up to the cathedral ceiling. "To the untrained eye, this may appear to be a remarkable art installation, a brilliant display of nature's wonder. But don't be fooled." Eyes twinkling, he jumps onto a golden exercise bike and pedals furiously. And as he does, the globes flash, an electric motor buzzes, and a hidden door slides open in the broad trunk. "In here is my top-secret project. Shhh, not a word to anyone."

The kids step through the tree hollow and enter a red-glowing pentagonal room. Pig paintings of all shapes and sizes are stacked against the walls, and calming classical music wafts through the air.

Fergus trots up to a central table and gazes over a basket of eggs positioned beneath a lime-green pyramid frame and a dangling heat lamp. "This is my fertility-boosting incubator." Under the warm red glow of the light, he inspects each egg through a magnifying glass. "I call it the pyramidubator."

"I've got a fertility truck at home," states Ollie, poking his finger in the air.

Pippa scrunches one eyebrow. "Don't you mean a utility truck? *Fertility* means being able to have babies."

"That's right," says Fergus. "And with my pyramidubator, not only will more eggs hatch due to increased fertility but also the magical pyramid powers, combined with a precise temperature setting and the soothing music of Mozart, guarantees the chicks will be hens. *Hee-heee!* Imagine that, nothing but egg-laying hens!"

Archie's face lights up. "So that explains why my chickens are sitting under Mum's pot plant pyramid. They're trying to boost their fertility."

"So Banjo was right," says Pippa. "They want to have baby chicks."

Bok bok bok bok, clucks the rooster in the cardboard box.

"And now they can," says Archie, tapping the lid with a cheeky glint in his eye.

Pippa points at the pyramidubator. "Look! One of the eggs is hatching. There's a crack!"

A tiny beak pokes through a small hole, and ever so slowly, a cheeping yellow chick hatches from the shell.

"Aww, it's so cute, a spring chicken," says Pippa.

"Eeew, it's so slimy, a wet goo bird," says Ollie, screwing up his face.

As the chick stumbles and falls, flapping its tiny wings, Archie takes one hand off the rooster box and helps the bird to its feet with his little finger.

Seizing the moment, the rooster bursts through the lid and flaps around the workshop, squawking hysterically. It flutters up to the rafters and bumps into the dangling lamp, which swishes in circles, flashing red light around the room.

Fergus places a protective bucket over the baby chick and eggs as the rooster continues its flapping frenzy. *Bokurrk, bok-bok bokuuurrk!* It flies into the art studio, knocks the canvas off the easel, runs through the paint palette, darts over the pig painting and escapes out a window. Flapping and squawking madly, it dashes across the yard.

In hot pursuit, the kids scream and shout, "Come back, come back! We won't hurt you!"

Unflapped by the madness, Fergus collects his painting, now covered in rooster footprints, and places it upside down on the easel. "Perfect," he says with a self-satisfied smile.

Observing the chaos from the deck, Banjo rests back in the armchair and strums his guitar, chuckling to himself as the kids chase the rooster into the forest.

EIGHTEEN

THE KEY

A few hours later, Archie arrives home with his rooster safely back in the cardboard box. The kids had caught the flighty bird by laying a trail of honey joy crumbs sourced from the depths of Ollie's parka.

He steps onto the back veranda and tiptoes over Kimba, curled in a ball, fast asleep on the doormat. *Nobody's home,* he thinks, peering through the window. *Better get the spare key.*

Along the way to the nearby water tank, where the key is hidden, a hen darts across the path and sits under the pyramid. Archie drums on the rooster box, *tap-tap-ta-tap-tap*. "Just wait till you see the surprise I've got for you, you cheeky chook."

The hen fixes her googly eyes on the boy, whom she doesn't trust much given his history of stealing eggs, and responds with an indignant, *buuuurrrk*.

Archie leans under the wooden tank stand and grabs the key from a protruding nail. "Got ya."

On his way back to the house, the rooster flutters its wings and shuffles around in the cardboard box. "Relax, matey. Once Kimba's inside, you can explore the garden and eat lots of yummy grubs. You're going to love your new life here." With the rooster box tucked under one arm, Archie steps over the sleeping dog and directs the key to the keyhole. But his aim is off, so it clanks on a metal strip surrounding the lock.

Kimba wakes in surprise, eyes sparkling at the sight of Archie—and he jumps in jubilation, scraping his paws against the box. The noises and vibration startle the rooster, which bursts through the lid in a clucking clamour, knocking the key from Archie's grasp. "Aargh!" In a reflexive action, he thrusts out a hand to catch it. Unfortunately, the whizzing silver object flicks his fingertips, then bounces off his belly, rebounds off a raised knee, ricochets off one desperate extended foot and spins out of control towards the ground . . .

Tink.

It strikes the decking and bounces . . .

"No, don't fall down the crack!"

Tink.

It tips the edge of a decking board and slips through a gap, disappearing under the house into a shadowy world, a world where Archie has never ventured before.

Meanwhile, perched up a tree, the shiny black rooster surveys the yard, contemplating his options for survival and a better life. Down below, a black-and-white Egyptian Fayoumi hen clucks with an air of excitement and gazes up lovingly at the handsome dark stranger.

Enjoying the female attention, the rooster flies onto the tip of the lime-green pyramid, puffs out his chest and calls to let the hens know he's here to stay, *cock-a-doodle-doo!*

Back at the veranda, sealed all around by impenetrable railway sleepers, Archie pushes two sticks through a gap in the decking and clamps them onto the key. "That's it . . . Easy does it . . . Come on . . ." As the key rises from the grimy underworld, it wobbles and slips a little. He squeezes the sticks tighter, so tight they flick sideways. In that frustrating moment, the key drops back to the dirt and slides under a dry leaf. "Huh! Where's it gone . . . ? Oh, this is hopeless."

To make matters worse, an annoying whining mosquito circles Archie's head.

"Urgh, get away!"

The pesky insect lands on his forehead.

SLAP.

"Yes!" Triumphant for winning round one, Archie flicks the squashed mosquito off his palm and kneels beside Kimba. "If Mum and Josephine don't get home before dark, we'll be eaten alive by mozzies. We've gotta get the key. Come on, let's find a way under."

On the lower side of the garden, Archie crouches in a flowerbed of daffodils and peers beneath the house through a wooden lattice. "Uh-oh, Kimba, we've got a problem. The gaps are too small. I can't fit through."

For Kimba, the situation is hardly a problem. Playing in dirty places and roaming the garden are among his favourite activities. And in the spirit of fun and adventure, he sniffs under the lattice, wags his tail in a flapping fury, and digs.

"What is it? What have you found?"

The digging stops. Kimba sneezes twice and lifts his head, revealing a hole just big enough for Archie to crawl through.

"Good dog! You found a way in. You wait here while I fetch the key. I don't want you stepping on a nail. Okay, boy. Stay."

Urrrmph, moans Kimba, flopping to the ground with his nose between his paws.

After Archie squeezes through the hole and sits under the house, his head bumps on the floorboards above. "Ouch!" He falls onto his hands and knees, wincing in pain, and crawls uphill towards the veranda. At first, the dank air, cobwebs and dusty dirt turn the key quest into an uncomfortable, tedious chore. However, Archie soon realises the underworld is a gold mine of ancient relics—metal springs dangling from a torn cot mattress, a box of old records, and a rusty iron wheel, half-buried in the dirt.

Further on, he discovers a rectangular object protected by a cotton sheet, leaning against a house stump. *I wonder what's under here.* He lifts the cover and reveals an oil painting of a sailing boat with a crow perched on the mast. *Ooh, this'll look great in my room. I'll grab it on the way out.* He throws the cover back over and continues around a broken armchair, where, in the distance, behind a small hill, appears an orb of white light. *What on earth is that? What would glow under the house?*

Fantastical thoughts whizz around Archie's mind as he heads for the light, slithering along a sheet of corrugated iron. *Maybe it's an alien spaceship or a giant glow worm? Perhaps a swarm of fireflies?* His thoughts are interrupted by a battered leather suitcase lying flat on the ground, blocking the way. He blows off a layer of dust and runs his palms over a collection of stickers. One in particular catches his eye—a man and a woman riding a camel overlooking the Giza pyramids. Desperate to explore inside, he pushes, pulls and twists the latch mechanism. It doesn't budge. *Darn it. Must be locked. There's gotta be some way to open it.*

As he searches for a tool to prise it open, the glowing light grows brighter as if calling him. Spellbound by the strange phenomenon, he commando-crawls up the hill to discover its source. At the top, kneeling in the dirt, he pauses in amazement. "Holy guacamole! You've gotta be kidding me!"

A short distance from the veranda, illuminated by sunlight streaming between the decking boards, stands a mind-popping, mountainous mound of bright white chicken eggs, tapering upwards in the shape of a pyramid!

Archie scrambles down the hill and kneels goggle-eyed in front of the miraculous egg stack. *Wow, there must be over two hundred. This would've taken months to build. I guess those Egyptian chickens were laying eggs after all. Woohoo! I'm gonna make a fortune selling these at the Kallista market!*

Just then, a beam of sunlight strikes a single egg at the peak of the pyramid.

Mesmerised, Archie draws closer, his eyes swirling with intrigue and desire. As his fingertips reach for the glowing treasure, Banjo's voice echoes in his mind, *Now listen up, fella. You're not gonna get a Supergoose by stealin' from a chicken.*

Having not yet learnt the value of an Elder's wisdom, the bike-obsessed kid ignores Banjo's advice and takes the egg. He reaches for another but stops short, gasping in horror as the pyramid collapses in a catastrophic crumble. Eggs fly, implode, bounce and explode. Jagged eggshells whizz past his ears as green slime sloshes all over the place. Soon the air thickens with a rotten egg stench worse than a fish in a gumboot on a summer's day.

"Arkak-kak-corrr-ararar," he gags, choking, coughing and convulsing from the wretched smell. Intoxicated, nauseous, green-faced and red-eyed, he crawls under the decking, presses his lips into a gap and inhales the fresh air.

Ready for action once more, Archie kicks dirt over the rotten eggs and lies under the veranda, scrabbling through dry leaves and muck in search of the key. But all he finds are clothes pegs, odd socks, a torn doll's dress, and other bits and pieces of rubbish that had fallen through the gaps over many years. Flustered and frustrated, he drops his head into his hands. "Oh, where are you, you silly key?"

At that instant, something sticky and slimy rubs against his leg. *Yikes! What's that?*

Could it be a rat? a snake? a giant earthworm?

Slowly Archie twists around to see. And there, lurking in the underworld, stands a freakish creature, a grotesque beast wrapped in cobwebs like an Egyptian mummy in a horror movie. "Eeew, Kimba, stop it that tickles!

The tail-wagging ball of cobwebs smells something more interesting than Archie's leg and scampers away from the veranda. A few snorts and guttural growls later, he drags out a pull-string doll and lies next to Archie, proceeding to thrash it about and crunch into a chubby pink thigh.

Concerned the plastic may contain harmful chemicals, Archie grabs the doll. "Drop it!"

Kimba chomps onto a plastic ring at the back and tugs hard.

Zzzzzzzzzzzzzzip.

The pull-string extends to its entire length. As the string retracts, a mechanical buzzing starts. Kimba's ears prick up in surprise when a cute baby voice says, *Stop it, that tickles, hehehe-hahaha. You're my best friend. Stop it, that tickles, hehehe-hahaha. You're my best friend.*

"You're gonna be a dead dog when Josephine finds out about this," says Archie, waggling his pointer finger. "She's been searching for that doll for years, you naughty boy."

Eeeeeeeeeeeee. A whining mosquito circles overhead. Within seconds, millions of the annoying insects appear, attacking every patch of bare skin, dive-bombing from all directions, swarming in a blood-sucking frenzy.

Archie peers through the decking. “Oh no, it’s nearly dusk.” *Slap, Whack, Slap, Squish*. “I’ve gotta find the key fast!”

Unfazed by the mosquitoes due to his thick fur, Kimba catches the scent of more doggy treasure and digs below the veranda. Dirt flings all over Archie’s face, and a dust cloud obscures his vision.

“No! Bad dog. You’ll cover up the key. Urgh, I’ll never find it now.”

Grrrrruff Gruff, ruff ruff ruff!

“What have you found, boy? Another doll?”

Kimba pauses.

As the dust settles, a silvery glint catches Archie’s eye. “There it is!”

Ruff ruff ruff! Kimba resumes the treasure hunt.

Seconds before the flying dirt covers the key, Archie dives for the prize with outstretched arms and lands belly-first in the dust. “Got ya!”

Proud as a pony, Kimba clenches a humungous mouldy bone between his teeth and heads for the exit.

“Oi, wait for me!” calls Archie. He grabs Josephine’s doll and scrambles back to the exit, collecting the painting and a few records along the way.

Back at the door, the dusty, dishevelled boy slides the key into the lock, taking extra care not to drop it this time. While stepping inside, the rooster crows in the background, *cock-a-doodle-doooo!* Archie grins. *At least the hens can make baby chicks now*. And although he has nothing to sell for his new bike, Archie has learnt a valuable lesson: Never steal eggs from clucky chickens!

PART THREE

NINETEEN

THE WATER TANK

On a blazing hot summer's afternoon in Archie's garden, a rotund blowfly, travelling at a leisurely pace, buzzes around Kimba. *Chomp!* He snaps it up with his lightning-fast jaws and gulps it down in a single gulp.

Archie shakes his head in disgust and strides over to the water tank. Curious as to how full it is, he leaps onto the wooden tank stand, stretches up on his tippy toes, and knocks twice on a metal corrugation.

DONGGGGGG. DONGGGGGG.

A hollow boom vibrates through Archie's chest and rings out across the garden. "There's no water at this level, Kimba. I'll try further down." He raps his knuckles on the next corrugation, descending methodically, hoping for the sweet sound of a dull donk—an indication of water.

DONGGGGGG

DONGGGGGG

DONGGGGGG

Just past the halfway point, the hollow booms continue. Every knock tells Archie the tank is closer to empty.

DONGGGGGG
DONGGGGGG
DONGGGGGG
DONK!

"Ooh, I like the sound of that." Archie's cheek presses against the tank. The cool metal provides more proof of the water level. "Good news, Kimba. The tank's not empty yet."

A solitary crow calls high in the searing blue sky. Archie peers up anxiously, searching for clouds. *It better rain soon or we'll run out of water.*

Indeed, this would be a disastrous situation for him and his family as they depend on the tank water for such things as showers and baths, toilet flushing, washing dishes, brushing teeth, and drinking.

A sweat bead rolls down his face and drips into a bone-dry terracotta bowl below the tank's tap. Kimba licks the droplet from the dish, dangles his tongue halfway to the ground, and pants.

Archie pats him on the head. "Let's get a drink, fella. You look thirsty."

In the kitchen, Kimba nudges a plastic bowl along the floor to Archie's feet and gazes up, licking his dry lips and nose as he whines, *arrooo, arroorooo.*

"Be patient. I'll get your water in a sec. I've just gotta find a glass." Above Archie's head stands a stack of dishes piled halfway to the ceiling. A tall gleaming glass is positioned right at the bottom, jammed under a dinner plate and a carving knife. It's the only one left in the house due to a recent spate of breakages. The thirsty kid wants to enjoy a refreshing drink from a clean glass because all the mugs have jagged edges and murky pond-green glazes. He also likes to see what he's drinking—and for good reason.

"Stand back, Kimba. This could be dangerous." Archie weaves his hand around the sharp knife and under the plate. Then, as if playing a game of supersized pickup sticks, he grabs the glass and whips it out, missing the blade by a bee's nose. The towering dishes teeter, threatening to crash to the tiled floor. Fortunately, the pile just clunks as it settles into a new, somewhat stable position. "Yes!" he cheers, triumphant for beating the odds.

Aroorooo, whines Kimba, pleading for a drink.

"All right, it's coming." Archie swivels on the tap and places the water bowl in the sink. After a few seconds of gurgles and splutters, tea-coloured, gum leaf-smelling water fills the glass and overflows into the bowl. "There you go, fella. Some refreshment."

While Kimba takes a drink, Archie holds his glass to the light, illuminating ten or more mosquito larvae wriggling up, down and all around the amber liquid. *Ooooh, lots of wrigglers today. Must be the hot weather*.

Josephine enters. "Eeew, you're not going to drink those wrigglers, are you? Why don't you strain them out?"

"No need. They're an extra source of protein," says Archie, raising the glass to his lips. *Glug, glug, glug, glug.* "Aaaaahh, that's better!" He wipes a stray wriggler from his chin and refills the glass with a fresh batch.

"Gross," says Josephine. "By the way, Mum says we need to save water. Otherwise she'll have to pay someone to fill the tank. Remember last time that happened? The water truck cost so much we got no pocket money for six months. So don't waste any, okay?"

"Yeah, yeah, don't worry. I want the pocket money as bad as you. I'll start flushing the toilet with a bucket of bathwater. That'll save some. And I'll pee on the lemon tree that we just planted. Dad reckons lemon trees love being peed on coz it gives them nitrogen and stops their leaves turning yellow."

"Too much information," says Josephine, walking off.

Archie tops up Kimba's water bowl. "Drink up, boy. We've gotta prepare my fishing gear. I'm going fishing with Pippa and Uncle Broos tonight, and I want to catch a ripper!"

TWENTY

THE HORRENDOUS HOLE

Beep! Beep! Archie waves goodbye to his mum, slings a fishing rod over one shoulder and trundles up Pippa's long driveway lined by tall camellia bushes.

Near the top of the drive in a small workshop beneath the raised weatherboard house, Pippa's dad, Broos, chops his spade into a dirt bank and tosses a mound of soil into a steel builder's wheelbarrow.

Broos is digging under the house to expand the workshop into a storeroom. You see, having three children—Pippa (the youngest), Lottie (the middle one) and Saskia (the eldest)—he needs extra space for storing their bikes as well as his tools and ever-expanding stock of fishing gear.

Broos's love of fishing started when he was a young boy growing up in the Netherlands. At the age of eight, he and his dad rowed a wooden boat into the middle of a lake and caught a massive fish—a monster pike. Such a thrill it was, he's been obsessed with fishing ever since.

Archie dumps his gear near the front door and wanders under the house to see what Broos is up to.

The dimly lit workshop smells of freshly dug earth and sweat blended with the sweet, spicy aroma of cinnamon and cloves (owing to Broos's liberal application of Dutch-inspired aftershave).

A sunbeam streams through a crack in the wall, highlighting the floating dust specks. The light strikes a framed photograph of a man dressed in wooden clogs and a boy wearing black-rimmed glasses, holding a whopper of a fish.

Dirt sprinkles onto Archie's shoes. He looks up to find Broos, just ahead, chopping his spade into the hard bank. "Hi, Uncle Broos." Although Archie and Pippa are not cousins, he calls her dad "Uncle" due to the closeness of their families.

Broos swings around in a spritz of cheer, his eyes twinkling through a pair of thick black-rimmed glasses, his swirly dark-brown hair dripping sweat onto his builder's overalls.

"I'm ready for fishing," continues Archie, allowing no space for Broos to answer. "I hope we catch a big one, like in that photo. Who are those people anyway?"

Broos removes the picture from a hook, wipes it with his sleeve and gazes lovingly at the photo. Then, speaking in a thick Dutch accent—where every "th" becomes a "d" or a "t" and every "s" becomes a "sh" and every "v" becomes an "f"—Broos says, "Dat'sh me and my farder wid my firsht big catch. He wash a fery great fisherman becaush he could tink like a fish!" Broos hangs the photo back on the hook and passes Archie a shovel. "Here you go, little man, you can giff me a hand digging."

Honoured to help Broos dig, Archie thrusts his spade into the dirt. "So how do you think like a fish?"

"Dat'sh a good question, Archie. To tink like a fish, you'ff got to imagine what it'sh like to be a fish. How dey feel. What dey are shcared of. What dey need. What dey want mosht."

"What do they want most?"

"Wormsh! Big fat juicy wormsh!" replies Broos with a broad toothy smile.

Archie nods, and he and Broos continue digging and talking about fishing until an impressive mound of soil overflows from the wheelbarrow.

"Dat'sh a good job. You're getting big shtrong mushles," praises Broos, resting his shovel against the dirt wall. "Dat'sh enough digging for now. We better shtart preparing for our fishing trip. But firsht we have shome business to attend to." He reaches into a pocket and hands Archie a crisp five-dollar note. "Here'sh shome pocket money for all dat digging. Don't shpend it all at once."

"No, I won't. I'm saving every penny for a new BMX bike. Thanks, Uncle Broos." Archie slips the money into his shirt pocket alongside a bundle of used tissues.

A rooster calls in the distance. Broos glances at his watch. "Oh by gosh, look at da time. Pippa better get home from acro-baticsh shoon or she'll mish da fishing trip." He takes a white bucket and lid from a shelf. "Follow me. I'ff got shome-ting shpecial to show you."

Near the driveway, shaded by blue hydrangea flowers, Broos crouches beside a square concrete slab. "Okay, mushles, giff me a hand pushing."

They slide the weighty slab to one side, revealing a hole in the ground. The unsavoury pit, also known as a septic tank, is where all the toilet waste goes for natural decomposition.

A pungent pong rises from the hole, strong enough to knock the head off a hippo. About an arm's length down, squillions of striped purply-red worms churn and squirm in smelly brown sludge.

Archie thrusts his sleeve to his nose. “Eeew, do they really like it in there?”

“Oh yesh, da little crittersh love it. Look how happy and fat dey are! Here, let me show you.” The crazy Dutchman rolls up his sleeves, plunges his hands into the pit and slops a writhing pile of worms into Archie’s hands. “Dere you go. Juishy tiger wormsh for our fishing trip tonight.”

“Umm, errr, thanks, Uncle Broos.” The feisty creatures wriggle in Archie’s cupped hands and curl around his fingers.

Pippa skips up the driveway in her acro dance gear and bounds over to Broos and Archie. “Eeew, Papa, I told you not to play with those worms. It’s disgusting.”

“Help me, Pippa! Quick, one’s crawling up my sleeve!”

She shakes her head, giggling. “No way! I’m not touching that stinky worm.”

“Here you go, put da little devilsh in dere,” says Broos, thrusting out the white bucket.

Archie unwinds the critters from his fingers, peels the escapee from his sleeve and plops them in.

Much to Pippa and Archie’s disgust, Broos plunges his hands back into the pit and slops three wormy handfuls into the bucket. “Dat should be enough for fishing. Now we giff dem a little shpray”—he rinses them under the garden hose —“and shomewhere to play”—he covers them with sweet-smelling soil from a flower bed—“and put dem away.” He clips on the lid and pushes the concrete slab over the hole. “Now go get changed, Pippa. We’ff got to get to our fishing shpot before da shun goesh down.”

Once Archie and Broos have washed their hands, they set to work packing the car with fishing rods, hooks, sinkers, a sharp knife, picnic blankets, torches, a lantern, buckets, a green net and the worms.

Broos stands by the car, scratching his head. "I tink we'ff forgotten shome-ting. Hmm, let me tink . . ."

A screen door bangs closed, and out pops Pippa's mum, Hilda, bouncing along in a white apron, yellow clogs and pointy Dutch hat. "Yoo-hoo!" she calls, speaking in a similar Dutch accent to Broos. "I'ff got sandwichesh, hot chocolate in a termosh and speculaash!"

Hilda enjoys wearing a traditional Dutch costume when cooking because it reminds her of happy times baking with her mum in the Netherlands. And as she says, "A happy cook makesh happy food, and happy food improvesh your mood!"

Pippa calls down from an upstairs window, "Mooie hoed, Mama, domme gans!" (*Nice hat, Mama, you silly goose!*)

Hilda honks, chuckles and waddles about, waving the basket of food around.

Broos smiles lovingly. "Niemand kan zo goed waggelen als jij, Hilde, mijn lieveling." (*Nobody can waddle as good as you, Hilda, my darling.*)

Unable to speak Dutch, Archie is confused and amused by the madness. Nevertheless, he can't wait to taste Hilda's sweet, spicy biscuits.

A few minutes later, Broos revs the car engine and sings out, "All aboard!"

Archie and Pippa squeeze between the fishing gear, and they head off on the thrilling night-time fishing adventure. Destination: a little creek somewhere in the hills.

TWENTY-ONE

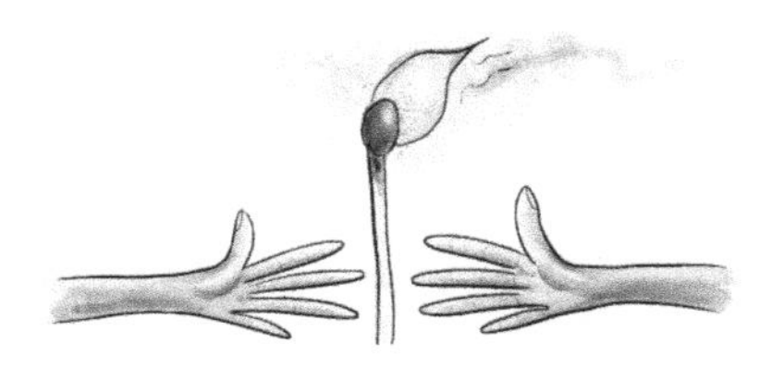

THE ART OF FIRE MAKING

As the sun vanishes behind the mountains and screeching cockatoos swirl in the orange sky, Pippa and Archie clomp along a forest track with fishing rods slung behind, buckets and torches jiggling by their sides.

"There's the creek." Pippa shines her torchlight at a slow-moving stream. The deep water, overhung by lush ferns, flows under a fallen dead tree, then meanders through white-trunked manna gums and smooth boulders submerged along the edges.

Thrash-thrash! The friends jump in fright as something lands in the wattle tree above their heads. The torch beam swings up through sprinkling yellow flowers to the leafy canopy. And there, tucked in the crook of a branch, sits a tiny fluffy creature with glowing moons for eyes.

"It must be a possum," whispers Archie.

"And there's a baby on its back. A real sweetie. Can you see?"

"Yeah, I see it. Aww, so cute."

Unaware of the creature, Broos jingle-jangles down the path and cracks a stick under his boot.

The startled animal leaps off the branch, and with its four webbed legs spread wide, glides over Broos's head. A few seconds later, leaves thrash from across the creek as it lands safely in a sassafras tree.

"Oh by gosh, what wash dat?" says Broos, ducking his head, eyes wide with surprise and intrigue.

"It might've been a sugar glider," says Archie. "I've seen them flying from tree to tree at my house."

"It's okay, Papa. Don't be scared. At least it wasn't a drop bear," jokes Pippa.

Broos makes a funny face and darts his eyes from left to right. "Not the drop bearsh! You know, when I wash a little boy, I—"

"Err, Papa, there's no time for stories. Don't we have some fishing to do?"

Slightly panicked, Broos glances at the sleepy mountains silhouetted against the pinky-orange sunset. "Yesh, you're right, Pippa. We'ff got to get wood for da fire before it getsh too dark."

While the kookaburras farewell the day with their rollicking laugh, the kids dump their fishing gear at a clearing beside the creek and race into the scrub to search for firewood. By the time the kookaburras' chorus fades, Archie and Pippa return from the bushes carrying bundles of sticks. They stack them near a circle of rocks and brush off their clothes.

Broos stumbles into the clearing and drops an assortment of logs onto the ground. "Dat should do da trick. Okay, who wantsh to learn how to build a hot fire?"

"Me! Me!"

"Marvelloush. Now lishen carefully," says Broos, kneeling beside the rocks, clasping a rolled-up newspaper. "Fire ish a fery dangeroush ting. You musht neffer build a fire wishout an adult and neffer effer when it'sh a total fire ban day or when dere'sh a big wind. Got it?"

Pippa and Archie nod as they crouch on the dirt.

"Exshellent. Now take shome newspaper, den scrunch it up into little ballsh and arrange dem in da middle of da rocksh like dish . . . Now shpread shmall sticksh and dry leavesh all over da top . . . Dat'sh da way. You shee, da key to a great fire ish to shtart wid da little-esht sticksh."

Broos strikes a match and lights the paper. "Fire alwaysh travelsh up. Sho ash da fire growsh, you put on bigger sticksh and bigger sticksh and den little logsh and big logsh until you have a fire sho hot it will burn anyting—even wet wood or a shoggy old boot!"

Once the little sticks are alight, the kids place bigger sticks onto the fire. Broos adds several small logs, followed by two larger ones. And before long, their happy faces glow brightly in the light of the roaring fire.

"Dat'sh how you build a hot fire," says Broos, smiling proudly with sweat dripping down his forehead.

The wind shifts direction and blows thick smoke into Archie's face, irritating his nose and triggering a humungous sneeze. "Ah, ahhh, ahhhhhchooooo!"

"Bless you," says Pippa.

"Gezondheid," adds Broos.

A snot bubble grows from Archie's nose. *Pop.*

Pippa laughs. "Errr, that's gross, you slime head."

Giggling, Archie fumbles for a tissue in his shirt pocket and accidentally drops the five-dollar note that Broos gave him for digging under the house.

"Hey, where did you get that from?" asks Pippa in a curious voice, half-giggling.

Archie stuffs the money back into his pocket. "Uh, your dad gave it to—"

"Ahem," coughs Broos, who, out of Pippa's view, shakes his head and waves his arms at Archie.

Clueless about the meaning of the animated gestures, Archie continues, "Umm, your dad gave it to me for helping him dig under the house today. We filled a big wheelbarrow right to the top. Didn't we, Uncle Broos?"

Instead of agreeing as expected, Broos sighs and glances down, squeezing his eyes shut in a pained grimace.

"What! He gave you pocket money?" says Pippa accusingly, her jaw dropping. Flushed red, she glares at Broos through slitted eyes. "Papa, you never give me money for doing odd jobs. I suppose you gave the money to Archie because he's a boy. Is that right . . . ? Well, it's not fair! How could you, Papa? How could you!"

Pippa slumps on a log and turns her back to the fire, arms crossed tightly. Not only has this act of treachery broken her trust in Archie and Broos, but it has also thrown into question her lifelong assumption that girls and boys are equal—an assumption now in jeopardy.

Flustered and ashamed, Broos searches his mind for a reply, an excuse of some kind. Yet there's nothing he can say to explain why he'd favoured Archie, except that he was a boy.

A wave of guilt thumps Archie in the chest. He feels guilty for accepting the money, guilty for getting Broos into trouble, and guilty for being a boy. Eager to ease his pain and make things right, he sits beside Pippa, smiling in a peace offering. But his gesture encounters an icy flinch as she tenses her shoulders and gazes at the stars, her place of solace.

After a few uncomfortable breaths, Archie says gently, "I'm sorry. When I took the five dollars from your dad, I didn't know I was getting special treatment."

It dawns on Pippa that her friend is innocent. "It's not your fault. I would've taken the money too. It's Papa who did the wrong thing. He's never even asked me to dig with him under the house, let alone pay me for it." She bursts into tears.

On cue, Broos, pale with guilt, comes over waving a five-dollar note. "Here you go, Pippa. Put dish money towardsh your teleshcope or shome-ting."

She refuses the offer and turns away. To be given money from her father, under a magical night sky, by the light of a cosy fire, is no consolation for her disappointment and pain.

Broos'll never forgive me, thinks Archie, glancing behind at the fire. A log falls. Orange sparkles fizz up into the night sky. As new flames envelop the log, an idea grows in his mind. *Of course!* Buoyed by the hope of a resolution, Archie bounds over to Broos and whispers in his ear, "The key to a great fire is to start with the littlest sticks."

Broos's face brightens, and he nods, indicating respect and gratitude for the good advice. Indeed, he needs to rebuild his relationship with Pippa one small step at a time, like when building a hot fire. And just as paper requires a spark to light, emotional wounds need apologies for healing to occur.

"Ahem," coughs Broos, sliding next to Pippa. "I'm shorry. I made a mishtake. I promish to neffer treat you unequally effer again. How about tomorrow we dig under da housh togedder? And we can feed da wormsh in da worm pit. I'll pay you five dollarsh an hour. How dosh dat shound?"

Pippa's mood lightens. "Uh, no thanks, Papa. Digging under the house is *not* my thing. And I don't like your smelly worm pit either. Her mind ticks over . . . But I'll dig with you in the garden and help repair the side fence that's falling down. As long as I get to use the drill and you pay me five dollars an hour—then I'll forgive you."

Bursting with happiness, Broos wraps his arms around Pippa. "It'sh a deal!"

"I love you, Papa," she whispers, sinking into the hug. Her mind ticks over once again. "Err . . . can I still have that five dollars?"

Smiling, Broos hands her the money, whips out his trusty silver harmonica and plays a happy Dutch ditty, *wawooo wawooo waweee wo—*

Splash! A fish belly-flops in the creek.

"Oh by gosh!" says Broos, whipping around, gazing at the rippling water. "Dat wash a big fish. I tink itsh going to be a good night for fishing."

TWENTY-TWO

NIGHT FISHING

Broos selects a fat wriggling worm from the bucket. "Watsh closhely, kidsh. Dish ish how you bait a hook. Firsht, let it crawl on your hand." He lays the worm on his palm. "Look at da little critter go! The direction it crawlsh is da head end. You shee, a worm neffer crawlsh backwardsh. Now inshert da hook below da head . . . shlide it along . . . poke it out halfway . . . and inshert da hook above da tail. And dere we have it—a wiggly head, a wiggly tail, and no hook showing!"

"So the fish won't get scared," says Archie, appreciating Broos's ingenious baiting method.

"Dat'sh right. Jusht a wiggly worm shaying, 'Come here, fishy fishy fishy'."

Pippa takes the rod, dodging the worm squirming helplessly on the end of the line. "Aw, Papa, I feel sorry for the poor worm. Doesn't the hook hurt?"

"Don't worry, dey can't feel a ting," assures Broos, whose love of fishing overrides his concern about the wellbeing of worms. He slops a handful of the slimy critters into an empty yoghurt container and hands it to Archie. "Da fire will be our meeting shpot. If you get losht, head for da light. And if you hook a fish, call out, and I'll bring over da net. And remember, whatsh the mosht important ting?"

"To think like a fish," reply Pippa and Archie in unison.

Broos nods. "Yesh. And what do da fish want mosht?"

"Worms," says Archie, holding up the container.

Satisfied with the lesson, Broos stomps off to find a good fishing spot, humming along the way, "Ho de-hoo, da-hoo da-doo, ho de-ho, da-do de-doo."

A few hours later, not a single fish has been caught. Archie and Pippa don't mind too much, because they love being in the wilderness, a place of magic and mystery.

Archie casts his fishing line high above the creek. The reel whizzes sweetly, and the worm plops into a deep swirling pool a short distance from Pippa's spot. He flips the bail arm over, tightens the line and rests the rod on a forked stick pushed into the earth.

Steam rises from the thermos as Pippa pours a cup of hot chocolate for herself and Archie. Whilst sipping the drinks, relishing the chocolaty flavour, they lean back against a smooth log and enjoy the peace and quiet.

Above the trees, zillions of stars sparkle in the clear night sky, accompanied by crickets chirping and pobblebonk frogs calling from the nearby swamp, *bonk bobonk, bonk bobonk, bonk bobonk, bonk bobonk . . .*

"I love being in the bush," says Archie, dunking a spiced Dutch biscuit into his drink.

Pippa gazes at the brilliant light of Venus. "Yeah, me too. The stars are so bright. It's so peaceful out here."

Hisssss! Rowweeeee! shriek two possums fighting from across the creek.

Biscuit sprays from Archie's mouth as he bursts into a giggle. "Yeah, real quiet."

While staring at the stars, contemplating the mysteries of the universe, Archie's rod tugs twice. Then, *whoosh!* It flings off the stick and rips along the dirt towards the creek. A second before vanishing into the water, he stomps on the handle, yanks it up and shouts, "I've got something!" The rod tip bows sharply and the line zips out from the reel.

Whizzzzzzzzzzzzzzzzzzzzzzzz

"It's a whopper, whatever it is!" He tightens the drag wheel to stop the line pulling out. But it has the opposite effect. The line slackens and the rod relaxes. "Oh no, I've lost it."

Whip-Twang!

The line tightens again. "No, I haven't! It's trying to swim away. I'm gonna reel it in."

"Okay, I'll get the torch," shouts Pippa.

To prevent the line from snapping, Archie walks downstream, stumbling over rocks and tree roots. Every time he winds the reel, the fish fights harder, whipping the rod down and around, stretching the line to breaking point. "Urrgh, arrggh, errggh! The line's gonna snap!"

"I'll get Papa. He'll know what to do," calls Pippa.

Near the water's surface, the fish thrashes, flips and tugs to break free.

"No, Pippa! You can't leave me here in the dark. I need you to hold the torch while I lift it onto the bank."

"Okay, okay." She shines the torch beam at the creek. The murky water swirls in a whirlpool, punctuated by tail thrashes and the sporadic glint of a fish eye.

Praying the line will hold, Archie raises the rod. The tip

bends sharply as a long black slithery thing emerges from the water, whipping and writhing in a frenzy. "It's an eel!" He swings the rod away from the creek and lurches across to a grassy clearing. "Yesssss! I've got it!"

In a violent outburst, the eel wallops its tail, flings off the hook and strikes the ground with a *whomp!*

The sight of the wet snake-like creature wriggling in the grass freaks Pippa out, and she runs screaming up a track with the torch, "Eeeeeeeek! I hate snakes!"

"Pippa, come back! It's an eel, not a snake!" shouts Archie, kneeling in the dark, wrestling the jaw-snapping, tail-whipping fish. Desperate, scared, confused, he presses the speculaas tin on the creature's slippery tail to stop it escaping. All he can see are its razor-sharp teeth, snapping in the starlight. "Uncle Broos! I've caught an eel! Help! Help!"

A few tail whips later, Broos's voice echoes across the bushland, "Hold on to da eel, Archie, I'm coming!" With his head torch bobbing and the net and bucket jangling, he rushes over, followed by Pippa holding a glowing lantern.

"Oh by gosh, good boy," says Broos. "It'sh a beauty. You hold it while I get it in da net." As he slides the net under the eel's belly, the panic-stricken fish bucks and backflips away from the metal rim, then slips out from under the tin and slithers frantically for the creek.

"Not sho fasht, you little critter!" cries Broos, streaking after it.

The eel shoots down the muddy creek bank.

Broos, the flying Dutchman, leaps into the air, swan dives over the bank, crash-lands on his belly and slides along like a tobogganing penguin. Leaves, mud and reeds scatter in a calamitous cacophony of crazy chaos.

Just ahead, as the eel touches its nose to the water and is

about to swim away, Broos swishes down the net and scoops it from the creek.

Pippa and Archie bend over in fits of laughter while Broos staggers up the bank with his glasses hanging off one ear, his hair covered in slimy leaves and his overalls dripping in mud.

"Oh by gosh, dat wash a closhe call," says Broos. He tips the eel into the bucket. "Well done, little man. Our firsht catch of da night."

Pippa holds the lantern over the slithering creature. "Are you really going to take it home, Archie? Those teeth are kind of freaky."

"Yeah, of course. It won't last long out of water, and I wanna cook it for breakfast."

TWENTY-THREE

FISH OUT OF WATER

The following morning, Florence bellows from the kitchen, "Arrrchieeee! What's this eel doing on my kitchen bench! Get up and do something about it right now!"

"Huh!" gasps Archie, waking in a panic. "The eel!"

Josephine peeks into the bucket and shrieks, "Eeeeek! I've never seen anything so disgusting."

Archie careers around the corner, sliding to a halt in his purple and green odd socks. "Sorry, Mum, I got home real late and put the bucket on the bench so Kimba wouldn't eat the eel I caught. I was gonna get up early and clean it for breakfast, but I slept in."

"I don't want to hear about it. Just get this thing off my kitchen bench RIGHT NOW!"

"Don't worry, I'll gut it in a jiffy. And then can you help me cook it for breakfast? Uncle Broos said eels are a prized delicacy in Holland. I can't wait to try some." Archie's mouth waters, imagining the long sausage-shaped eel tasting like salami or chewy cabana. "And you couldn't get any fresher—fresh from the creek last night."

"Oh, it's fresh all right," says Josephine, raising her eyebrows and pinching her nose.

Archie peers into the bucket, expecting to see a dead eel. Instead, he finds the slimy creature slithering around the muddy bottom. "What? Impossible! Fish can't survive out of water for that long. They usually die in minutes. I was certain it would be dead by now."

"Well, it's alive and kicking, and what are you going to do about it?" questions Florence. She proceeds to balance a dinner plate on top of the ridiculously high dish stack.

The plate wobbles.

Archie cringes, expecting the stack to crash to the floor. Luckily it doesn't. "Don't worry, Mum. I'll deal with it right now. I just need a sharp knife."

"Good. And when you're done, I'll fry it up in garlic and butter. We'll serve it with fresh dill from the garden and sourdough toast." Florence whisks a carving knife from the bottom of the dish pile, swipes its shiny silver blade back and forth across a sharpening rod, and hands it to Archie. "Don't take too long. Hilda and the girls are coming over for morning tea, and I don't want a stinky eel slithering around the house." She returns to the sink and dunks a saucepan into the dishwater. "And I need you to pick a container of blackberries, and sweep the paths, and feed the chooks, and dry the dishes, and clean the gutters on the—"

Swish. The bucket flies off the bench, and Archie hightails from the kitchen.

Florence whips around, spraying soapsuds against the wall. "Archie? Archie! Where have you gone!"

Safe in the bathroom, Archie examines the gleaming knife blade. Silvery reflections cast across his face as he ponders the kindest way to end the eel's life. Then he remembers Broos saying that before cutting off a fish's head, it's best to strike it above the eyes with a blunt instrument. That way, it goes unconscious and feels no pain. *Makes sense. I don't want the poor thing to suffer.* He searches in the cupboard and finds a heavy rubber mallet. *Perfect.*

And there he stands, the innocent young boy, holding a whopping hammer in one hand and a deadly carving knife in the other, gazing down at the muddy slithering eel. *Hmm, looks a bit grimy. Better give it a rinse first.* He lowers the bucket into the bathtub and turns on the tap.

"Stop wasting water," yells Florence from the kitchen.

"Don't worry, Mum. I'm only using a tiny bit to wash the eel so I don't get dirt in the fillets. I'm turning it off now."

Half covered in water, the eel swishes around the bucket—clean, happy and refreshed. Soon it slows to a slither, lifts its head and stares into Archie's eyes as if to say, *thank you.*

Astounded by the eel's resilience and touched by its spirited personality, Archie falls to his knees in silence and drops the knife . . .

CRASH-SHATTER-BANGALANGA-CLANKA-DONG!

A cataclysmic calamity booms from the kitchen as the sky-scraping dish stack crashes to the floor, shattering, clanking and bouncing amid Florence's distressed squeals and shrieks.

Seconds later, Kimba skids around the corner and leaps onto Archie's lap.

"It's okay, fella, you're safe now. When will she ever learn, eh? Just one too many plates on the dish stack."

Kimba sniffs the fish-scented air and pokes his nose into the bucket, licking his lips and growling, desperate to chomp on the eel and give it a good thrash about.

Water splashes and swirls in the bucket as Archie pulls him back. "No! Naughty boy. Leave it alone."

Thankful once again, the eel pokes its head from the water and gazes up, pleading for mercy.

With Kimba in his arms and the knife and mallet splayed across the floor, Archie thinks, *Poor thing. It's survived this long. How can I eat it now?*

TWENTY-FOUR

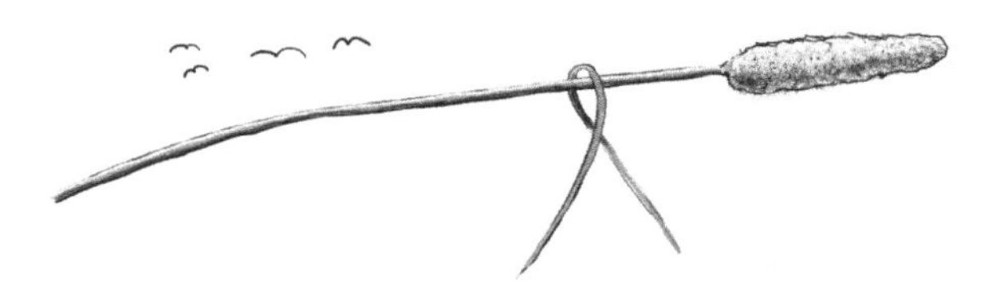

BOING BOING

Later at Fairyland, Archie picks a plantain stem topped with a cone-shaped seedhead and pokes it through another looped stalk. He tightens the loop and rips the first stem backwards, launching the seedhead into the sky. "Woohoo!"

In Ollie's usual extravagant manner, he launches several seedheads simultaneously, marvelling at their flight path as he relaxes back on soft clumps of freshly mown grass. "So you mean to say you've left the eel in a bucket in the bathtub? I'm not sure that's a good idea, Archie. If you're going to keep a pet eel, you have to create the right environment for it. Take my guppies and catfish, for example. To keep them alive and healthy, I've got a thirty-litre glass tank with an activated carbon filter, a quartz heater for wintertime, a variety of underwater plants to take up the nitrogen. And I feed them a portion-controlled diet of bloodworms, shrimp, leafy greens and the occasional live wriggler. To start with, you need to find a bigger space for your eel to swim around. A bucket's way too small. And you better feed it soon. They like a high protein diet, you know. In fact, according to the *Guppy Gazette*—"

Mischievous giggles sprinkle down the hill, interrupting Ollie's lecture. "What are they doing?" He peers up the meadow at Josephine, Pippa, Saskia and Lottie sitting in a bed of flowers, threading daisy chains.

Archie goes all tense. "Uh-oh. I think we're in big trouble."

"Huh? What trouble? What's going on?" blurts Ollie.

More giggles waft down to the boys as Pippa and Josephine saunter over in floral dresses, dripping in daisy chain necklaces, bracelets and garlands.

"Oh no, not daisy chains. No way," says Archie, preparing to bolt across the meadow.

"Get some perspective, man. Making daisy chains is fun. Consider it bushcraft," says Ollie, searching for a dandelion flower to thread.

"But, Ollie, you don't understand. Last time those girls got together, they dressed me up like a Barbie doll with a long blonde wig, a gold evening gown, bright red lipstick, glittery nail polish, high heels, dangly clip-on earrings and a pearl necklace. And it all started with daisy chains! I did it once, but I'm not doing it again!"

As the girls draw near, Pippa waves a bag of lacy dresses, dainty satin shoes and other mysterious items. "Oh, boys. Who wants to play dress-ups?"

Before Ollie and Archie can reply, the girls pounce, sliding daisy chains over the boys' heads.

Ollie grabs a white sash from the dress-up bag and drapes it over one shoulder. Together with the flower garland around his head, he sits proudly like a Roman emperor, trying unsuccessfully to keep a straight face.

"Hail, Caesar," says Archie, giggling. "No, no, wait." He sprinkles a bunch of dandelion leaves onto Ollie's hair. "Hail, Caesar salad!"

"An acquired taste, I'd say," notes Ollie, munching one of the leaves. "A little on the bitter side, but might be nice with some balsamic vinegar, fresh loquats and shaved Parmesan."

Lottie calls out in a cheeky voice, "Come over here, boys. We've got lovely red lipstick."

"And pink nail polish, your favourite," adds Saskia, wiggling the bottle.

Archie waves both hands and shouts, "Don't come near us with that gunk."

"No thanks," calls Ollie. "You wouldn't have green or gold by chance?"

"Hey, what are you doing? We'll end up dressed like Barbie dolls if you're not careful."

"I take your point, Archie. We all have a right to be ourselves, to feel comfortable in our skins. But you could lighten up a tad. It's just a bit of harmless body art, a bit of theatre and creative expression. Anyway, what's wrong with green and gold? They're the official Australian colours, an inspired colour palette derived from the golden wattle." Ollie scoops up a clump of green grass clippings. "The green comes from the glossy wattle leaves"—he gathers a bunch of dandelion flowers—"and the gold from the bright yellow flower balls." He dumps the lot on Archie's head. "*Wattle* you think of that, ay?"

"Ha, ha, very funny. *Wattle* you think of this!" Archie, giggling, tosses a handful of soft grass at Ollie's face.

Ollie calmly removes his dirty glasses, puffs the lenses clean, places them back on his head, gathers a fistful of clippings and chases Archie down the hill, giggling and shouting, "GRASS FIGHT!"

The girls join in the fun, laughing, leaping, lunging and lashing at each other with bundles of wispy grass.

"Take that!" shouts Archie, shoving a clump down Ollie's T-shirt.

As Ollie charges in retaliation, the grass spewing from his belly, Pippa ambushes him from behind and gleefully shoves a handful down his back.

"Arrrggghh!" screams Ollie, galloping after her up the hill.

Meanwhile, Josephine, Lottie and Saskia surround Archie and unleash a barrage of clumpy clippings, *boof-boof-babba-boof!*

Stunned but unfazed, he shakes off the grass and screams, "Boys against girls!"

Responding to the call, Ollie stuffs his pants with clippings and tears down the meadow, hollering, "I'm coming, Archie!" Unfortunately, having stuffed in one too many grass clumps, his pants pop open and fall down around his ankles, causing him to flip over and sausage roll down the hill.

"Uh-oh," says Archie, who, now surrounded by the girls and all alone, has no choice but to spin in a dizzy-whizzy while flinging out his remaining clippings.

As grass sprays in all directions, Ollie tumbles to a halt at Archie's feet, displaying a fine pair of red Smurf undies.

"Attack!" shout the girls, seizing the moment to launch a coordinated assault, forcing the boys to curl into balls on the ground and accept their fate:

Boof-ba-boof-ba-boofy-bubba-boof-da-doofy-boof-baboof!

Half-giggling, half-whimpering, Ollie pokes his hand up through the fluffy pile of grass clippings and waves a white hanky on the end of a stick. "We surrender! No more grass. No more. Please, have mercy, *hee-hee*."

With a ceasefire declared, the sweaty, red-faced kids flop onto the meadow and gaze at the sky. Slowly, three fluffy clouds merge into a giant rabbit. Between its ears appear five black cockatoos, flapping their majestic wings in slow beats. Their high-pitched wailing song echoes across the forest and valley below. *Queeeee-yah, queeeee-yah, queeeee-yah.* As they fly into the distance, silence descends upon Fairyland.

The kids breathe and dream.

They are happy.

Screech-Screech! Two crimson rosellas rocket overhead in flashes of blue and red.

Then from deep within the earth, a pounding, rhythmic vibration travels up through the kids' bodies, and a distant boinging sound grows louder and louder, *boing, boing, boing, boing, boing . . .*

The kids sit bolt upright, wide-eyed and bemused, listening and peering around.

"It must be a kangaroo. Kangaroos make a boing sound when they hop," says Ollie, whose only qualification in animal sounds is his consumption of early morning cartoons.

"Yeah, it must be a kangaroo," agrees Archie, being similarly qualified in such matters.

"Have you two gone barmy? Kangaroos don't make a boing sound in real life. That's a sound effect added to cartoons," asserts Pippa, who can't believe the idiocy of her friends.

Lottie, Saskia and Josephine nod in agreement.

Nevertheless, the boings grow louder and faster, shaking the ground:

boing

BOING

BOING

KA-BOOM, BOOM, BOOM!

Suddenly a six-foot-tall grey kangaroo explodes from the forest and bounces straight for the kids! Pippa flies left, Archie leaps right, Ollie flings backwards—everyone rolls, flips and scatters across the grass as the male boomer bounces right through them:

BOOM

BOOM

BOOM

KA-BOING!

The powerful bouncy animal leaps a wire fence and bounds into the bushes on the other side of Fairyland.

Archie sits up in a daze. "Umm, am I imagining things, or did that really happen?"

Everyone nods, for what they had seen and heard was real.

"Told you it was a kangaroo," boasts Ollie, spitting grass from his mouth.

Pippa lobs a plantain seedhead into Ollie's lap. "So, mister smarty-pants, kangaroos really do go boing-boing when they hop. Seems like you were right for once. But nobody will ever believe us. That was seriously weird."

Josephine picks a fairy puffball. "Well, there's one thing I'm convinced about"—she closes her eyes and blows the fairy seeds into the sky—"Fairyland is magical." She grabs some empty yoghurt tubs from a basket and passes them around. "Time to pick blackberries, everyone. Mum said if we pick enough, we can make blackberry jam."

"Yum," says Archie, taking a container. "And then I need to find worms for my eel."

"Has this eel of yours got a name?" asks Ollie.

"Yeah. Slimy. I'm calling it *Slimy*."

TWENTY-FIVE

A NEW HOME FOR SLIMY

Grab your hats, bathers and sunscreen, folks, because today is going to be a scorcher. A total fire ban has been declared, with the mercury set to soar above forty degrees Celsius.

Gale-force northerly winds will reach sixty kilometres per hour by mid-morning, which fire authorities warn will create the conditions for catastrophic bushfires.

Residents in the Dandenong Ranges are urged to keep roof gutters clear from dry leaves, remove vegetation from around the house and review evacuation plans. For more information, visit the CFA website.

Thanks, Sandy. Next on Mountain District Radio News, a report about a local funny bunny with her sights set on Hollywood—

Florence switches off the hairdryer, exits the bathroom, slaps on her oversized sunglasses, selects a bundle of empty shopping bags and rushes out the door. Unaware of the fire ban declaration, she clambers up the steps to the car and calls down to Archie, who's digging for worms in the compost heap. "Arrrchieeee! I need you to clear the garden and rake up any dead leaves. Josephine's inside rehearsing for a school play, so try not to bother her. I'm going shopping. I'll be back soon."

Florence's words enter Archie's ears like tinkling coins, and his brain goes *CHA-CHING!* You see, having recently secured an odd-job payment system with his mum, a request to clear the garden means good money—money he desperately needs for a new bike. So he waves and calls back enthusiastically, "Okay, Mum, I'll have it done before you get home."

"And do something about that eel, for goodness sakes," she yells, poking her head through the open window of an old white Volkswagen Beetle. Smoke puffs from the exhaust as the car springs to life. And after a couple of bunny hops and back-fires, Florence zooms down the road.

Meanwhile, Archie digs his spade into the compost heap and unearths a mishmash of rotten vegetables containing a splendid collection of squirming earthworms. "Aww, take a look, fella. Slimy's gonna love these."

In typical Kimba fashion, he ignores Archie's comment, instead preferring to roll in a hodgepodge of mouldy orange skins, eggshells, rotten mushrooms and other unknown smelly compost concoctions.

"No, don't roll in that! There's not enough water to wash you, you naughty dog. Stop it. Stop!"

Guilty as charged, Kimba squints and lowers his tail. Then he smells some burnt toast, and unable to resist his doggy instincts, woofs it down.

"What a dog," huffs Archie, returning to the house with his container of earthworms. "You stay, boy. You're too stinky to come inside. I'll give you a bath later."

Hearing the word *bath*, Kimba's eyes bulge, and he bolts under the tank stand to hide. The scruffy dog hates getting all soapy, fresh and clean. After all, he goes to great lengths to smell like a dead frog in a soggy sock.

In the bathroom a short while later, Archie dangles a fat worm above the fish bucket. "Eat up, Slimy. I don't want you getting sick or skinny."

The hungry eel thrashes its tail, leaps from the water and snatches the wriggly treat from Archie's fingers, gobbling it down in a flash.

As Archie prepares another juicy worm for Slimy, Josephine barges into the bathroom. "Eeew, yuck. That's disgusting. Can you please remove that slimy thing from the bath? I want to have a shower before I learn my lines. Why *do* you have a pet eel, anyway? It's weird."

"Uh, umm, err, well, you see . . ."

"Ah, forget it," she snaps. "There's probably not enough water for a shower, anyway. Urgh, I'm sick of this madhouse!" And out she storms.

"Don't worry, Slimy, she'll learn to love you someday. She just needs to get to know you better."

The eel swishes its tail, attempting to stretch out and swim. However, the conditions are too cramped for anything more than a wiggle and a whomp.

Archie takes the bucket by the handle. "Come on, let's find you a bigger, better home."

Later, having ruled out a few places like the bathtub, the tank and the hot water service, Archie wanders into the kitchen for fresh ideas. He peers into a square sink filled with lukewarm dishwashing water and extracts a pot coated in burnt porridge. *Yuck. Slimy's not going to like it in here.*

To the left is another sink, round and deep, used for washing salad greens. He scoops up a baby spinach leaf floating in a small amount of tea-coloured water. *We can always wash the salad in a pot,* he thinks. *This'll be perfect.* "Here we go, Slimy. Get ready for a slippery dip." He tips the bucket on its side. The eel slides into the sink with a slappy splash and a tail whump.

"Welcome to your new home, Slimy. Now you've got a lovely pool to swim around. And don't worry, this is just temporary. I'll find you something bigger and better soon."

Josephine wanders from her bedroom, reciting lines from an upcoming school play of Romeo and Juliet. "My only love sprung from my only hate! Too early seen unknown, and known too late! Prodigious birth of love it is to me, that I must love a loathed en—" She pauses outside the kitchen doorway, having spotted her brother's suspicious activity. "Uh, you've got to be kidding, Archie. You can't keep your eel in the sink. Are you insane? Mum'll go nuts when she gets home. And I'm never eating salad ever again. Urgh!" She storms into her bedroom and slams the door.

Despite Josephine's protest, Archie is happy that Slimy has a comfortable place to swim. So he turns his attention to other important matters—earning money for his new bike.

TWENTY-SIX

THE BONFIRE STACK

Under the shade of a straw hat, Archie drags a dead wattle sapling up the sun-baked garden path and throws it onto a mountainous pile of bushes, leaves, sticks, grass and gum tree branches. "That's the last one. A job well done, eh, Kimba? I reckon I've earned at least ten dollars so far."

While pondering more ways to earn pocket money, a hot north wind roars through the treetops, and a twig falls to the ground. He tosses it onto the stack and recalls Broos saying, *Da key to a great fire ish to shtart wid da little-esht sticksh.*

Brilliant idea, thinks Archie. "Mum'll be so pleased when I burn all this rubbish. She'll pay me another five dollars for sure. Whaddaya reckon, fella?"

Grrrrroowww, responds Kimba, biting into a green stick.

Little does the boy know, a total fire ban has been declared. And despite Broos's warning not to light fires without an adult, he decides to throw caution to the hot north wind.

Crouched below the towering bonfire stack, Archie shoves scrunched-up balls of newspaper under a bunch of dry twigs and leaves. The paper, which smells of last night's fish and chips, attracts Kimba's curious licking tongue. "No, you lick monster." He drags him back. "Eeew, you stink. Off you go, ya mutt. I'm lighting the fire now."

Kimba skulks away, tail drooped, and resumes chewing his stick in the shade of the nearby rain tank.

"Here goes." The match flares to life, but the wind blows it out. Archie strikes another, shielding it with his cupped hand while lighting the paper. Wispy white smoke spirals up into the air, followed by a small flame that creeps over a crinkly news article, turning it black and flaky. In seconds, the twigs ignite, and flickering flames extend into the leaves, bushes and bigger sticks piled high above.

As the growing flames leap and sparkle in a magical display, Archie steps back and wipes his sweaty brow. The escalating radiance tingles his cheeks and forces him to retreat a little more. His innocent watery eyes glow amber from the roaring flames. And as the fire grows larger than expected, his face twists into a grimace.

It seems the inexperienced boy has underestimated the flammable nature of gum leaves, especially on a scorching hot summer's day. The leaves contain eucalyptus oil, a volatile substance that explodes like petrol when exposed to a flame.

WHOOOSSSHHHHH.

Archie stares in wide-eyed terror as the piled-up gum leaves ignite into a fireball. Fanned by the blustery wind and fuelled by eucalyptus oil, the flames fizz and flare above his head, singeing his eyelashes and eyebrows.

Frozen in shock, Archie's mind replays Broos's wise words, *Neffer build a fire wishout an adult, or when dere'sh a big wind.*

A whippy wind gust blows off Archie's hat, and he clasps his cheeks in horror. *Oh no! What have I done?*

To make matters worse, an overhanging gum tree branch explodes into flames. The burning leaves flash and crackle in a fury as the fire shoots skyward—hissing, roaring, leaping. Intoxicating Eucalyptus fumes clog the air. Glowing orange embers float over to the leaf-littered roof gutters.

Could the house burn down? Could a devastating bushfire take hold?

Archie thinks not. Determined to save the day, he dashes across the yard through a maelstrom of fire, ash and smoke, coughing and rubbing his stinging eyes.

Over at the rain tank, under the wooden stand, he finds Kimba quivering in the hazy shadows.

"It's alright, boy, I'm putting the fire out." He attaches the garden hose, flicks on the pump, swivels the tap, twists the nozzle to jet-spray, and waits.

Gurgles reverberate inside the whirring pump. The hose whips from side to side on the dirt, and water spurts in a long powerful stream, high into the sky.

"Wahoo!" he cheers.

Then suddenly, for no apparent reason, the flow stops dead. The pump whines and burbles, straining under intense pressure as if it's about to blow.

Archie spins around and searches frantically for a solution. *Huh! There's a kink in the hose!* In a race against the flames, he leaps to the blocked section and squeezes the flattened rubber back into a tube shape.

SWISSSSSSHHHHHHH.

The water rushes through at such high pressure that it explodes from the nozzle and sprays in crazy circles. The hose flips about in a wild octopus dance, whipping and whirling around his arms, legs and head, creating a spaghetti mess-up of epic proportions.

Trapped and with the blaze spreading fast, Archie visualises the great Houdini escaping from chains. *I can do it. Just relax . . .* And through a sequence of wiggles and near-dislocations of various arm joints, he bursts free from the rubbery prison.

Hose in hand and Kimba by his side, he storms back across the yard. "Take that!" High-pressure water shoots at a fiery branch. "Yes, it's working!"

Splossshhhh.

Splisssshhh.

Swassshhhh.

Spsshhh-kak-kak-k-k.

The hose coughs and splutters, and the pressure drops to nothing once again.

Archie swings around to check for kinks, but all is clear. "Crikey, the tank's out of water!"

Fuelled by gale-force winds, the fire returns to its former glory, spreading in a ferocious free-for-all across the treetops. Dwarfed by the firestorm, no water, no hope, he drops the hose. As it strikes the ground, the intense heat stings his face, and tears pour from his reddened eyes. Another tree explodes into blinding orange flames that rip across the sky, popping like firecrackers.

With Kimba clutched in his arms, Archie searches for an escape. But a raging wall of fire blocks every direction he turns. Black smoke masks the sun, transforming day into night. Gasping for air, he tucks Kimba under his shirt and gets down low, continuing to search for an exit, praying for a miracle.

But there is no escape route, only fireballs exploding and ballooning all around.

And then—

Honk, honk! WOOWOOWOOWOO! A fire truck speeds up the road, complete with red and blue lights flashing, horn honking and siren blaring.

Called by worried neighbours who spotted the smoke and floating embers, the fire engine screeches to a halt on the road above Archie's house. Four firefighters spring out and rush around the truck. They quickly unravel a thick hose, and after turning a dial and flicking a chunky lever, a booming pump starts. Suddenly gushing water blasts to the fiery treetops. The flames leap and lurch, pop and fizzle, but they're no match for the torrent of water. Seconds later, the fire is extinguished. The smoke clears, and the sun shines through the trees, creating a spectacular rainbow as the water rains down through the sky and onto Archie's blackened face.

A screen door bangs in the background. Josephine sloshes across the garden, tears streaming, fearing for her brother's safety. "Archieeee!" The sight of the sodden kid, unharmed, standing in a puddle, lights her face in relief. "Thank goodness you're okay. I was so worried when I heard the siren. What happened out here? Where's Kimba? Is he safe?"

Kimba pops his head out from under Archie's shirt and licks his chin. "Oi, that's enough. Hop down, you soggy mop."

As Josephine crouches to cuddle Kimba, she notices a packet of wet matches pressed into the mud. "Oh, my God, what did you do? It's a total fire ban, and you're playing with matches?"

"I didn't know it was a fire ban. I just lit the bonfire to—"

"Bonfire! On a day like this? Are you crazy? You're gonna be toast when Mum gets home." The sound of Florence's Volkswagen climbing the hill catches Josephine's attention.

"You got into this mess on your own, so you have to face it on your own." She hands Kimba over and hurries back inside.

Amid the ballyhoo, Florence pulls up behind the fire truck and bursts from the car in hysterics. "What's going on! Archie! Where are you? Where's Josephine and Kimba? Is everyone okay? What on earth is the fire brigade doing here?"

Archie retrieves his soggy hat from a puddle and waves it about. "Here I am. It's okay, Mum. We're all safe."

At first, Florence waves back in a flurry, happy and relieved. Then, as she gazes around at the bonfire remains and charred trees towering above the house, her mouth falls open, her eyes swell, and she screams, "ARRRRRCHHIEEE! You're grounded for SIX MONTHS!"

Although Archie expected not to be paid for clearing the garden, his mum's words come as a devastating, heart-crushing blow. *If I'm grounded for that long, I'll miss out on Chestnut season and never get my bike. Oh, what am I going to do now?*

While a fireman debriefs Florence on the situation, a jet-black crow swoops up through a billowing steam cloud and flaps over to the leaf strainer of the water tank.

Seeing the bird pecking and scratching in the leaves gives Archie a brilliant idea. "Follow me, Kimba. I've got a plan to get back in the good books with Mum."

A kid on a mission, he sloshes through muddy puddles and steaming ash and fronts up to a firefighter checking for spot fires. "Errr, thanks for putting out the fire. I'm really sorry for lighting it. I didn't realise today was a fire ban, honestly I didn't. My sister just told me."

The firefighter removes her yellow hard hat. "What's your name, son?"

"M-m-my name's Archie," he says anxiously.

"That was a dangerous stunt you pulled, Archie. Fire ban or

not, there's no burning off allowed this time of the year. It's too hot and dry. You could've set the whole of Sherbrooke Forest on fire, burnt your house down, even lost your life. I hope you've learnt a valuable lesson."

"Yes, I have. I made a big mistake. I'll never burn off in the summer or on a fire ban day ever again. I promise."

"Glad to hear. And what else have you learnt?"

"Um, not to light a fire in a strong wind or near trees. And not without an adult."

"That's the ticket." The firewoman crouches down and inspects him for injuries. "You all right? Any burns?"

"Yeah, I'm okay. No burns, apart from my singed eyelashes and eyebrows."

"Well, you'll look like a hairless clown for a while. But don't worry, they'll grow back. Looks like my job's done here. The fire's out, nobody's hurt, so we'll be off then."

"Wait," says Archie. "I was wondering if you could help me with another problem?"

The firewoman glances at the boy through squinted eyes, curious as to what the request might be.

Back at the truck a few minutes later, the fire crew drag their hose to the rain tank and insert the nozzle through the leaf-strainer opening. After a wink from the friendly firewoman, Archie twists open the valve and clean water gushes into the hollow tank.

Florence clambers down the steps, carrying two bulging brown paper shopping bags, babbling excitedly along the way. "Oh, my goodness! Are you filling the tank for free?"

The firefighters nod and smile, happy to be of service.

"Thank you, thank you! That's wonderful! We need water so badly. It's been such a dry summer, and funds are a bit low at the moment. Oh, and while you're at it, could you give the garden a good soaking too? The ferns need watering desperately." As Florence continues down the steps, she beams at Archie, elated to have a full rain tank and four firefighters to do odd jobs around the garden.

"And don't forget to water the pot plants and the lemon tree!" she adds, smiling sweetly at the fire crew.

Archie punches the air. "Yes! I'm back in the good books. She can't ground me now."

Excited by the happy occasion, Kimba jumps onto the tank stand and sprays water everywhere as he shakes.

"Hey, I'm wet enough, you soggy mop. Well, at least you're clean. The fire hose did a great job. I don't need to give you a bath now."

Hearing the word *bath*, Kimba's eyes bulge. And before Archie can do anything, he leaps off the tank stand and scurries under the house to hide.

"Come back, you crazy dog! I said I *don't* need to give you a bath."

The screen door to the house creaks open in the background as Florence trundles inside to pack away the groceries before they perish in the heat. A moment later, she shrieks from the kitchen. "Eeeeeeeeeek! Arrrrchie! What's this eel doing in my sink!"

Rocks grow in Archie's shoulders. Due to all the excitement, he'd forgotten all about his pet eel. *Perhaps the kitchen sink wasn't such a good home for Slimy. Darn it. Looks like I'm back in the bad books.*

Just then, gurgles and gloopy bubbling sounds emanate

from the tank. Archie peers through the round opening and marvels at his smiling reflection in the voluminous water swirling near the top.

Once the tank overflows, the fire crew withdraw the hose and spray the garden, including the lemon tree and the pot plants as instructed. Then, with the efficiency and speed of an elite Special Forces team, they pack up their gear and charge back to the truck, fearing Florence will order them to do more odd jobs. And with sirens blaring to hasten their escape, they roar down the road.

Archie jumps into a deep puddle. The warm water lapping at his ankles triggers a brilliant idea—a plan to solve the *Slimy* situation and secure his freedom to pick chestnuts with Pippa and Ollie next autumn.

A few hours later, Archie shovels out the last pile of dirt from a newly dug hole. He sits down, legs out straight, and swings both arms around to test the size. Satisfied by the space, he lays black plastic across the bottom and up the sides, then secures it in place with rocks along the edges.

Finally, standing beside the hole, hose in hand, Archie announces, "And now for my big finale!" He turns the nozzle. Fresh, clean water gushes out in a long stream. And before long, the pond is full, ready for action. "Here you go, Slimy. Home sweet home."

The eel splashes into the water and swims around in circles, frolicking about while exploring the new environment. After a few minutes, it drifts up and down the pond's edge, slipping and sliding on the plastic.

"What is it? Are you hungry?" Archie dangles an earthworm. "Is this what you want? Here you go. Come get it."

Ignoring the offer, the eel pokes its head above the water and gazes around as if searching for something—something it needs more than anything else in the world.

TWENTY-SEVEN

FAREWELL TO A FRIEND

Hunched over by the pond, Archie wonders, *How can I make Slimy happy?*

"What's wrong, little fella?" comes a voice from behind.

"Banjo! You gave me a fright. What are you doing here?"

"Your mum invited me for dinner. She cooks a good chicken soup, she does. Best soup I ever tasted."

A wind gust rushes through the gum trees above. Soon after, black ash snows down from the sky and lands on Banjo's hat and shoulders. "That's some serious burnin' off ya been doing, young fella."

Archie glances down with an ashamed sigh. "Yeah, I've learnt my lesson."

"So what you doing out here by the pond, lookin' so glum?" asks Banjo.

"I'm trying to cheer up Slimy, the eel I caught down at the creek. Can you see him? There he is, behind that leaf."

"Yeah, I see it. Oooh, a nice fat one. Good bush tucker that eel. You gonna cook it up?"

"No, Banjo. I can't eat him. He's my friend."

"We'll have to stick to chicken soup then, eh?" Banjo sits on a rock beside the boy. "Anyway, best not to eat this one. She's got unfinished business—women's business."

"What? Slimy's a girl? How can you tell?"

"She's too big to be a male eel. They're smaller and skinnier. And see those large eyes. She's a female alright."

"So why do you think she's sad? I feed her the best worms. And I made this great pond, so she has plenty of space to swim around. But no matter what I do, she's unhappy. Oh, Banjo, I feel sad for her."

"Well, if your heart's sad, your spirit's sayin' ya on the wrong track." Banjo closes his eyes and inhales the warm northern wind, scented with burnt eucalyptus leaves and distant lands. "You know where that eel come from?"

"Yeah, from a creek not far from here."

"No, I mean where she was born?"

Archie shakes his head.

"That eel, she come from the warm waters of the Coral Sea, long, long way away, right up the top of Australia where that big north wind blowin' from. Her mother and father, their spirit still up there."

Water thrashes in the pond as Slimy whips her tail and leaps into the air.

"She's a good swimmer, that one," continues Banjo. "She swam all the way through the ocean, up the rivers and over the swampland until she found her way into the little creek you caught her in."

"How do you know she came from the Coral Sea?"

"That's where all the eels come from. It's the way of the world."

"Wow," gasps Archie. "No wonder she survived in a bucket without water for so long. She's a real battler."

"*Hee-hee,* she's a tough one alright."

As the two ponder Slimy's epic journey of survival, a breeze whispers through a casuarina tree shading the pond, its airy secrets prompting Banjo to gaze up. "Hey, whaddaya think that wind sayin'?"

Archie shuts his eyes and listens for a hidden message.

Shhhhheeeeeeoooooowwwwoooooeeeeeee.

"Umm, it's windy?" he says with a cheeky chuckle.

Banjo smiles wryly. "Ah, that's a tricky answer. You gotta listen with ya heart, not ya ears." He closes his eyes, takes a long breath and exhales slowly, "*Haaaaaaa.* I think that wind sayin', 'Come home, Slimy, come home'."

"So you think she's searching for a way back home?"

"That's right. All the eels gotta swim back to the Coral Sea if they want to have a family of their own. Those big sad eyes sayin', 'I want to go home to have my babies.' But to get there, she'll have to slither over dry land to the nearest creek. That'd be Sassafras Creek, right?"

Archie nods.

"Yeah, well, she'll never make it in this heat. And she knows that. So she's stuck here in this pond of yours."

A dark cloud lifts from Archie's heart. "I know how to help Slimy now."

Banjo pats him on the shoulder. "That eel, she lucky to have a friend like you."

The following morning, Banjo, Broos, Florence, Josephine, Pippa and Archie assemble beside Beagley's Bridge, where Sassafras Creek meanders through lapping ferns and dense forest. Dappled sunlight peeks through the horizontal gaps of the mountain ash, waltzing on the water, sparkling in ever-changing patterns as they crouch by the creek's edge.

While Broos plays his harmonica and Banjo sings a farewell song, strumming along on his guitar, Archie submerges his bucket into the cool flowing water.

Slimy swishes around a few times and gazes at Archie for a fleeting moment. Then, with a brisk tail flick, she torpedoes into a deep dark pool of water.

"She's happy now," says Pippa.

"Farewell, Slimy. Have a safe journey home," says Archie.

Josephine touches his arm. "You did the right thing. She's going to make a good mum."

Everyone sits in silence under tall shady ferns, listening to the trickling stream and the whistle-whip of whip birds in the forest.

Wondering where Slimy might be, Archie swishes his hands in the water. The coolness is a soothing balm to summer's heat and a distraction from the loss of a friend. Upstream, a bright yellow leaf slides down a tiny waterfall and swishes over and around smooth rocks until it floats into Archie's fingers. He raises it to the sun. Golden light glows through its semi-transparent membrane. Excitement buzzes. *At last, chestnut season is coming . . .*

PART FOUR

TWENTY-EIGHT

BAGARAMADRAMA

"Up you get, boy. We're picking chestnuts today," says Archie, ruffling Kimba's fur.

The scruffball leaps onto an open book on the floor and sniffs a photograph of Houdini escaping from a tangle of rope.

"Oi, off that. There's no time for reading. The others'll be here soon, and we've gotta find a bag to carry the chestnuts."

Distracted by a mysterious odour, Kimba crawls under the bed and drags out Archie's vinyl school bag. First he sniffs it, then he growls and thrashes it around in his clenched jaws.

"Let it go, you daft dog." Archie rips it from his teeth and peers inside. "Eeew, yuck, mouldy peanut butter and sultana sandwich." As he rummages around, gooey slime squishes between his fingers, and his hand pushes through the soggy bottom. "Uh-oh, I think I need a new school bag." Brown sludge oozes from the hole and slops onto the floor. "Aw, gross. I was wondering where that banana went."

Quicker than a licking lizard, Kimba gobbles the mushy fruit. A stomach gurgle later, after a brief convulsion, he spews it onto a half-finished school project and gulps it back down.

Archie screws up his face in disgust. "I'll pretend I didn't see that. Come on, let's keep looking. This bag's no good for chestnutting."

Following a thorough search around the house, all Archie finds is an ancient backpack with gaping rat holes at the bottom, and his long-lost Dr Who scarf, knitted by his nanna. Disappointed and bagless, he slumps on the couch, plonks his feet on a coffee table and wraps the scarf around his neck five times. *Oh, what am I going to do?*

A car horn sounds in the distance, followed shortly after by a *tap-tap-ta-tap-tap* at the front entrance.

Archie swings open the door.

"Morning, squire," says Ollie. White clouds puff from his mouth as he wipes his new navy-blue moon boots on the mat. "Brrrrr, it's freezing out here."

Pippa rubs her red knitted gloves together and steps inside. "It's going to be a beautiful day for chestnutting once the mist rises and the sun comes out."

"Great," says Archie, closing the door. "I've been watching the trees over the past week. It's the perfect time for picking. The nuts have just started dropping by the bucket load."

Ollie throws a package onto the coffee table. "I got the paper bags you wanted. One hundred should be enough for our stall, don't you think?"

"Yeah, they're perfect. Now we've only got one problem to sort out."

"What . . . problem?" questions Ollie. "Last time you had a problem, we were nearly eaten alive."

Archie slumps on the couch and sighs. "I can't find a chestnutting bag. Without something big and easy to carry like a backpack, we won't be able to collect enough nuts to make any decent money."

"Wait a minute. I might have the answer," says Ollie. He unzips a hidden sleeve pocket and extracts a seemingly endless stream of brown knotted string.

Pippa lifts an eyebrow. "A string bag? You've got to be joking. The chestnuts will fall straight through the gaps."

Disappointed his parka couldn't save the day, Ollie stuffs the stringy mess into the Abyss. "Sorry, there's a bag drought at the moment. Haven't seen a decent one in months."

"Me neither," says Pippa. All I've got is this." She flings her cotton overnight bag onto the couch.

"This is a disaster," says Archie. "The chestnuts only drop for a few days. We'll miss out if we can't find a good bag. Then we'll have to wait a whole year till they're ripe again. I can't wait that long for my new bike."

"Hey, what's that up there?" says Pippa, pointing to a large white plastic bag on a high shelf above the piano.

"I dunno, probably some of Mum's old junk."

Ollie wiggles his finger. "Don't be so quick to judge, my friend. In my experience, the most valuable things are found in high places. It's a fundamental truth."

"Okay. I doubt it's anything, but I'll check it out." Archie leaps onto the piano, stretches up on his toes and peeks under the plastic. "Holy rigatoni, you're right. It's a brand new backpack. Perfect for chestnutting!"

Florence bursts from the bathroom in a cloud of billowing steam, dressed in a pink shower cap and baby-blue bathrobe.

"Hey! What are you doing up there! That's my new bag for my European study trip. Can't I keep anything from you kids? Don't you dare use that bag for picking chestnuts! Get down from there right now!" She grabs her clothes from a drying rack and storms into the bathroom to get dressed.

"But, Mum," yells Archie, jumping down from the piano, "what will we use for chestnutting? I've looked everywhere. I can't find any bags large enough without rat holes."

Florence explodes from the bathroom in a cloud of talcum powder. "Well, what will I use for my study trip if you ruin my bag? I can't afford another one, and I'll fail the subject if I miss the trip. Can't you use baskets or your school bag?"

"No! We can't use baskets. They're too small and hard to carry. And my school bag's busted. We're planning on picking heaps, so we need a big bag that's easy to carry."

Florence rushes around the house in a tizzy. "Oh, where are my keys? I have to get the car to the garage. It's on the blink again and I'm running late."

Keen to cool things down, Archie scans the usual locations and digs down a crack in the couch. "Found ya keys!"

"Oh, good boy." She whisks them from his hand.

"By the way, Mum. We need a lift to Belgrave early in the morning to sell our chestnuts."

"Okay then. Let's hope the car's working or you'll be walking." Florence pecks Archie on the cheek and smiles at Pippa and Ollie. "Now, be careful chestnutting. And DON'T TAKE MY BAG or there'll be BIG TROUBLE! I'm in a rush. See you later, kids."

"But, Mum! You forgot to take off your—"

BANG.

The front door slams.

"—shower cap," says Archie, cringing.

Ollie assumes a relaxed position on the couch, placing his moon boots on the coffee table and a crochet blanket over his thighs. "Perhaps we won't need a ride tomorrow morning. I mean, without a bag, we might as well play Chinese checkers by the fire or do some baking."

"No way," responds Archie. "We've got a lot riding on today —your computer, Pippa's telescope, my BMX. I've been waiting all year for chestnut season. I'm not giving up that easy. And anyway, we do have a bag." He whisks the crochet blanket off Ollie's legs and clambers up onto the piano. "See. All we have to do is replace Mum's backpack with this lovely blanket"—he swaps them over—"and berzinko, we've got the perfect bag for chestnutting."

Archie jumps down and lays the backpack on the floor. Everything about it says high-quality: the sleek brown fabric, mouldable frame, and quick-release buckles. "What a beauty. Check out the padded waist strap. It'll take the load off our shoulders so we can carry heaps of chestnuts."

"Err, didn't your mum say *not* to take her bag?" says Pippa. "You'll be in serious trouble if she finds out."

Ollie nods furiously. "She'll go berko, for sure. Didn't you see the wild look in her eyes? This European study extravaganza means the world to her. Your bread will roll if she discovers you've taken her backpack for chestnutting."

"Head. Your *head* will roll," grumbles Pippa.

"Don't worry. As long as we return the backpack before Mum gets home, she won't even realise it was missing. Anyway, it's just a bag. What could go wrong?"

Ollie and Pippa shrug their shoulders and say in unison, "Yeah, I suppose you're right. What could go wrong?"

TWENTY-NINE

BANANA PASSIONFRUIT

"Last one there's a mouldy peg!" hollers Ollie, bolting down the lane towards Fairyland.

"Let the goofball go," says Archie, ambling along with Pippa and Kimba. "So, as I was saying, after we pick some banana passionfruit, there's a shortcut that'll take us to the best chestnut trees in the—"

"Hey, wait!" Pippa spots Ollie waving frantically in the distance. "What's he up to now? We better go see."

They race down the lane and stare goggle-eyed at a bold red sign attached to a gate blocking the way that says:

PRIVATE PROPERTY

TRESPASSERS WILL BE PROSECUTED!

Archie yanks a chunky brass padlock attached to a chain. "What! Who would do this?"

As Pippa peers over the sign, gazing longingly at the grassy meadow, the colour drains from her cheeks. "They can't block off Fairyland. It's our special place."

Tears well in Ollie's eyes, and his lips quiver. "B-b-but what about our g-grass fights? H-h-how will w-we survive without our grass f-f-fights at Fairyland?"

"I don't know," says Pippa. "And how will we survive if we can't pick banana passionfruit or thread daisy chains or spy on dancing lyrebirds or make secret fairy wishes? And I love our grass fights, Ollie. I can't imagine a better place for grass fights than Fairyland." She pounds her fists on the barrier. "I hate this sign!"

"Yeah, what a joke," says Archie. He pelts a handful of mud at the sign. *SPLAT!* Brown goo oozes over the word PRIVATE.

Pippa and Archie share a cheeky glance, and without saying a word, unleash a barrage of sloppy splodge-balls.

SPLATTER

WACKA

SPLODGETY

GOOP!

Ollie crosses his arms and hangs back, preferring to stay out of trouble.

Kimba, *keen* for trouble, sniffs a gatepost, lifts his leg and widdles.

"Good dog. That's exactly what I think too," praises Archie, finding a smile. "Hey, Ollie, remember last autumn when you squeezed a humungous banana passionfruit into your mouth, and you laughed so hard the juice squirted out your nose? *Hee-hee*, it was hilarious."

A dash of cheeky pride streaks across Ollie's face, and joy beams from his widened eyes. But then the bitter reality sinks in. Fairyland is no more. His eyes droop, the light fades, and a tear rolls down his cheek. "I was looking f-f-forward to the juicy b-b-banana passionfruit. I've been waiting all y-y-year for them to ripen."

"Come on, don't be sad. Let's go pick some," says Archie, straddling the top railing with his legs dangling down each side. "We can climb over. It's easy."

"But, but we can't. Fairyland's p-p-private property now. We'll be p-p-persecuted for t-t-trespassing."

"Prosecuted," corrects Pippa. "I think it means getting in trouble with the police."

Ollie blows his nose on a hanky and responds sarcastically, "Oh, well, that's all right then. I can see the headlines now: 'Crime spree! Three youths jailed for picking banana passion-fruit at Fairyland'. If that's the kind of publicity you want, go ahead, trespass if you must.

"How about this for publicity?" Pippa slaps more mud on the sign and smears it all over the words with both hands. "Now the sign says Mud-Splat-Gloopy-Goo. That means *you're welcome* in my book."

"That's right," says Archie, leaping onto the Fairyland side. "See. No persecution. No prosecution. Nothing."

"Yet . . ." says Ollie, raising his eyebrows in doubt.

Pippa sits sidesaddle on the gate. "How do we even know the sign's legal? Fairyland belongs to everyone." She swings her legs over and crunches on the gravel next to Archie.

Unimpressed and alone, Ollie drops his head and traipses up the lane.

"Hey, where are you going?" calls Archie.

"To the main road. I'll have to dodge cars and trucks, but it's the only sensible way to The Patch now. I'll meet you at The Patch Store in about an hour. If you're not in prison, that is."

Ruff Ruff Ruff Ruff, barks Kimba, bouncing up and down at the gate. His nose pokes through a gap, and his paws scratch on the wire as he whimpers, *uurh uurh uurh*.

"Come on, boy. Up! Up! Come on. Jump over. You can do it," encourage Archie and Pippa.

The scruffy mutt runs back up the lane, turns spritely, sprints at the gate and leaps into Archie's outstretched arms. "Good dog. You did it! Now sit down while I clip on your lead. You can't chase lyrebirds at Fairyland."

While plodding up the lane, Ollie mutters to himself, "Welcome shmelcome. Next I'll be bailing them out with my computer savings. 'Told you so', I'll say."

"Eeeeeeeeek," comes a squeal from Fairyland.

Ollie freezes, expecting the worst.

"Hahaaa! Got you!" echo the happy voices of Archie and Pippa racing around the meadow, throwing grass at each other.

As if hypnotised by the familiar playful sounds, Ollie's eyes grow large and dreamy.

"Climb over! Everything's fine!" calls Pippa, leaping for joy. She cartwheels through the dandelion flowers, then picks a fairy puffball and blasts the seeds to the sky. "See, it's still Fairyland! Nothing's changed."

"And the banana passionfruit are ripe," shouts Archie. "It's a bumper crop, Ollie. Woohoo!"

A gentle breeze carries the fairy seeds up the lane.

Mesmerised by the fluffy aerial display passing overhead, Ollie's posture straightens, his cheeks turn rosy, and he gallops down the lane, clambering over the gate as he shouts, "Wait for me! I'm coming too!"

Together in Fairyland, the friends gaze up at the long, fat banana passionfruit dangling from the vine, nestled among shiny leaves and dazzling pink flowers. Some of the fruit are green or purple. The prized ripe ones are bright yellow, which means they are sweet and juicy.

"Oooh, *it is* a bumper crop," says Ollie, rubbing his tummy. "Goody goody yum-yum."

After tying Kimba's lead to the wire fence, Archie plucks a plump banana passionfruit from the vine and slices it down the middle with his fingernail. "Mmmm, smells like mandarins and apples." He rips it apart and gobbles down the orange jelly pulp and crunchy black seeds. "Aw, yum. It's so juicy."

Ollie, having selected the fattest, yellowest specimen he can find, chomps off each end, and using the skin as a supersized straw, sucks out the entire contents in one stupendous slurp, *thhhhuuuwwwwooorrrruuuuooooop*. "Mmmm, bananary."

While the boys search for more, peeking behind leaves for yellow surprises, Pippa climbs the fence. "Hey, guys, there's heaps of ripe ones up here. We can save them as snacks for later. I'll throw some down. Here they come, ready or not!"

The boys scramble to action, catching the flying fruit with heroic leaps, spectacular dives and gallant lunges. Once they have nothing less than a truckload, Ollie stuffs them into his parka until it bulges like a bloated pufferfish.

"Watch out!" calls Pippa, jumping down from the fence. She lounges on the grass and devours a scrumptious banana passionfruit, unfazed by the juice dribbling down her chin. "So, Archie, which chestnut trees shall we pick from first?"

"I say we start at the Twelve Apostles."

"The twelve what?" says Ollie.

"Twelve enormous chestnut trees, all in a row. They're incredible. I've been picking chestnuts there since I was little. We can walk straight across a paddock to the trees. They drop bucket loads of huge nuts every day, so we should have all the chestnuts we need before lunch. That'll give us plenty of time to sneak Mum's bag back before she gets home. Then we can paint signs and weigh and bag the chestnuts ready for selling tomorrow."

"I'm so excited. I can't wait to pick those lovely chestnuts," says Pippa.

Archie springs to his feet. "Won't be long now. Come on, Kimba, time to go." Just as he unties the lead from the fence, the spirited hound spots a field mouse and dashes across the meadow in a barking fit.

"Stop! Come back, you crazy dog!" hollers Archie in hot pursuit.

"Wait up!" shouts Pippa, screaming behind.

Ollie tries to run, but his parka is so stuffed with banana passionfruit he hobbles along like a bouncy sumo wrestler. "Hey, wait for me, you pongo-bongos! I don't know the way to the Twelve Impossibles!"

THIRTY

THE BIG DIPPER

"Not far now," says Archie. "Once we reach the bottom of this hill, it's only a short walk to the Twelve Apostles."

Pippa peers over the edge. Coated in white frost, the grassy slope plunges at a giddying angle to the misty valley below. "Ummm, how do you suppose we climb down this hill? Or should I say *cliff?*"

"That's not a cliff. That's an icy grass slide," says Ollie, whose yearly skiing trips with his parents makes him quite an expert on the matter. "I'll grant you it's a hairy-scary launch and a tasty eighty percent gradient straight down to the bottom. She's a smooth run though. Not impossible with the right equipment."

"If only we had a boogie board or something slippery to slide down on," says Pippa, glancing around. Her eye catches the sheen of Florence's new bag. "Hey, what about the back-pack? It's even got a grip handle."

"Are you kidding? It'll only take two of us, and if it rips on the way down, I'm dead meat. Wait a sec. How about this?" Archie drags out a fallen fern frond from the bushes and places it by the slope. "Here goes . . ." *Crunch.* The brittle leaves crumble to pieces under his bottom. "Nah, that won't work."

"Nice try, Archie. A superb display of quixotic quackery. But I think this situation calls for something a little more hi-tech." Ollie reaches inside a chest-high pocket and pops out a banana passionfruit. "No, no, wait." He reaches in again and extracts a compact first aid kit. In addition to bandages, safety pins and a pair of tweezers, it contains a space blanket neatly folded inside a tiny packet. "If we're going to rocket down this fun-plunge, we'll need something spacey." He shakes the blanket out, displaying a surprisingly large silver sheet.

"You're a legend. This is perfect," says Archie, sliding his hands down the shiny, slippery surface.

"Hang on. There's one blanket and three of us. How's that going to work?" questions Pippa.

"No problemo," says Ollie, whipping out his Swiss Army Knife. He flips out a pair of scissors and cuts the sheet into thirds. "One for you, one for you, and one for me. Now we're ready for our very own space race."

Archie wraps the sheet around his legs and dangles his feet over the precipice. Then, with Kimba held tightly, he wiggles closer, and they launch down the slope. "Geronimo!"

"Whoopee!" cheers Pippa, flying after him.

Inspired by his favourite Winter Olympic Games event, the luge, Ollie sits on the silver blanket, grips a grass tuft on each side, glides back and forth a few times and explodes down the slope via a whippy push-off. "Whoopidee-doopidee!" He lies back in a plank, toes pointed, and gazes up at the clouds as he rockets down the hill, screaming, "Whooaaahh!"

Halfway to the bottom, shooting along, the kids' cheeks stretch backwards like wobbly slime balls hurtling through space at light speed.

High in the cloud-dappled sky, a flock of yellow-tailed black cockatoos glance down, wondering what the mysterious silver objects might be.

"Watch out! Rabbits!" shouts Archie, sliding towards a rabbit mound sloping up into a ski jump. "Whoooooaaaaa." They swish over the ice-coated rise and fly through the air. Legs, arms and paws akimbo, they plummet to earth and crash land in a soft onion weed patch.

"Look out!" screams Pippa, twisting and twirling in a spectacular aerial display, her shimmery space blanket streaming behind. Just before impact, she dives into a forward roll and tumbles into the padded backpack.

"Banana split!" yells Ollie, barrelling through the onion weed with banana passionfruit exploding and flinging from his pockets. *D-d-d-d-SPLAT-d-d-d-d-SPLAT-d-d-d-d-SQUELCH.*

Coated in fruity juice, the goofball rolls to a stop on his back and stares up, smiling at the cockatoos circling overhead.

While everyone lies in silence, dazed but unharmed, the pungent pong of crushed onion weed wafts all around in the chill air. Too strong for Kimba's sensitive nose, he sneezes twice and then leaps after a passing white butterfly.

"Talk about shortcuts. That was unreal," says Pippa.

"I'm officially naming this slippery dip the Banana Split," declares Ollie, proceeding to lick his glasses clean. "Mmmm, passionfruit with a hint of onion. Not bad, not bad at all."

Archie flicks off a clump of onion weed from his mum's backpack and stands up. "This way, you gooseberries."

"Hey, who are you calling a gooseberry, you stroopwafel," jokes Pippa, bumping Archie's shoulder as they cross a quiet country road.

THIRTY-ONE

THE TWELVE IMPOSSIBLES

"Welcome to the Twelve Apostles," announces Archie proudly.

The kids peer down a meadow, where, blanketed by a white mist, stand twelve grand old chestnut trees, all in a row, their leaves glowing golden in the morning light.

"Wow," gasps Pippa.

Ollie inspects the trees through his binoculars. "I had my doubts, Archie. But I must say, you've hit the jackpot this time. Methinks we are going to be rich."

"Let me see," says Archie. The image blurs, then sharpens as he zooms in. "Yep, the trees are loaded . . . Huh! What is that?" A wooden post creeps into view, then a wire and more posts. "Oh no, you've gotta be kidding me. There's a barbed-wire fence blocking the trees!"

"I thought you'd been collecting chestnuts here for years?" says Pippa.

"Yeah, me, Josephine, and Russell used to come here when I was a little kid. We walked straight across the paddock to the trees—no fences, just grass and mud."

Mooooo, bellows a cow from the paddock.

“They’re the Twelve Impossibles now,” declares Ollie. “Only fools and desperadoes would collect chestnuts from those trees. Cows are dangerous creatures, you know. They kill more people than sharks.”

Pippa hops up and down, pointing at the paddock. “Look, it’s Leo and Neville!”

The bullies fall to their knees in the distance and toss out handfuls of chestnuts from a bulging army-green duffel bag. They glance behind, faces ghostly white as if being chased by a wild beast.

Archie presses the binoculars to his eyes. Leo and Neville spring to their feet and continue running across the paddock with the bag. “They’re freaked out by something. I wonder what they’re running from.”

A raging black bull emerges from the mist—a hulking ball of muscle and power—snorting and bellowing as it charges for the boys.

“Arrgghhh!” screams Leo, who, predicting a gruesome end, throws the bag over the fence before leaping the wire in a single bound.

Neville follows, but his jeans catch on the barbs, leaving him dangling mid-way, legs kicking about helplessly.

Closing in fast, the charging bull angles his horns at Neville’s defenceless body and roars, *MOOOAARRRGGGHHH.*

“He’s gonna be rammed! Quick, we better do something!” screams Pippa.

Ollie waves his red jacket in a frantic, theatrical display. “It’s not working. We’re too far away.”

With his options running out and death imminent, Neville whips off his jeans and flops over the fence, plunging face-first into a squishy warm cow patty.

White clouds of air puff from the bull's nose as it headbutts the wire and stomps on the frosty grass.

The bullyboys head for the road, Leo stumbling along with the duffel bag on one shoulder, and Neville jogging in his yellow polka-dot boxer shorts, flashing his pale knobbly knees above the mist.

Beep. A countdown timer starts on Ollie's digital watch. "It's my estimation that in one minute, twenty-three seconds and twelve milliseconds, we'll cross paths with Leo and Neville, and as I'm not in the mood for a confrontation, may I suggest we—"

"Ruuunnnn!" shouts Archie.

The friends hotfoot it down the road and head up a gravel lane to safety.

"So what's your next big idea?" says Ollie in a cynical tone, slowing to a fast walk. "Perhaps we should pick our noses instead of chestnuts?"

"At least we'll get something," jokes Pippa.

"Come on, cut me some slack, you two. How was I to know the Twelve Apostles were fenced off and patrolled by a bull?"

"But aren't you the Chestnut King? You should've known," says Pippa with a wry smile.

"Yeah, perhaps I was a little off my game."

"So where's our next stop, Sire?" asks Ollie.

Archie grabs a stick from the ground and wallops a stone, sideswiping it into a ditch. "I've seen a great chestnut tree on Clarkson Avenue. There's just one problem—"

"There's more than one problem," says Ollie, clasping a long stick, bounding to Archie's side. He parts his feet and grips the stick in professional-golfing style. "You see, your stance is all wrong, and your swing is a complete mess. You've got to move your feet wider apart, bring your arms in a bit, follow through in a nice arc. And you must always keep your eyes on the rock. Got it?"

"Uhhh, thanks for the golf lesson. But I mean, there's a problem with the chestnut tree on Clarkson Avenue."

Ollie swishes his stick through the air. "What's the catch this time?"

"Well, I heard the owner hides rabbit traps under the tree to stop kids collecting the chestnuts. One false move and the metal jaws will—"

SNAP. A golf ball-sized stone whizzes up the centre of the lane. After a brief gloat, Ollie peers over his glasses at Archie. "Did you say rabbit . . . trap?"

"Yeah, it's probably just a rumour. I doubt it's true."

"I wouldn't be so sure about that," comments Pippa. "The other day at school, Claire Thickett told me about a dog that went missing near Clarkson Avenue. It was gone for a whole week. Everyone thought it was dead or lost until the poor thing turned up with one leg missing. Claire said it got caught in a rabbit trap and escaped by gnawing its own leg off."

"Aww, that's horrible. The poor dog," says Archie, stroking Kimba's head.

Ollie drops the stick. "That settles it. Chestnut season is officially over. There's no way I'm picking chestnuts if there's any chance of hidden rabbit traps. This chestnutting madness has gone too far. I'm going home to make honey joys instead."

"Honey joys? Have you gone bonkers?" says Archie.

"No. I'm thinking as clear as a cow."

Pippa shakes her head. "Well, that explains everything."

"As I was saying," continues Ollie, "I've been working on a honey joy recipe using maple syrup, organic coconut butter and a hint of orange essence. We can make a mega batch to sell at our roadside stall. They'll be gluten-free and paleo, so they'll go down a treat with the tourists. What do you say? No barbed wire. No rabbit traps. No charging bulls. Just yummy, sweet honey joys!"

"Err, how are they honey joys if there's no *honey* in them?" says Pippa. "And anyway, Claire and I sold them at the school fete last summer. No one bought any till we lowered the price to five cents. We'll need to sell thousands to make the same money as selling chestnuts."

"She's right," says Archie. "Now listen. We can't give up chestnutting yet. There's other good places we can try. I know a great tree near the Kallista Church. It's a bit of a hike from here, but there's no barbed-wire fences or rabbit traps—and I promise, Ollie, no cows or bulls."

THIRTY-TWO

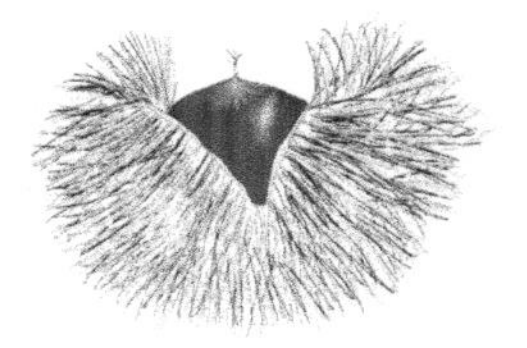

ALL WELCOME

The friends trek up a hill through the forest, past Clarkson Avenue, down Tom Roberts Road and into the little town of Kallista, where they arrive at a white weatherboard church.

Under the shade of two magnificent chestnut trees growing near the church front lawn, Archie leans his mum's backpack against a wooden sign that says:

ALL WELCOME

As Ollie gazes under the trees, a dead leaf flutters across the barren ground. "I thought you said the chestnuts were dropping by the bucket load. I'm *so* glad we hiked all this way for nothing. Bravo, you've hit the crackpot this time."

Archie kicks an empty chestnut burr across the dirt. "Rats, we got here too late. Someone's already collected the nuts." He points to a metal rake resting on a mountainous heap of green and brown chestnut burrs. The spiky casings are usually filled with four or five chestnuts, but the piled-up ones are empty. "Looks like a professional job too."

"Chin up. There's bound to be a few nuts lying around. Let's pick what we can," says Pippa.

"Yeah, we might get half a kilo if we search real hard."

Ollie scouts around the trunk and finds a shiny dark brown chestnut under a leaf. "Ooh, ooh, I found one! Take a look. It's a beauty."

"Nice one," says Archie, opening the bag. "Our first nut of the day. A hundred thousand more like that and we'll be set."

Keen to get involved, Kimba drops a stick at Archie's feet and peers up, eyes bulging and twinkling, begging for a game of fetch.

"Great idea, Kimba. Stand back, everyone. I'm gonna try something." Archie gazes at the tree, eyes scanning the canopy. Then he tosses the stick at a cluster of spiky chestnut casings on a high branch. "It's a bullseye. Watch out!"

Everyone scrambles for cover as five green burrs plummet to the ground, along with a smattering of loose chestnuts clickety-clacking down through the leaves and branches.

While Pippa and Ollie dash about collecting the nuts, Kimba fetches the stick, drops it back at Archie's feet and peers up with those eager eyes, hoping for another toss.

"Hang on, boy, I've gotta collect the nuts first." Archie stomps on a burr, expecting lovely plump chestnuts to pop out. But instead, the long spikes pierce the thin sole of his old desert boot, and sharp pain zaps through his foot. "Oweeee!" He collapses beside the ALL WELCOME sign and rips off his boot and sock.

"You might need these," says Ollie, offering a pair of tweezers from his first aid kit.

"Thanks. Aww, ouch, they really sting." While Archie plucks the spikes from his foot, he calls out, "Hey, who's got good shoes for stomping on burrs?"

"Me," says Ollie, pointing to his moon boots. "They've got thick cleated souls for extra grip, spongy rubber inserts and a fluffy lining—comfy, warm and can stomp on anything!"

"Mine are pretty good too," says Pippa, testing her high-tops on an empty casing.

"Great. How about you two do the stomping, and I'll knock more down with the stick?"

Ollie crushes a burr under his moon boot and smiles as if possessed. "Let the chestnutting games begin."

"Take cover, everyone. Here goes." *Whoosh.* Archie's flying stick strikes a loaded branch, and a chaotic cascade of burrs and loose chestnuts plummet to the ground.

Squealing in excitement, Pippa and Ollie run in from the side and collect the chestnuts lying on the dirt. Then they jump around stomping on the casings, popping out more to collect. Handfuls of nuts pour into Florence's backpack, which now sits up all on its own.

Although the stick method is a slow way to pick chestnuts, the system works brilliantly for a few minutes until—

KA-BOOF! A priest wearing a black robe bursts through the wooden church doors, wielding a broom, screaming to high heaven, "Arrrrrrgggghh, these chestnuts are church property! Skedaddle, you kids! You're trespassing!"

Archie, Pippa, Ollie and Kimba run helter-skelter as the priest chases them round and round the tree, waving his broom, shrieking, "Scram, you little devils!"

Archie grabs the backpack, swipes his boot off the grass, whisks Kimba under one arm and escapes down the road with the others. While hobbling over jagged stones on one bare foot, he shouts, "Head for Beagley's Bridge!"

THIRTY-THREE

THE MOUNTAIN SPRING

The frantic kids race past Beagley's Bridge Picnic Ground and follow a narrow forest track alongside Sassafras Creek. Twenty or so minutes later, all red, hot and sweaty, they collapse at a mountain spring. The crystal-clear water, flowing out from a high rocky bank, cascades over moss and dainty ferns growing in the cracks.

Archie steps across loose wet pebbles to the spring and dangles his head under the icy water, splashing his face and soaking his hair and neck. "Ahhhh, that's better."

Pippa unbuttons her woollen jacket, rips off her shoes and dips her aching toes in the stream. Once her feet are nice and cold, she slips and slides up to the spring and drinks from her cupped hands. "Delicious. I've never tasted water so good."

Kimba joins her side and laps from a puddle to his heart's delight.

Still reeling from the church fiasco, Ollie pokes a twig into Archie's arm. "No rabbit traps and bulls, hmm? Didn't mention the crazy chestnut-picking priest. Mental note: add to the chestnutting safety list—no bulls, no cows, no rabbit traps, AND no priests. Any other surprises up your sleeve?"

Archie averts his eyes. "I honestly thought we could pick at the church. I've picked there before without any trouble. And the sign did say All WELCOME. You saw it for yourself."

"Well, it appears everyone's in the chestnutting game these days," replies Ollie, stretching his calf muscle on a log. "It's tearing the community apart." After completing both legs, he clambers over the slippery rocks, falling to his knees several times. Finally reaching the spring, his mouth opens wide and he guzzles the water, allowing it to dribble down his sweaty neck. "Mmm, tastes like autumn with a hint of moss, essence of fern and overtones of volcanic rock." His eyes flash wide. "Brainwave! Why don't we fill recycled bottles with the spring water and sell them beside the road instead of chestnuts? We can call it *Hilly Water*. No, no, how about *Activated Hills Water*? Yes, that'll do the trick."

Archie unwraps a peanut butter and sultana sandwich and lounges on a clover patch beside the babbling creek. "Listen. I'm telling you, we can make a fortune selling chestnuts. We can't give up yet."

Ollie and Pippa take a sandwich each from the backpack and find a comfortable spot on the clover.

"Actually, these are pretty good," says Ollie, munching on a peanut butter-coated sultana. "I had my doubts, Archie, but you're on to a winner here." He brushes his fingers across the white clover flowers. "Who wants to help me find a four-leaf clover? It'll bring us good luck if we find one. We could do with some luck, methinks."

"I'll help." Pippa rolls onto her tummy and sifts through the clover. "My teacher Miss Corrigan says that in Irish folklore, each leaf of a four-leaf clover has a different meaning. The first encourages faith, the second provides hope, the third is for love, and the fourth brings luck. Oh, and anyone who finds one will have the power to see forest fairies too."

"Well, that's a bonus," chuckles Archie.

"Could come in handy," says Ollie. "They might even know where to find a decent chestnut tree. Hey, speaking of Irish things, I'm learning an Irish song in choir."

"What? You didn't tell us you were in a choir," says Pippa.

"Yeah, I just started in the Hilltop Singers. We're learning a song called 'Danny Boy'. It's based on an old Irish folk tune." He hums the melody for a few bars and then bursts into song:

"Oh honey joy, your flakes, your flakes are calling,
From tree to tree and down the mountainside.
The summer's gone, and the chestnuts they are falling,
Oh honey joy, it's you, it's you that I must find."

Continuing in a booming operatic voice, he builds to an almighty crescendo, "OH HONEY JOYYYY—"

Archie play-tackles him to the ground. "Stop! Great singing, but we'll find chestnuts even if it takes us all night. So get those honey joys out of your noggin, okay?"

"Alright, alright," says Ollie, giggling as he wrestles Archie on the clover. "Here, have some honey joys in *your* noggin." He rubs Archie's hair, making it go all frizzy and extra spiky.

Pippa nudges Ollie in the side, prompting the play fight to end. "I never knew you had such an amazing voice."

"Gee, thanks," he replies, blushing.

Now sporting a wacky electric-shock hairdo, Archie throws Kimba a bread crust and relaxes back on the clover, exploring his mind for more chestnutting options. "I found a whole forest of chestnut trees on Georges Road the other day. They'd be perfect to pick from, except two German shepherd dogs patrol the property. We might get a few nuts on the nature strip, but we'll be eaten alive if we jump the fence."

"What about the trees opposite Kallista Primary School, you know, near the Mechanics Hall?" says Ollie.

"Yeah, nah. I checked them out when I was walking home from school the other day. There's too much shade from gum trees. The chestnuts'll be scrawny."

A crow swoops down from the sky and lands in a blanket leaf tree. The woolly white undersides of the leaves contrast against the crow's shiny black feathers as it hops along a branch, searching for insects.

"Hey, Archie," says Pippa, studying the crow, "the other day when I was exploring along the creek near my place, I saw a ginormous chestnut tree in the middle of a grassy field. Do you know it?"

"No, I've never explored down there. Does anyone own it?"

"It looked abandoned. Seemed like no one was bothering to collect the nuts, except for a couple of crows. And the fences were falling apart, so I doubt if there were any cows or bulls."

Ollie interjects. "What about priests? Any priests? I can't take any more priests today."

"Don't worry. There were no priests. I promise."

"Phew. Well, that's all the safety boxes checked."

Archie slings the backpack over his shoulders and jumps to his feet. "Great. It's unanimous then. Show us the way, Pippa."

THIRTY-FOUR

THE ABANDONED TREE

Crouched in weeds and long grass behind a rickety barbed-wire fence, Ollie peers through his binoculars at a spectacular chestnut tree in the middle of an overgrown meadow. "It's a big one, no doubt about that. Might be a dud though. I mean, with all those nut-pecking crows, there mightn't be any good chestnuts left for us."

"Give me a look," says Archie, grabbing the binoculars. "What are you talking about? The tree's loaded. There's heaps of good ones on the ground too."

Pippa takes a turn, adjusting the focus as she pans around. "Aww, how cute . . . three bunnies eating grass."

"I suppose if it's safe for bunnies, it's safe for us," says Ollie. "Although I'm not so sure we should pick here. I mean, how do we know it's abandoned?"

Archie gazes through the rusty barbed wire. "Well, the grass is overgrown, and there's no signs of raking or picking of any kind. I agree with Pippa. It looks abandoned. Clearly nobody's caring for the place. The chestnuts will rot if they're not collected soon."

"If *Nobody's* caring for the place, why's the grass overgrown?" says Ollie. "Perhaps we should talk to Mr Nobody and ask permission to pick the nuts."

"No, Ollie. What I'm saying is, *no one* owns the tree."

"Oh, I see what you're saying. So, Mr Nobody, who cares for the place, works for Mr No one, who owns the tree. In that case, let's have a chat with Mr No one. I'm sure he'll be very interested to know that Mr Nobody's been slacking off, leaving the nuts to rot in the long grass."

"But *no one* is NOT a Mr anything!" screeches Archie, flushing red in frustration.

"Ah, so he's a she," says Ollie. "My apologies. Then let's go talk to Ms No one and see if—"

"STOP!" shouts Pippa. "This is crazy. Nobody's talking to anyone. Got it?"

Ollie appears befuddled. "Who's *Anyone*?"

"I have no idea," says Archie, shrugging his shoulders.

Pippa flits her eyes to the sky, then pulls the wobbly fence wires apart, squeezes through and swings around. "Well? Is Anyone coming? Or is she too busy talking to *Nobody* on behalf of *No one?*"

"This is getting a little confusing," says Ollie. "Oh well, at least we agree no one owns the tree."

"Exactly," says Archie, leaping the fence.

Ollie presses down the top wire and flings one leg over. Regrettably, his hand slips and the wire springs up between his legs—*TWANNGGGG!* "Help," he squeaks.

"Oh, Ollie, you're such a wally," says Pippa.

While leaning on Pippa's shoulder, Ollie unhooks a barb caught in the crotch of his pants. Once freed, he flops onto the grass in a heap and says in a high-pitched voice, "I'm okay. No permanent harm done."

Pippa wrenches him up, and the friends leave the safety of the fence line. Soon the meadow's open space engulfs them, the stark light, the wispy air, views all around. Halfway to the tree, voices of doubt chitter-chatter in their minds. *What if someone does own the tree? What if we get caught?*

Ruff ruff ruff, barks Kimba, rushing after a rabbit.

Spooked by the barking, ten or more crows burst from the chestnut tree and swirl across the sky in a raucous rabble before settling on the wobbly fence posts.

Pippa skips ahead of the boys and twirls under the tree, enchanted and thrilled by the thousands of dazzling golden-brown chestnuts lying among the fallen autumn leaves. "I've never seen so many chestnuts. This is a dream come true!"

Archie scoops up a handful of the nutty delights—so fresh, so shiny, so big and round—and tosses them into the air. "Yippee, we've hit the jackpot!"

"Golden nuggets. Golden nuggets. We've found the golden nuggets," chants Ollie in a zombie's voice.

With no time to lose, the friends scurry around collecting the precious treasure, tossing them into the backpack by the handful. Before long, the bag is half full, and everyone takes a well-needed rest.

Ollie props himself against the backpack and chews on a long blade of grass, closing his eyes, allowing his mind to empty . . . "Brainwave! How about we roast the chestnuts and sell them for twice the price? We'll make the same amount of money as a full backpack. That way, we can finish now and head to The Patch Store for light refreshments. What do you say? Hey? Hey?"

Pippa's foot swishes through the leaves. "We've pretty much collected all the nuts on the ground." She tosses a stick at a high branch. It strikes a bunch of burrs, and two chestnuts topple down. "It'll take us forever to knock them down with sticks. So unless we find another good tree, what choice do we have? Perhaps we should consider roasting them."

Ollie points his finger to the sky. "Another brainwave! I could whip up a nice bush spice mix to give them an exotic gourmet touch. Then we'll sell them for thrice the price. I can see the sign already: *Spicy Nuts to Fill your Guts!* What do you think, Archie?"

"Well, it's a good idea. But the thing is, the Italians travel from the city to the hills to buy fresh chestnuts—the fresher, the better. They use them for making cakes and all sorts of things for Easter. We might sell a few roasted ones to tourists, but the Italians are the best customers coz they're crazy about chestnuts."

"How do you even know the Italians will come tomorrow?" asks Pippa.

"Trust me. They always come during chestnut season. And always on a Sunday morning because they know us kids will be selling them on the side of the road."

Ollie lifts the backpack. "Well, in that case, we better find a way to fill the bag. We don't want to disappoint the Italians, now do we?"

THIRTY-FIVE

THE BULGING BACKPACK

Archie gazes up at the chestnut tree. "Hey, Ollie, have you still got that—"

Swish. The ever-prepared lad extracts a pocket umbrella from his parka and clicks it open, revealing a green frog with bulbous eyes popping up at the top. "Meet my new improved froggy force field. I call him Doink."

"Brilliant," says Archie. "How about you two hide under Doink while I shake down the chestnuts?"

With everyone in agreement, Archie scoots up the trunk and straddles a loaded branch mid-way up the tree. "Watch out, here goes!"

As he shakes the branch back and forth, thrashing the leaves, hundreds of chestnuts rain down through the canopy in a chaotic clatter before bouncing off the umbrella.

"Okay, it's safe," calls Archie, pausing for a moment.

Ollie and Pippa scurry around, collecting the loose nuts scattered on the ground. To maintain quality control, they reject any that are scrawny or pale and unripe. Once finished, they stomp on the burrs, popping out chestnuts in a fun-filled popathon. "Yippee! Wahoo!"

After several hours of shaking and picking and picking and shaking, Florence's backpack bulges with the biggest, ripest, freshest, most tastiest shiny brown chestnuts imaginable—a sack of golden treasure.

Pippa grips the bag from the top, straining with all her might to lift it off the grass. But all she manages is a hair width at best. "Umph." She plonks it down with a thud. "How are we going to carry them home? The bag's too heavy."

"Let's try lifting it together," suggests Archie. "Okay, on the count of three. One, two, three, LIFT!"

Working as a team, they raise the backpack above the knee-high grass and hobble over to the fence. Kimba trails behind, sniffing rabbit dung along the way.

"Yes, we're doing it," says Pippa, her arms shaking from the heavy weight.

"Keep going," encourages Archie. "We're nearly—"

BANGGGGG-Shhhhhhhhhhhh comes a cracking gunshot that reverberates high above the kids' heads.

A shadow casts across the field as the alarmed crows flutter off the fence posts, darkening the sky in a plume of swirling black feathers.

The friends freeze in terror, their faces ghostly white, eyes bulging, hearts leaping.

Stan, a short, potbellied farmer with a rifle slung over one shoulder and rope coiled under his arm, storms across the paddock. Having spotted the children from his nearby farm, he's on a mission to punish them for picking chestnuts from his neighbour's tree.

Trapped against the fence and weighed down by the heavy backpack, the kids await an uncertain fate. Random thoughts flash through their minds: *Will he call our parents? the police? Will we be persecuted? prosecuted? branded as criminals? sent to prison?* Not knowing what to do or where to look, they stare anxiously at the ground.

Stan's boots pound rhythmically on the grass, growing louder and more terrifying by the second. Until finally, a furious voice cuts through the air, "WHERE DO YOU THINK YOU'RE GOING WITH THOSE NUTS? EH! EH! This is Mr Crow's farm. Those nuts belong to him!" He rips the backpack from the children's fingers. "It's just as well I spotted you kids. YOU'VE GOT NO RIGHT stealing Crow's chestnuts!"

Kimba growls and tugs at Stan's trouser cuff.

The sight of Florence's new bag in the man's grasp turns Archie's skin deathly grey. *Mum'll freak if I lose her backpack. I'll be toast if I go home without it.* Voice trembling, heart thumping, he responds, "B-b-but that's my mum's new bag. H-h-how will I get it back?"

Stan shakes and kicks his leg, attempting to free himself from Kimba's clenched teeth. "Get off, ya mongrel!" In a sly move, he loops the rope around the gallant dog's neck and yanks him off his trouser cuff. "You can collect ya bag and ya dog from that house over there." He points to an orange brick house way off in the distance. "The main road'll take ya there. Look for the name CROW on the letterbox."

The kids stand dazed while Stan stomps back across the paddock with the backpack over one shoulder and Kimba being pulled along on the lead. "Crow's gonna have your guts for garters when he gets a hold of you lot!" he shouts. "There's nothing more he hates than thieving vermin!"

Kimba growls and pulls at the rope, but there's no chance of escape from the irate farmer.

"Kimmmmba!" wails Archie at the top of his voice.

"Let our dog go!" screams Pippa. "You have no right to take him! Let him go, you meany!"

"G-g-g-guts f-f-for garters," stammers Ollie. "I don't understand what it means. B-but it doesn't sound healthy."

"Who is Old Crow anyway?" says Pippa.

Gripped by worry, Archie sits on a rock, clasping his head. "I'm not sure. I've never met him, but he sounds real mean."

Pippa crosses her arms tightly. "Well, I'm not scared of Old Crow or that horrible farmer. Besides, they can't do anything to us. Right? We're just kids."

"G-g-g-guts f-f-for garters, g-g-guts f-f-for garters," blubbers Ollie.

Archie's stomach churns with dread. *Is Kimba safe? Will I get Mum's bag back? What will Old Crow do to us?* The agonising questions whirl around his head, pressurising his aching brain. But there are no answers, just confusion and turmoil.

While the kids sit hunched over in harrowed silence, pondering what to do, a crow lands on a fence post and drops a chestnut from its beak. As it pecks at the nut, Banjo's happy face appears in Archie's mind, and magically, the fear and anguish evaporate. Buoyed by renewed courage and clarity, he uncoils his body and jumps to his feet. "We've got no choice. We have to face Old Crow."

THIRTY-SIX

OLD CROW

As the friends walk along the road to the orange brick house, the same crow as before lands on a power line above their heads and calls solemnly, *arrh, arrrrh, arrrrrrh.*

"I think that crow's trying to tell us something," says Archie.

Ollie listens to the call. "Don't go to Mr Crow's house. He's a madman. That's what it's saying."

"Mad or not, I'm not leaving without Kimba and Mum's bag," says Archie.

Around the next bend, they approach a rusty letterbox with the name CROW painted on the side in rough white strokes.

Pippa takes a deep breath. "Whatever happens, we stick together. Okay, everyone?"

"Agreed," says Archie. He pushes open the creaky metal gate, and side by side, the kids tiptoe down the concrete path.

Just before reaching Mr Crow's front steps, a howling wind sweeps across the yard. Blood-red autumn leaves flutter over their heads, and the gate swings back and forth, *eeek, eeek, eeeeeeoowwwrrrr . . .*

BANG! It slams shut with a loud clang.

Pippa jumps and pats her pounding chest. "Oh my gosh, I nearly had a heart attack."

"Yeah, me too. That was pretty freaky, eh, Ollie? Ollie . . . ? Hey, where's he gone?"

The nervy lad crawls out from behind a conifer bush, smiling sheepishly. "Just testing our emergency escape system. Can't be too prepared, you know."

"Up you get, bugalugs," says Pippa, yanking him to his feet.

The trepidatious trio continue down the path and step onto a brown-tiled porch.

Dead leaves swirl around Archie's feet as he approaches the door. Riddled with anxiety, taking shallow gulps of air, he raps his trembling knuckles on the solid wood.

The friends hold their breath, staring at each other, eyes like moons, listening for signs of Old Crow.

All is silent.

Then something bangs inside the house. Is Crow coming? The banging continues in random patterns. An accompanying wind whistle reveals the answer—a loose window shutter. Everyone exhales, relieved that nobody came, disappointed the agonising suspense must continue.

Frustrated by the situation, Pippa taps on an amber window beside the door and peers through the hazy bevelled glass. She squashes her nose on the cold surface. "All I can see are shadows. Nothing's moving. I don't think he's home."

"Maybe he's round the back," says Archie, growing in confidence and nerve.

Ollie nibbles his fingernails and jabbers, "Umm, err, how about I wait here in case Mr Crow comes this way?"

"Okay," agrees Pippa. "If we're not back in fifteen minutes, call for help."

The two friends slink down a path alongside the house and enter a slate courtyard featuring a rotary clothesline in the middle. Tied to the half-rusted winding crank is a rope flapping in the breeze.

"Hey, that's the lead the mean farmer used to steal Kimba," says Archie, inspecting the loose end. "Look, there's bite marks. He must've escaped by chewing through. No wonder Kimba likes my Houdini book—he's an escape artist."

"Clever dog," says Pippa.

"Yeah, but where's the scruffy mutt gone? I hope he's okay. He could get lost in the forest or hit by a car. Or a vicious dog might attack him."

"Don't worry, he's streetwise. Remember how he handled Okka? And he'll sniff his way home if he needs to. If there's one thing I know for sure, Kimba can take care of himself."

"I suppose you're right. He's a tough dog."

"Come on, let's find Old Crow and get your mum's bag back. Then we can go find Kimba."

Archie nods, and they continue along a gravel driveway to a steel farm shed, big enough to be an aircraft hangar.

Pippa pokes her head inside. The air smells of farm chemicals, chicken manure, dirt and diesel fuel.

As Archie enters, he accidentally kicks over a metal bucket. A startled pigeon flutters off a crate of flower bulbs and lands on a grubby red tractor. "No sign of Old Crow. But check that out." Mounted horizontally on the wall is a rifle, similar to the one used by Stan.

Wind whistles through the creaky iron roof, sending shivers down Pippa's spine. "Urrrgh, this place gives me the creeps. Let's get out of here."

They head down a garden path to the back veranda of the house and step onto the decking.

"Huh!" gasps Pippa, stopping in surprise.

"What the!" blurts Archie.

Propped against the screen door is Florence's bulging backpack, and perched on top, half-buried in chestnuts, a note.

Archie bounds up to the bag and reads the message:

"Dear Crow, I caught some kids stealing your chestnuts. They're coming for the bag and the dog. Call me when you get home. Regards, Stan."

A wild look streaks across Pippa's face. "Let's pour the nuts all over the veranda and stomp on them. That'll teach those meanies a lesson!"

"But, Pippa, if we take the lot, we can return Mum's bag and still sell the chestnuts tomorrow. It's a win-win. Come on, whaddaya reckon?"

"You're right! Besides, we were the ones who picked them."

"Yeah, the nuts would've rotted if we hadn't collected them. There'll be heaps on the ground tomorrow for Old Crow if he wants them. Quick, take a strap. We better hurry."

Around the front of the house, Ollie throws a pinecone at an unsuspecting garden gnome—*donk*. *"Hee-hee,"* he chuckles, watching it wobble. As he prepares for another toss, hoping to knock the little fellow over, an urgent whisper from behind catches his attention.

"Ollie, Ollie! Quick, help us carry the bag! Grab a strap," urges Pippa as she and Archie struggle down the sideway with the hefty backpack.

"Huh! What? How? But!" jabbers Ollie, thunderstruck by the insanity of the situation.

Arms aching, Archie adjusts his grip on the bag and eyeballs Ollie, pleading for help as he staggers along. "Crow's not home, Kimba's run away, and we found the chestnuts by the back door. Come on, Ollie, give us a hand. Hurry up!"

"Have you two gone completely nutty? We'll be caught for sure, turned into sausages or worse!"

"No, we won't," says Pippa, pausing for a rest behind a large white-painted rock. "There's a secret track over the road, behind those lilly pilly bushes. I ride my bike along it all the time. No one'll see us. Come on. What are you waiting for? Help us carry the bag!"

Ollie glances around nervously. "Oh, all right." His arm hooks under a side strap. "I tell you what, we should get danger money for this chestnutting business."

While Ollie babbles on about spring water, honey joys, persecution and other such things, the kids flee across the street and crawl under the lilly pilly hedge, dragging the pack behind them. On the other side, safe from passing cars, they stagger along the path to where it meets the main road. Exposed and in danger, they take cover behind a row of clumpy agapanthus plants.

Archie peeks between the long shiny leaves. "Okay, after we cross the road, we'll take the track to The Patch School. Can we get to your place from there, Pippa?"

"Yes, I know a shortcut through the wetlands. We won't even need to cross another road to get there."

"Excellent. Sounds like a plan."

"A mighty fine plan indeed," says Ollie, "but"—he removes a small round mirror from his parka and attaches it to a stick via a blob of used chewing gum—"first we need to cross the road. If Old Crow and Mr Guts-for-Garters come along, we're in deep sheep."

Pippa raises both eyebrows but says nothing.

In classic detective style, Ollie extends the mirror out from behind the leaves and spies up and down the street. "Quick! Hide! They're coming!"

Bodies fly in a chaotic clamber for cover as an orange van whooshes past.

Once the coast is clear, Archie pokes his head out from under an agapanthus clump, his hair dripping in slime from the gooey squashed foliage. "Phew. I thought we were goners."

"Whoops, false alarm," says Ollie, wiping slime from the mirror. "Better safe than sorry." He checks for more cars. "All clear. Go, go, go!"

They hobble over the road and down a track littered by yellow birch leaves, passing below the school and across the wetlands to a fast-flowing stream that cuts off their path.

"This way," says Pippa, leading the boys to a bridge formed by a fallen tree. They slide along the trunk on their bottoms, dangling their feet above the rushing water while dragging the backpack across. Over the creek, the path turns into a muddy bog that weaves through shady tree ferns. The first few steps are hard going, the mud sucking in their shoes as they walk. A wooden plank, semi-submerged in the sludge, provides relief and takes them to twenty or more stone steps that ascend to drier terrain and open sky. Waist-high sword grass licks at the ill-defined path, threatening to cut their arms and fingers. A few metres on, they enter a cleared section covered in ivy, weeds and decaying tree stumps. Hazy blue mountains beam in the distance. At the top of the hill, the kids clamber over a dilapidated fence and head up Pippa's driveway through a corridor of pink and red camellia flowers.

"We made it," says Pippa, inhaling the comforting aromas of home.

Upon reaching the house, the exhausted kids guzzle water from a garden tap and collapse in a heap at the front door, ripping off their jackets to release the steamy hot air.

Archie rubs his aching thighs. "Aw, my legs feel like jelly."

"Oh, yeah, what flavour?" says Ollie. "I wouldn't mind some myself. Lime jelly. Mmmm."

"May I suggest," says Pippa, waggling her finger, "that you stay away from excess sugar and artificial colours. You're hyper enough." She opens a wooden trunk and removes a jumble of clogs and gumboots. "Let's pour the chestnuts in here. It's the perfect hiding spot."

They tip the backpack on an angle. The chestnuts flow out in a river of gold, quickly filling the trunk.

"Wow, look how many we picked," says Archie, having exceeded his best expectations.

Pippa plunges her hands into the chestnuts and trickles them between her fingers. "They really are golden nuggets."

"Nothing but trouble if you ask me," says Ollie. "How are we going to sell them without Old Crow and Mr Guts-for-Garters catching us, hmm? Have you thought about that, Mr Chestnut King? Or should I say, Mr Chestnut Bandit?"

Archie pats Ollie on the knee. "Lighten up, buddy. We'll wear wigs and sunglasses so they won't recognise us. And we're not bandits. It's not our fault Stan and Old Crow wanna keep all the chestnuts."

"And priests," adds Pippa.

"Exactly. Everyone realises chestnuts are worth something now. When I was little, the farmers didn't even pick them. It was us kids who knew they were valuable. And now *we're* the bandits? Hah! Nobody asked us if it was okay to fence off the trees. They could've left a few good ones for us to pick from. It's only fair."

"I suppose you're right. We are the future after all," says Ollie. He selects a large chestnut, rubs it under his sweaty arm, buffs it to a high gloss and holds it up to his pearly white smile. "Click! Chestnut selfie, get it? *Hee-hee.* Hey, can I keep a few? I've got an idea for a new recipe. Chestnut strudel with apple, cinnamon and rosewater. Yummm."

"As long as we get the first taste," says Pippa.

"Yeah, we can all keep a few," agrees Archie. "We'll need some for roasting at Fergus's party in a few weeks."

Ollie rubs his hands together and grins with a naughty glint in his eye. "Oooh, I can't wait, exploding chestnuts."

Archie shuts the trunk. "Get your skates on, you two. We've gotta search for Kimba. I'm really worried about him." He holds open the backpack. "Shove your jackets in here in case we get cold."

THIRTY-SEVEN

KIMBA

"Kimmmba . . ." call the kids as they traipse across the grounds of The Patch School. "Kimmba

Kimmmmba

Kimmmba."

On the road high above the playground, a brown Holden Kingswood cruises to a halt.

"Don't look now. I think we're being followed," says Archie.

Pippa peeks up the steep grassy hill. "Oh my gosh, you're right. I feel like we're in a creepy movie. Those meanies must want the chestnuts real bad."

"It's not about the nuts," says Ollie. "Otherwise they would've picked them themselves. This is personal. Old Crow and Stan want our heads because they think we swindled them. It's basic psychology. Good old-fashioned retribution, that's what we're dealing with." He swivels around and strides back across the playground, continuing his rant in a louder voice. "We can't search for Kimba along the road now. They'll string us up by our toenails and turn our guts into garters, whatever they are."

"Wait, Kimba's up there somewhere," says Archie, catching up and walking by Ollie's side. "We've gotta keep searching till we find him. Don't worry about Stan and Old Crow. I have a plan for those mean old gronks."

Ollie pauses with raised eyebrows. "Another one of your bear-brained schemes, no doubt."

"Harebrained," says Pippa, approaching. "Schemes or no schemes, I hope we run into those meanies so I can give them a piece of my mind."

"No, no, your approach is all wrong," says Ollie. "The first rule of conflict resolution is to attack the problem, not the person. I myself like to start with a compliment to soothe the opponent's nerves and build rapport. Mr Crow and Stanley just need buttering up so they feel better about themselves."

Archie blows a raspberry, *bththththtthurrp*. "How's that for an approach?"

"Looks like I'm coming," says Ollie, feeling that his negotiation skills will be required yet again.

Up on the road, the friends continue calling, "Kimmba

Kimmmba

Kimmmmba"

When they reach The Patch Store, the rumbling Holden Kingswood cruises past and stops just ahead, blocking the way.

The kids stand frozen, their pale faces illuminated by the glowing red brake lights.

The engine switches off.

All is silent, apart from a chainsaw buzzing in the distance and a man sweeping autumn leaves onto a smoky fire near the store. *Swish, swish, swish.*

The farmers emerge from the vehicle and slam the car doors, one after another, heavy and deep.

Mr Crow, a skinny man wearing a blue terry-towelling hat and brown chequered shirt, approaches with quick strides and a scowl on his bony face.

Stan, intoxicated by vengeful thoughts, nods and mutters to Mr Crow, "Yep, them's the brats who stole your nuts."

As the farmers draw near, two long shadows engulf the trembling children. They gaze up, squinting from the hazy afternoon sun glowing around the men's silhouetted figures.

"You kids are a bunch of SWINDLERS!" barks Mr Crow, waggling his grubby finger about. "What gives you the right to trespass on my farm and pick my chestnuts, eh? Eh! And not only that, you steal them twice! Such a cheek! What've you got to say for yourselves, eh?"

"Um, I think you've got the wrong kids, mister. We didn't take your nuts," insists Archie in fake innocence.

Stan's eyes and chest swell. "What do you mean you didn't take Crow's nuts? You're the kids all right. I remember ya scrawny little faces." He points to the bulging backpack attached to Archie's shoulders. "What's in the bag then, eh?" And with smug checkmate eyes, he says to Mr Crow, "That's the bag. I'm as certain as a roast on Sunday. I took it from them, out by the tree."

Mr Crow clenches his fists. "I'm gonna have your guts for garters, you little thieves. Now show us what's in the bag!"

"If you insist," says Archie. He slides the backpack off his shoulders, unclips the top flap, tips it upside down and shakes vigorously.

Stan and Mr Crow fix their beady eyes on the bag, glaring like hungry hyenas, sensing victory. But their predatory glares turn to wide-eyed stares, when, instead of chestnuts, the kids' jackets tumble out, toppling onto the bitumen in a heap.

Archie wiggles the pack a little more, dislodging a small object that twists and twirls through the air . . .

Chink. It strikes the bitumen and whizzes around in a blur.

The farmers freeze in anticipation of sweet victory, tantalised by the possibility it may be a chestnut, the very evidence needed to incriminate the kids, to punish them to the full extent of their powers.

Gradually the mysterious spinning object winds down, slower, slower, slower, until finally, it grinds to a halt.

Mr Crow and Stan's eyeballs pop, their jaws drop, and their brains go flip-flop. Because resting on the road is not a chestnut, but instead, Ollie's ballerina figurine doing a pirouette, smiling with her bright red lips and sparkling eyes.

Pippa nudges Ollie and giggles.

Trying not to burst into hysterics, he whispers back, "I told you she'd come in handy someday."

Eyes glowing red, the farmers switch their gaze to the kids, who stare back with sweet angelic grins, shoulders shrugged.

Mr Crow lurches at the children. "Why, you little—"

Ollie raises his left hand, interrupting Crow's tirade, and scanning for something to compliment, says in a pleasant, calm voice, "I must say, that's a lovely shirt, Mr Crow. Flannelette is so versatile and soft against the skin, isn't it? Now, I'm sure we can sort out this little misunderstanding. A few minutes ago, I saw two boys, named Neville and Leo, walking suspiciously down by the school. And it just so happens they were carrying a large bag of chestnuts. They must be the swindlers you're looking for. It's a simple case of mistaken identity, that's all."

"Yeah, so leave us alone, you mean old farts," curses Pippa under her breath.

The veins in Stan's temples bulge, and his eyes flare. "What did you say?"

Ollie intervenes nervously, "Ummm, what she said was, 'Leave us alone. There's a cold draught'." He points to the pile of jackets. "Err, we better rug up. You know, it's a bit draughty. Brrr, there's a chill in the air, don't you think?"

Pippa and Archie cross their arms and pretend to shiver. "Yes, brrrr. It's so cold. We really should be going. Our parents will be worried about us."

"And may I ask," continues Ollie, taking matters a little too far, "what's a garter?"

Just before Mr Crow and Stan explode once more, Fergus and Banjo screech to a halt in the army jeep.

"Hey, kids! We picked up a hitchhiker," says Fergus in a jolly voice.

A wet black nose pokes through Banjo's arms.

"Kimba!" squeals Archie.

"He's been up to some kind of mischief, I reckon," says Banjo, chuckling. "Found him running amok at Baynes Park with a pretty white poodle."

Fergus slaps the side of the jeep. "Hop in, kids. I'll give you a ride home."

Archie stuffs the jackets into his mum's bag, and the friends pile into the back seat.

"Can you take us to my house?" says Pippa.

"Okay, buckle up!" The gears crunch and Fergus roars away, honking his rooster horn, *COCK-A-DOODLE-DOOOO, HONK-HONK-HONK!*

The befuddled farmers stand in the billowing diesel smoke, shoulders sunken, chests deflated, peering down at the smiling ballerina.

THIRTY-EIGHT

THERE'S A SILENT T IN CHESTNUTS

"Hoo-de-doo," sings Hilda as she whips up a fresh batch of speculaas in her kitchen. "A little sugar, a little spishe, mixsh it all togedder and dey taste sho nishe."

Pippa rushes through the door and slides across the flour-coated tiles. "Hi, Mum, can I please borrow the kitchen scales? Remember I'm staying at Archie's house tonight. We have to weigh and bag the chestnuts for selling in the morning."

"Of courshe. Jusht let me give dem a little clean firsht." Hilda inflates her chest and blows on a silver tray attached to the scales, puffing a cloud of flour all over Pippa's face. "Hoo-ho-hoo, whoopsh-a-daishy." Using an apron corner and a dab of spit, she wipes Pippa's powder-white cheeks. "Dat'sh better. Marvelloush."

"Errr, thanks for that. Sorry, gotta go." Pippa whisks the scales off the table and heads for the door.

"Yoo-de-hoo! You'ff forgotten shome-ting!"

"What do you want, Mum? I'm in a hurry. We're going to Fergus's place to make signs for our stall. He's waiting in the jeep with Banjo."

"You forgot to pack your pyjamash and toot-brush. You kidsh will need shome energy too." Hilda gazes lovingly at a pile of freshly baked biscuits.

While Pippa scoots off to gather her things, Hilda stacks a generous serving of almond-filled speculaas into a tin decorated with windmills and tulips.

Around the front of the house, the boys transfer the last few handfuls of chestnuts into the backpack and hoist it into the idling jeep.

COCK-A-DOODLE-DOOOO, HONK-HONK. "All aboard!"

"Wait for me," shouts Pippa, jumping in with her goodies.

Back at Fergus's place, the friends skip through the giant lizard entrance, led by the kooky man himself, strutting proudly along the path. "Follow me, kids. You'll find everything you need in the art studio: paints, brushes, plywood. And there's a stack of egg cartons under the workbench. You can use them for palettes." He trots over the bridge and enters the wacky house through a cockatoo-shaped door. A second later, he pops out an oval window and shouts, "Watch out for the chickens. They've been acting a bit odd lately." He swishes back inside, departing with a "Bokuuurrrk!"

Banjo chuckles to himself as he moseys up the path behind the kids. "Those chickens are acting a little bit strange alright. Almost as strange as that crazy man Fergus—"

"Chook attack!" hollers Ollie, ducking as a chicken flutters over his head, fluffing his hair into a bouffant.

Perched on the silver rocket's pointy tip, the rusty-brown bird puffs out its chest, flaps its wings, points its beak skyward and calls, *crrroak-ca-doodle-squawwwk!* Another one leaps onto the fun-parlour mirror and calls, *crrroak-ca-doodle-squawwwwk!* And one by one, twenty or more other young chickens find high vantage points, filling the neighbourhood with a cacophony of croaky crowing calls.

"They must be the chicks we saw hatch in Fergus's pyramidubator," says Pippa.

Archie scoops Kimba into his arms. "Yeah, but why do they sound so weird?"

"Those young fellas are learnin' to crow," says Banjo.

"You mean to say they're all roosters?"

"That's right. Every last one of 'em. *Hee-hee*. That Fergus, he silly fella. That fancy pyramidubator of his turned 'em all into roosters. Got the music wrong or somethin'. He big boss rooster-man now!"

Archie flaps his arms and galumphs about. "Cock-a-doodle-doo, here comes Fergus!"

"But what will he do with all those roosters?" asks Pippa.

Banjo wanders off, chuckling to himself. "Well, he'll have to sell 'em or cook 'em up. Mmmm, gonna make good soup, those roosters."

"Cock-a-doodle stew," jokes Ollie.

"Come on, let's make the signs. It's getting late, and we've still gotta weigh and bag the chestnuts," says Archie.

Ollie glances over his glasses. "And return your mum's backpack before she realises it's missing."

On the curved wooden deck overlooking Fergus's garden, the kids dump their painting gear and spread out a large canvas tarp. An outdoor couch serves as the perfect spot for Kimba, who leaps up and curls into a ball for a well-needed snooze.

Archie selects a rectangular sheet of plywood from the pile. "This is perfect for a chestnut sign. We can paint one each."

"Go ahead," says Ollie, "paint signs if you must"—he reaches into a pocket and plonks a black velvet beret on his head—"but I'm in the mood for art!"

"Hey, where'd you get that funny hat?" says Pippa, giggling.

"What do you mean, funny? I think it's quite stylish. I found it in Fergus's studio on the skull of a dancing skeleton. Can't paint without a beret. Gets the artistic juices flowing."

"Hang on, you're missing something." Using a pointed brush, Pippa paints a black curly moustache and goatee beard on his face. "Perfect. Now you look like my favourite Dutch artist, Rembrandt."

Archie cracks up laughing. "Show us your best stuff, Mr Rembrandt."

The goofball squeezes out an entire tube of green paint, *pthhhhhuuuurrrrrrrroooooop,* followed by a bunch more:

Red, *pthththooooopth.*

Yellow, *pthhhaaarrp.*

Blue, *pthhheeeepthth.*

Silver, *pthhawwwpop.*

Orange, *pthhhoooop.*

Purple, *pthththeeeep.*

Gold, *pthhwuuurrp.*

"Whoopee, let's paint!" squeals Pippa.

In a sudden giggly-squiggly frenzy, brushes splish, splosh, splat and paint flip, flop, flaps all over the plywood. And after a good fifteen minutes, the masterpieces are finished: three fabulous kaleidoscopic CHESTNUTS FOR SALE signs.

Archie steps back to inspect their handy work. "Oh, Ollie, you've spelt chestnuts wrong! It's got a silent *T* after the *S*."

"What? But that's your sign," insists Ollie.

Armed with a brush covered in dripping red paint, Archie lunges forward, swishing his weapon through the air. "On guard, my friend. We'll settle this with paint!"

In swashbuckling style, Ollie swishes his brush back and forth. "May the best slam win! *Hee-hee*."

Pippa rolls her eyes and adds a *T* to the sign. "Drop your weapons, lads. I've fixed it."

"Oh . . . Touché," says Ollie, lowering his brush.

"Hey, while the signs are drying, let's search for tadpoles in the pond and play on the flying fox," says Archie. "Then we can head to my place and bag the chestnuts."

THIRTY-NINE

BAGS OF GOLDEN TREASURE

Later that night in Archie's bedroom, after a delicious meal of gado-gado, the friends tip the chestnuts out all over the floor, creating a mountainous spreading pile.

For Kimba, the empty backpack seems like the perfect place to settle for the night. So he circles on the soft padding and curls into a tight ball.

Archie lies on his tummy and fiddles with Hilda's scales, sliding the counterweights back and forth to test how they work. "Huh? These scales are in pounds. Does anyone know how many pounds make a kilogram?"

"I think it's about two pounds to one kilogram, but I'm not exactly sure," says Pippa.

Ollie taps a miniature calculator keypad on his digital watch. "Wait a minute. One kilogram is equivalent to a thousand grams, and one pound is sixteen ounces. So, if I divide one thousand by sixteen, the answer is sixty-two point five. Umm, err . . ."

"Nice try, Ollie. But think about it. One kilogram does *not* equal sixty-two point five pounds," asserts Pippa. "We need to know how many grams are in a pound to work it out. Hey, Archie, have you got an exercise book with a conversion table at the back?"

"Yeah, somewhere in my cupboard, but it's a big—"

Pippa opens the tall closet, and an avalanche of books, board games, puzzles, cricket pads, footy boots, magic tricks and stamp albums tumble onto the floor. "Um, on second thoughts"—she shoves everything back and slams the door—"how about we make one-pound bags? It'll be easier."

"Yeah, the customers won't mind as long as we tell them," says Archie. He scoops up some chestnuts from the pile and drops them onto the stainless-steel weighing dish.

Ollie straightens his glasses and slides the one-pound counterweight into position. Next, he aligns his eyes with the balance indicator and checks the result. "Five more should do it . . . No, that's too many. Take three off . . . No, no, put one back . . . Yes, that's one pound exactly."

While Pippa holds open a brown paper bag, Archie pours in the chestnuts. Then they weigh and bag another lot, continuing the process long into the night until the mountain of chestnuts is converted into one hundred bulging paper bags of golden treasure.

"Wow," gasps Pippa. "I can't believe how many we have. And there's even some leftover for your strudel, Ollie."

"Brilliantissimo. And if there's any leftovers after tomorrow, I'll make chestnut mousse with finger-lime sprinkles!"

"Hang on. What do you mean, leftovers?" says Archie. "We'll sell them all, don't you worry about that. We just have to follow the—"

"Arrrrrchieeeeee! Have you taken my backpack?" bellows Florence from the lounge room, having discovered her precious possession has been replaced by a blanket.

The kids tried sneaking the bag back when they arrived at Archie's house, but Josephine was in the way practising the piano, so they figured they'd return it later.

Footsteps thunder across the floorboards and Florence bursts into the bedroom, waving the crochet blanket in anger. "Where's my bag for Europe? I TOLD YOU NOT TO TAKE IT CHESTNUTTING!"

Archie reaches behind his back, shoves Kimba off the bag and whisks it around to the front. "Here's your backpack, Mum. I only borrowed it for a little while." He brushes off a strand of onion weed and a clump of dog hair before handing it over. "See. It's still perfectly good for your study trip."

Florence clasps the bag lovingly to her chest, smiles wryly and rushes out.

"Phew, that was lucky. If only Mum knew what her bag went through today."

"Yes, that bag went on quite a journey, quite a journey," repeats Ollie, stretching up his arms and yawning.

"And so did Kimba," says Pippa, cuddling him in her lap.

Archie rubs his droopy eyes. "I'm tired. Let's hit the sack. We've got an early start tomorrow."

Ollie stares misty-eyed at the pile of chestnut bags. *Thump*. He falls asleep on the floor.

FORTY

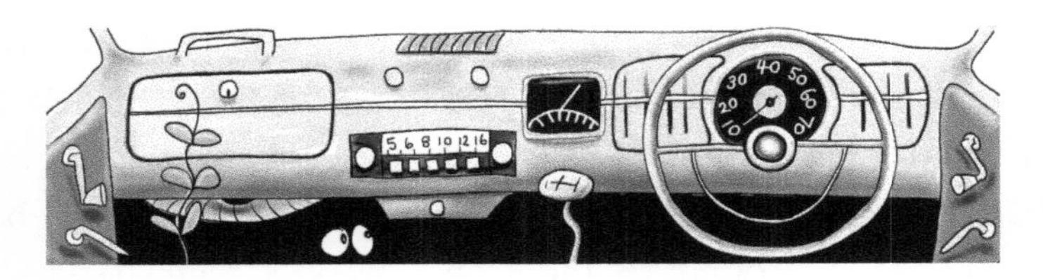

START YOUR ENGINES

Early the following morning, Archie, Pippa and Ollie cram into the freezing cold Volkswagen, all packed and ready for their roadside chestnut stall.

Florence turns the ignition key, *rrr-rrr-rrr-rrr-rrr-rrrow-clunk*. She strokes the dashboard and says calmly, “Come on. Good little car. Please start.” She tries again, *rrr-rrr-rooo-roorr-r-clunk*. “Urgh, stupid car! I just had it serviced yesterday.” She pumps the accelerator pedal and tries once more, *rowww-rooooow-click*. “Grrrr, this is hopeless. Everybody out! I need you to push so I can do a roll-start.”

“Yayyyyy! I love roll-starting!” cheers Archie as he and the others race to the rear of the car.

“One, two, three, PUUUSSH!” shouts Florence.

The kids push so hard their faces turn purple. But the car doesn’t budge an inch. So they spin around and press their backs against the chrome bumper bar. As they heave and strain, gripping their feet on tree roots and half-buried rocks, the wheels groan and squelch through soggy leaves, mud and crunchy gravel.

Florence calls out excitedly, "It's moving. Keep pushing, kids, PUUSSSHH!"

The car rolls faster and faster. After one final heave, it passes onto the road and continues down the hill unassisted, followed by the squealing kids running behind.

Keen for a thrill ride, Archie jumps onto the bumper bar and clings on tight. "Yeeeee-heeee."

"Everyone hop in!" shrieks Florence, waving her arm out the window. Although Archie is visible in the rearview mirror, she can't stop or slow down because the old car must reach forty kilometres per hour to have any chance of a successful roll-start. "Arrrrchieee! GET OFF!"

Just before the car strikes a pothole, Archie leaps off the bumper bar and rolls to safety in a buttercup patch. "I'm okay! Hurry up and jump in!" he calls to Pippa and Ollie as they scream past in pursuit of the runaway car.

Legs a blur, Ollie sprints alongside the Volkswagen, flings open the passenger door and belly-flops onto the back seat, bouncing headfirst into a box of chestnuts.

"Watch out!" shouts Pippa as she dives into the car, somersaulting over a sign and sliding into a folded-up picnic table.

"Nice dive," says Ollie. "Didn't point your toes though. Lose a point for that."

"Listen, you wackadoo, there's no time for competitions. We're losing Archie. We've got to do something!"

To encourage his friend, Ollie waves furiously out the back window and squashes his nose and lips against the glass in a slimy sea-slug, pig-snout display.

"Wait for me!" screams Archie, sprinting down the road, drifting further behind by the second.

Pippa thrusts her head out the side window. "Run faster, Archie, RUN!"

For fear of slowing the car by braking, Florence enters a hairpin bend way too fast, squealing the semi-bald tyres as she swerves around the corner.

Unable to keep pace, Archie realises the only solution is to take a shortcut. So he jumps over a bank and storms down a vacant bush block, whipping through bracken ferns and around bendy saplings. Charged with superhero powers, he leaps a boulder, flies over a fallen tree, vaults over a neighbour's fence and streaks down a grassy slope past a clothesline, over a frog pond, through a vegetable patch and down a series of steps to a gravel driveway that takes him back to the road just as the Volkswagen speeds past with Pippa hanging out the window, screaming, "Jump in, Archie! JUMP IN!"

Parallel to the car, sprinting along, Archie grabs the door handle. "Woooooahhh!" The door swings wide open, leaving him clinging on for dear life.

"Hang on!" squeals Pippa, stretching out her hand to help.

The rolling car descends the final, steepest section of the road, creating a wind thrust that pushes the door closed. Just before it slams shut, Archie lets go and catapults onto Pippa's lap. "I made it. Phew!"

With the end of the hill in sight, the pressure is on. You see, if the Volkswagen arrives at the bottom before starting, they'll be stranded. And with no way to reach their prime selling spot, the kids' chestnutting dreams will be over for another year.

"Quick, Mum. Start the car! We're running out of hill!"

"Okay, okay, hold on to your horses. We're nearly there!" Florence fixes her desperate, panic-stricken eyes on the speedometer. And at the exact moment the needle hits 40 kilometres per hour, she stomps on the clutch, yanks the gear stick from neutral to third and screams, "Buckle up, kids!

Here we go!" Following a silent prayer, she lifts her foot off the clutch, pumps the accelerator pedal and turns the ignition key.

Seconds away from the bottom of the hill, the car lurches forward, and in a fit of jerks and convulsions, the engine springs to life, *VRROOOOM*.

"Yee-heee! Good little car. I knew you could do it," says Florence, stroking the dashboard.

The kids cheer and wave their arms out the window as they head for the best chestnut-selling spot in the hills.

FORTY-ONE

THE SEVEN GOLDEN RULES

At the entrance to Sherbrooke Forest, near the home of Puffing Billy, the Volkswagen emerges through thick fog and skids to a halt in the gravel beside a bus shelter. The friends unpack the idling car, and Florence speeds away. Shadowed by a backdrop of mountain ash trees shooting up through the mist, the kids stand next to a disorganised pile of chestnut-selling stuff.

"Thank goodness we're the first ones here," says Archie, puffing out clouds of cold air.

A whip bird calls in the distance. Ollie gazes at the fog-swamped forest and switches back to the desolate road. "Listen, my friend. All the sane people are in bed. We're the only pongo-bongos crazy enough to be in Belgrave at seven o'clock on a freezing Sunday morning."

Archie winds his Dr Who scarf around his neck and glances up and down the road. "Don't be so sure. We're not the only kids trying to sell chestnuts in the hills. And not everyone knows about the seven golden rules."

"Really? Oh, they're common knowledge," responds Ollie. "Everybody knows about the seven golden rules." He gazes up aimlessly, twiddles his thumbs and taps his moon boots on the gravel. "Err, Archie . . . what *are* the golden rules?"

"Oh, common knowledge, eh? Well, if you want to know, they're the seven golden rules of selling chestnuts. It's taken me years to work them out. If we follow them, we're sure to make a fortune."

"Okay, so what are they?" says Pippa.

"Well, *number one,* you've got to make the stall look pretty. We're not just selling chestnuts, we're selling a cultural experience. The tourists love a bit of local colour and pizazz. *Number two,* be patient. You never know when there'll be a rush of sales. *Number three,* refuse any offers to buy the lot for a bargain price, because it's always a bad deal. *Number four,* sell the best, freshest nuts. Quality is king in the chestnut game, especially for the Italians. *Number five,* be honest about the weight of the bags. Nobody likes a cheat. *Number six,* set up the stall where there's lots of tourist traffic and parking space. And lucky last, *number seven,* arrive early so other kids don't steal your spot, and if the spot's taken, move on. Got it?"

Pippa grabs one of the painted signs. "What are we waiting for then? We better start decorating our stall to make it look pretty. I'll lean this against a pole up the road so the cars see it as they approach."

"Perfect," says Archie. "It'll give them time to pull over. I'll put this one down the other side. That way we've got both directions covered."

While Pippa and Archie hurry off to display the signs, Ollie unfolds the picnic table legs. The first three flick out nicely, but the fourth one has a rusty hinge that won't budge. "Hi-yah!" He karate-kicks the leg with his moon boot. It straightens with a jolt, jamming his bootlace in the hinge as it locks into position. "Pongo-bongo." Hopping on one leg, he kicks, pulls and yanks wildly, then loses balance and flings backwards onto the upturned table.

A few minutes later, Pippa and Archie return to find their silly friend lying on his back like a stranded beetle, flailing about, trapped by the collapsed table legs. “Help. I’m stuck. Somebody get me out of this thing.”

Archie topples over in hysterics. “Distinguished guests and bald-headed babies! Behold, as Ollie, the great escape artist, attempts a world first—drum roll please—to escape from a picnic table!”

“You might want to work on your act, you goof,” says Pippa, fixing the table and helping Ollie to his feet.

In an attempt to salvage some pride, Ollie brushes himself off, combs his dishevelled hair and slips a white chef’s apron over his head, fastening it with a tidy bow at the back. Then he flings a red-and-white chequered cloth over the vinyl table and arranges the chestnut bags into neat rows. “Tuscany meets Belgrave. Yes, I like it,” he says proudly.

“With a touch of the Netherlands,” adds Archie, passing out the last of Hilda’s speculaas. While munching on the treat, he places the empty windmill tin behind the chestnuts. “We can use this for the money.”

“And we need to make a table sign,” says Pippa. She grabs a blank sheet of paper and writes CHESTNUTS $5 A BAG, using a different coloured marker for each letter.

“Wait,” says Ollie, munching on an almond flake. “We need more colour and pizazz.” He draws squiggles around Pippa’s sign using fluorescent orange and yellow highlighters, adding a smiling chestnut with a talking bubble that says, I’M FRESH! “Now that’s what I call pizazzy.”

“Nice work,” says Pippa, taping it to the table. “There we go. Done. Cultured enough for you, Archie?”

Archie leans the third plywood sign against the stall and steps back. “Yeah, looks great. No one’ll miss us, that’s for sure. All we need now are customers.”

Two kookaburras land on the bus shelter roof and laugh, *kookoo-ca-ca-ca-caa-kookoo-kookoo-ca-ca.*

As Ollie bides his time waiting for customers, shivering in the cold, he puffs out a swirling ball of misty white air. “Ha! Did you see that? I made a woolly sheep.” He blows out another cloud that dissipates above his head. “Ha! A wombat!”

“Hey, someone’s coming,” says Pippa, pointing to headlights approaching through the foggy forest.

Ollie clasps his cheeks and ducks under the table. “It might be Old Crow and Stan! Quick, grab the wigs!”

FORTY-TWO

UNHEALTHY COMPETITION

A scratched-up Ford F100 ute pulls over onto the gravel about twenty metres up from the kids' stall.

Pippa runs her hands through her long hot-pink wig. Archie swivels his spiky mullet into position, flicking the tails out from his collar. And Ollie slides on a curly brown disco wig, complete with a stick-on moustache and canary-yellow 1970s sunglasses.

"That's not Old Crow and Stan. It's worse. That's Leo and Neville!" says Archie, cringing in anticipation of the dramas about to unfold.

Dressed in skinny jeans, hoodies and black beanies, the bullies unload the makings of a chestnut stall from the tray of the idling ute. Once unpacked, the F100 roars off, skidding its tyres and pinging stones against the metal bus shelter. Left standing in a haze of dust and exhaust fumes, Neville and Leo rub their hands together and begin setting up their stall.

"Amateurs," mutters Ollie, straightening his moustache and zipping up his puffy red parka. "Don't they realise skinny jeans are no good in the cold? You need a layer of air for insulation. Such fools."

Archie shakes his head. "I don't believe this. It's pretty obvious—when you set up first, it's your spot, and if the spot's taken, you move on. We arrived first, so those bullyboys have no right to be here."

But Leo and Neville don't care about golden rules or chestnutting etiquette. Their philosophy of life is dog-eat-dog, a world where people will do anything to succeed, even if it means harming others.

"So much for the seventh golden rule," comments Ollie. "It just goes to show, rules without enforcement are nothing but puff fizzle."

After completing their set-up, Leo and Neville pour themselves hot chocolate from a tartan thermos and lean back in camping chairs, sipping their drink while chuckling at Ollie, Pippa and Archie dressed in their goofy disguises.

"Urgh! We've gotta do something about this. I'm gonna go talk to them," says Archie.

Before he takes a step, Pippa blocks him with her arm. "Oh, no you're not. There's safety in numbers. We're doing this together. Right, Ollie?"

"Eeek," he squeaks.

Pippa's eyes widen. "Right . . . Ollie?"

"Yes, yes, yes, I'm coming. After all, you'll need a good negotiator. Hate to see you get into trouble again with that snappy tongue of yours."

Pippa pokes out her tongue and says smartly, "It's called being assertive."

Strengthened by their solidarity, the friends arrive side by side at the bullies' stall.

Archie steps forward. "Hey, you two. This is our spot. We got here first. Why don't you find somewhere else to sell ya chestnuts? We'll all do better that way."

In a deliberate act of disrespect, Leo silently unpeels a small gold-foil chocolate Easter egg, then pops it in his mouth and says while chewing, "Get lost. It's a free country. You can't make us move, especially dressed like that. What *are* youse, some kind of roadside circus act or somethink?"

Pippa backflips on the spot, thrusts her hands to her hips and says proudly, "Yes. That's exactly what we are."

Stunned by the impressive performance, Neville nudges Leo. "Gee, that was pretty good, don't you—"

Splat! Leo stomps in a muddy puddle and splatters brown water all over Ollie's apron. "Nice bib, mop head."

"Hor-horr," chuckles Neville.

Unfazed by the humiliation attempt, Ollie withdraws a hanky from his parka and tries to wipe away the stain.

"Aww, not coming off, eh? What a pity," smirks Leo, revealing a black hole from a missing front tooth. He pops another Easter egg in his mouth and rolls the foil wrapper into a compact ball as he chews.

Blood rushes to Pippa's head, and she crosses her arms. "Aww, lost a tooth, have we? Serves you right for eating too many lollies. And you're not supposed to eat Easter eggs until next Sunday, didn't you know?"

"Actually, smarty-pants, lost the tooth bumping heads at footy practice. And I'll eat me eggs whenever I like. In fact, after today, we'll be buying a bucket load more. Right, Nev?"

Neville smiles like a pirate, also displaying a missing front tooth. "Aye-aye, me matey. We'll be getting a mighty stash."

He places a set of fake lolly teeth in his mouth and says in a muffled voice, "Who needs real teeth when you've got these."

"Exactly. So why don't you pack up and move on? This is our spot now," snarls Leo, lunging forward.

"Now, now, gentlemen," says Ollie in a soothing voice, his moustache half falling off. "I'm sure we can all sell chestnuts today. I mean, look around. This bus stop is big enough for both stalls. Let's take a positive approach, perhaps draw a line in the gravel, giving each team an equal share of the space. Whaddaya say, fellas? Win-win, that's my motto."

Not even bothering to reply, Leo thumb-flicks the foil ball at Ollie's chest. "Go ahead, draw ya stupid line. But it won't matter, coz you ain't sellin' nothin' today." He points to a misspelt cardboard sign that says, *CHESNUTS $2/Kg*, messily written in thick black marker. "Beat that price, ya losers."

An open paper bag on the table catches Archie's eye. The chestnuts are large and shiny, an indication of high quality. *They must be from the Twelve Apostles*, he thinks.

Unimpressed by the situation, Pippa retrieves the gold wrapper and tugs Ollie's arm. "Let's go. They're not worth the trouble."

Archie slumps his shoulders and walks off. "Yeah, this is a lost cause."

Halfway back to their stall, Ollie draws a line in the gravel. "That'll keep the riff-raff out."

"Maybe," says Archie. "But it doesn't change the fact their bags are bigger than ours and less than half the price. And their chestnuts looked awesome. We can't even say we've got a better product."

"Oh well, we have to lower the price. It's the only sensible solution," says Ollie. "Competitive market forces are at work, my friends. What we're dealing with is healthy competition."

"More like *unhealthy* competition, if you ask me," says Pippa, frowning.

Archie nods. "Yeah, it's not healthy, it's criminal. Those drongos are selling them way too cheap. If we match their price, we'll hardly make any money, especially split three ways. There's gotta be some other way."

Pondering the problem, Pippa gazes beyond the gravel line. "Hang on a sec. Check out their stall: no colour, no love and absolutely no pizazz. They haven't even bothered using a tablecloth. And those grubby cardboard signs are no match for our masterpieces."

"And they can't spell," adds Ollie. "*Tut, tut, tut*. Don't they know there's a silent *T* in chestnuts?"

"You're right," says Archie. "When it comes to the first golden rule, we win hands down. There's more to competition than price. Let's leave our chestnuts at five dollars a bag and see what happens."

"Ooh! Ooh! Look!" jabbers Ollie, bouncing in excitement, pointing to a man and a woman dressed in fancy exercise gear, jogging in their direction. "Customers!"

Everyone flits around, adjusting the bags, checking the empty money tin, trying to appear keen but not desperate.

Neville springs from his camp chair, waving the sign, shouting, "Two dollars a bag! Freshly picked! Best prices!"

As the joggers approach, they glance with perplexed expressions at Archie, Ollie and Pippa's wacky wigs and the five-dollars-a-bag sign. And in that split second, they change course and head for the bullies' stall.

Archie stomps his foot. "I can't believe it. They're buying two bags!"

"Don't worry, here comes another customer!" says Pippa. A silver car turns off the road and parks nearby.

While Leo counts the jogger's money, Neville galumphs across the gravel, thrusting the cardboard sign above his head, tempting the customer with their bargain price. Yet again, the sale goes to the bullies.

Over the following hour, the friends watch helplessly as two more customers ignore their fancy stall, preferring Neville and Leo's bargain prices.

Overcome by disappointment, Ollie plonks his head on the table. "It's all over, red clover. We've been outplayed."

Pippa flings her wig into a box under the table. "Old Crow and Stan are the least of our troubles. People couldn't care less about our pretty stall or good spelling. They just want the lowest price."

"She's right," says Ollie, peeling off his moustache. "It seems our fancy stall makes no difference. So much for pizazz. Methinks you can cross the first golden rule off your list, Archie-boy."

"Not yet. I'm guessing those customers were locals. It's too early for the tourists. They're the ones looking for colour and pizazz. And don't forget we've still got rule number two up our sleeves—be patient." Archie gazes up the road with a far-off searching look in his eyes and says in a determined voice, "It's not over till the Italians arrive."

FORTY-THREE

THE VALIANT CONVOY

"Valiants!" says Archie, pointing at three cars approaching in the distance. "It's the Italians for sure. They love Valiants. Hold on to your hats, things are about to get real crazy."

"Well," says Pippa, "it wouldn't be a normal day in the hills without some kookiness." She sucks in her cheeks, curls her tongue and crosses her eyes.

The convoy continues down the road—the first car, a broad olive-green sedan (a Valiant Ranger); the second, a long baby-blue station wagon (a Valiant Safari); and the last one, a white deluxe model featuring a silver emblem sticking up from the bonnet (a Regal AP6).

The lead car flashes its indicator, and one by one, the vehicles crammed with Italians of all ages, pull over onto the gravel a few metres down from the kids' stall.

Two men exit the Valiant Ranger. One is short with serious eyes, a shiny bald patch on his crown and a round tummy bulging under a tucked-in shirt—that's Luigi. The other is tall and slim with wild wispy hair, bushy eyebrows and a big friendly grin—that's Federico.

Desperate to attract the Italians, Neville hops and leaps about while frantically waving the shabby $2/Kg sign. However, being men of culture, style and good taste, Luigi and Federico swagger over to Archie, Ollie and Pippa's fancy, colourful stall.

"Buongiorno, bambini," greets Federico. "Is-a beautiful day to pick-a your nose-a." He sniffs a yellow rose protruding from his cream jacket pocket. Having just immigrated to Australia, Federico's grasp of English is rudimentary and often muddled.

The kids giggle as Federico continues, "We come-a today, me whole-a family, to look-a for good castagne. Capisci?"

Archie points to the chestnuts. "Yes. We understand. You want cast-an-yeh."

"Yes. Castagne. How-a you say?"

"Chestnuts," says Pippa, smiling.

Federico's eyes light up, and his hands dance in the air. "Ah! Ches-a-nuts-a, ches-a-nuts-a, I love-a the ches-a-nuts-a."

Luigi checks out the bags and says in a serious but polite voice, "How much are the ches-a-nuts-a, mate?"

"They're five dollars a bag," answers Archie confidently.

Appearing concerned, Luigi picks one up and passes it from hand to hand. "How much this bag-a weighs?"

"They're one pound exactly," says Ollie. "Not a nut less. Not a nut more. I can vouch for that, weighed them myself."

"Small-a bags for five-a dollars," says Luigi, passing it to Federico, who peeks inside to inspect the quality of the nuts.

Federico beams. "I am-a good nut. Very big-a nut." He sniffs the chestnuts. "Ah, yes! I like-a this nut very much-a. Very good nut for-a me family."

Slowly, Luigi takes a chestnut from the bag and glances at the kids, his eyes narrow and suspicious. "When-a you pick-a them, eh?"

"We picked them yesterday. You couldn't get any fresher," insists Pippa.

The men launch into a passionate Italian conversation, flinging their arms every which way, until finally, Luigi steps forward. "We give-a you twenty dollars for the lot-a. Is a good-a deal, *no?*"

Ollie gawks at Archie. "Take the deal! Take the deal!"

"No, wait. Remember the third golden rule," says Pippa.

Arms crossed, Archie says firmly, "Sorry. No deal. They're high-quality chestnuts. Five dollars a bag is a fair price. We went to a lot of trouble picking them."

The men resume their discussion, thrusting up their arms, huffing, puffing and bantering in Italian until coming to a new agreement.

Once again, Luigi approaches the stall, his heated emotions masked by a friendly, businesslike grin. "Okay, my friends. You make-a me poor-a man. But I like-a you bambini. So I give-a you thirty-five-a dollar for the lot-a." He flashes the money and slaps it on the table. "We take the lot-a for thirty-five-a dollar. Is a good-a deal, *no?*"

In perfect unison, Archie and Pippa shake their heads from side to side like laughing clowns at a country fair.

In disbelief, Ollie grips his face and drags down his lower eyelids.

Never before has Luigi encountered such hard-bargaining kids. Usually the buy-out deal works a treat. Surprised and flushed red, he swallows his pride, shrugs his shoulders and swipes the money from the table. "Okay. You have your-a way, and I have my-a way."

As the Italians head over to Leo and Neville's stall, arguing along the way, Pippa draws several deep breaths to slow her pounding heart. Archie wipes his sweaty palms on his pants.

Ollie gnaws on his worn fingernails. And together, they watch from a distance as the negotiations unfold.

First, Neville offers the men a bag of chestnuts from the table. Federico and Luigi inspect the nuts, and after a brief argument, flash thirty-five dollars at the boys.

Leo nods, smiling cheerfully as he accepts the money.

Neville punches the air in celebration. Then he stacks their entire chestnut stock into two large boxes and passes one to Federico and one to Luigi.

The men carry the nuts back to their car, grinning proudly. And one after another, the Valiants depart, vanishing into the forest in search of a good picnic spot.

Leo and Neville pull down their signs, tip out the hot chocolate dregs, fold up the table, collapse the camping chairs and pile the stall into a heap under the bus shelter.

"Ha-haa! Look what we've got, losers!" calls Leo, waving a fistful of money.

Archie wrings his hands, trying to ignore the taunts. "Good. Now the market forces are back in our favour."

"Competition's not our only problem," declares Ollie. He whisks out a pocket book from his parka titled *101 Marketing Tips for Your First Million Dollars*. "It says here that a successful business must consider supply and demand." A car whizzes by on the lonely road. "We've got the supply, but where's the demand? Now the Italians are out of the picture, who's going to buy our chestnuts, hmm?"

While everyone ponders the question, Puffing Billy whistles in the distance, *Woooo-Awoooo-Awoooooo,* and the bullies strut over, whispering to each other as they kick stones across Ollie's line.

Leo approaches the stall with his usual smirk and gawks into the empty biscuit tin. "No money, eh? Aw, that's too bad.

Don't worry, we know how to move chestnuts. Show 'em, Nev."

In a nasty pre-planned move, Neville rams his knee against the picnic table. A hinge collapses, the table falls, and the chestnuts crash to the gravel. "They're moving now, *hor-horr*."

"See. It's not that hard," says Leo, sniggering.

Suddenly Neville's eyes bug out, and he jiggles on the spot while tapping Leo's arm. "The Italians are coming back. We'd better scram!"

FORTY-FOUR

WHAT GOES AROUND COMES AROUND

The Valiant Ranger swerves off the main road, tyres squealing, and skids to a halt near the kids' stall. Luigi and Federico burst from the car, shouting and waving their fists. Seconds later, the Valiant Safari arrives in a long gravel skid, blocking Leo and Neville from escaping into the forest.

Luigi shouts, "Stop-a! Stop-a! You sold us rotten castagne and put-a rocks in the bags-a. Money back you give-a, or you'll-a be sorry!"

"Did you hear that?" says Ollie. "The fooligans put rocks in the bags to cheat on the weight."

"That's terrible," says Pippa. "They must have rocks in their heads."

Archie fixes the table leg. "Yeah, and there's nothing more the Italians hate than rotten chestnuts and being ripped off."

The bullies flash past, followed by Luigi, Federico and a procession of angry Italians: mums, dads, uncles, aunties and children—all shouting and screaming.

"Serves them right, those bullyboys," says Archie, enjoying the pandemonium.

Ollie circles a hanky around the lens of his glasses. "What goes around comes around, I suppose."

Pippa tapes the sign back in place, positions the money tin on the table, and crawls on the gravel to salvage the fallen chestnuts.

In the background, the AP6 Valiant cruises out of the forest and parks beside the bus shelter. The car's shiny white Duco and silver emblem gleam in the morning sun.

As Pippa scoops up the chestnuts, golden light glints across her face. She glances up and sees an Italian nonna sitting in the backseat of the car. *It just might work.* And with that thought, she polishes a large chestnut on her sleeve and heads towards the Valiant.

"Hey, where are you going?" calls Archie.

Pippa swishes around. "It's secret women's business." She approaches the car and smiles at a little girl peeking through a Venetian blind in the rear window.

The girl points and shouts, "Nonna, Nonna, una ragazza è qui." (*Nanna, Nanna, a girl is here.*)

An electric window winds down, revealing the nonna with a headscarf framing her wrinkled face. "Buongiorno, signorina."

"Hello. I mean, buongiorno," answers Pippa, presenting the chestnut on her palm. "Would you like to sample a chestnut? It's fresh. We picked them yesterday."

"Molte grazie. Thank you," says the nonna. She holds the nut to the light and assesses its shape, sheen and colour. She moves it to her nose and inhales. She bites into the thick outer skin, and after peeling it away, scrapes off the inner membrane. She chomps into the white nut, closes her eyes and vanishes into a world of memories—a time when she and her friends ventured into the chestnut grove near her family home in Italy, playing hide-and-seek, climbing the trees and collecting nuts (which they often nibbled raw), enjoying their crunchy texture and earthy, nutty flavours.

Pippa watches in earnest, awaiting the nonna's verdict on the quality of the chestnut.

The nonna stops chewing and smiles so brightly her eyes sparkle, her cheeks form rosy balls, and her gold-capped teeth glimmer in the light. "Eccellente! Eccellente! Beautiful."

Everyone in the car cheers, "Evviva! Evviva! Nonna ama la castagna!" (*Hooray! Hooray! Nonna loves the chestnut!*)

Dozens of hands, young and old, reach out as the nut passes from one family member to another, each person taking a nibble of the prized delicacy before handing it on.

Meanwhile, Leo and Neville burst from the forest and sprint towards the regal AP6, followed in hot pursuit by the parade of angry Italians.

The nonna closes her eyes, traces a cross on her chest, whispers a prayer of forgiveness and thrusts open the door.

BOOF! BOOF!

The bullies slam into the barricade and collapse in a jellied heap on the gravel. Stunned but unharmed, they spring to their feet and dash for a steep embankment.

BOING! BOING!

They crash into Luigi's bouncy round tummy.

Federico and his family members crowd around—a sea of angry eyes, standing tall in solidarity.

Still catching his breath, half bent over, Luigi says in a friendly, somewhat threatening voice, "We don't want to hurt-a you. Just-a give us the money back-a. Then you go your-a way, and we go our-a way."

Leo, the smart-aleck, pats down his clothes and says arrogantly, "Aww, sorry. We lost it." He turns out an empty pocket. "See. Must've fallen out me jeans."

Federico holds up a marble-sized stone. "Now listen, me friend. We no like-a to pay for rocks-a. We want-a honey, or Luigi he break-a your rose-a."

Scrunching one eyebrow in confusion, Neville responds, "Honey? We got no honey."

"As I said," continues Leo, "we don't have ya honey or ya money. And anyway, Nev let you sample the nuts. You didn't have to buy them. A deal's a deal, mate."

"I not-a your mate, *mate*," says Luigi, clenching his fists. He lunges for Leo's shirt pocket to search for the money.

Just then, a police car cruises past.

"Help! Police! Help! Help!" shouts Leo, deliberately making a scene in the hope the Italians will back off.

"Very well-a," says Luigi, keen to avoid an escalation of the situation. "We let-a you go this-a time, but—"

"NO, NO, NO, NO, NO!" comes a wild, hoarse voice from inside the white Valiant.

"It's okay, Mama," says Luigi. "We let-a them go this-a time. They not-a worth-a the trouble."

"Ah, shut up-a ya face," barks the nonna, clambering out of the car with a rolled-up newspaper in one hand. "I'm-a no scared for little boys-a or polizia. What for-a you scared, eh? We done nothink wrong-a." She stands chest height to the bullies, pointing with angry jerks. "You make-a me sick-a with your rocks and rotten castagne. Give-a me the cash, you bad-a boys!"

Leo shakes his head. "No cash. You *comp-re-hen-day*, old lady? Money fall out down there. Probably gone by now, picked up by someone or blown away."

The nonna explodes, waving her arms about. "What-a you say? Hallo? Hallo? You hear me? Where-a you from, eh? Eh? I call-a your mama, tell her you crooks-a. Now give-a me the money!" She whacks them with the floppy rolled-up newspaper.

Whack, Whack, Slap.

"You bad-a boys!"

Whack, Slap, Slap.

"Bad-a, bad-a boys!"

Whack, Whack, Slap, Slap.

Leo's beanie falls off following a swipe to the head, and the thirty-five dollars flutters to the ground.

"Ah, see! Cash-a." says the nonna. "Now get out-a me face, you bad-a boys!"

"Whoooaarrrrrggghhhh," they scream, haring off into the forest, totally freaked out by the fierce nonna.

WHOOP, WHOOP, WOOO, comes three short siren blasts as the police car pulls up next to the rabble of Italians. A policewoman leans out the window in Pippa's direction. "Is everything okay?"

"Yes, everything's fine."

The policewoman speaks into a CB radio, then turns to the nonna. "Any problems, miss?"

A sunray illuminates the nonna's angelic face, creating a halo above her head. "Si, si, si." (*Yes, yes, yes.*) "Everythink is-a beautiful."

"Si, si, si," says Federico in a jovial voice. "I just dropp-ed me funny."

Satisfied that all is well, the police officers leave the scene.

Meanwhile, Federico and Luigi crawl on their hands and knees to gather up the thirty-five dollars. As they stumble to their feet, the nonna slaps them with the newspaper. "Scemi, scemi." (*You stupid fools.*) "Look, nothink! No castagne to roast on the fire! How I make-a Easter cake with no castagne, eh?" She holds up the sample nut. Her face softens. "Taste."

Federico takes a bite. Three chews later, he dances in a circle, hand on heart. "Mamma mia, mamma mia. Magnifico!"

Serious as usual, Luigi pops the last chestnut piece into his mouth and chews. Slowly, his blank face transforms into pure joy, and he turns to Federico. "Is-a beauty, mate!"

"Yes!" replies Federico, kissing Luigi on each cheek. "Is-a beauty, mate!"

The nonna's persuasive eyes point in the direction of Pippa, Archie and Ollie's pretty stall.

FORTY-FIVE

CHESTNUTS IN MY SOUP

"Get the money tin ready, you guys! We're about to make a killer sale," says Pippa, rushing back to the stall.

The Italian men swagger over as if enjoying a Sunday stroll in the forest.

Federico stops in front of the fold-up table, gazes up at the blue sky and draws a deep breath. "Haaaaaah. Is a beautiful day for a run in the forest-a." He points to the trees and back to his chest. "You see? I run like a goat-a. Chase-ed those bad-a boys for selling us rocks and old-a castagne. Nonna, she scared-a them away. Nonna, she scary lady. They run away—*peep peep peep peep*—scared like-a da rabbit." Eyes twinkling, he gazes at the children. "You look-a after me family, and I look-a after your-a family."

Luigi picks up a bag. "No rocks-a?"

"No rocks. And they're all super fresh," says Pippa.

A bright smile shines on Luigi's round face. "Okay. We take-a fifty bags. Is a good-a deal, *no?*"

Lost for words, the kids nod all at once and form a huddle to work out the price.

Archie whispers, "So, fifty bags times five dollars is . . ."

"Well," says Pippa. "Fifty times ten is five hundred, so if we halve that, we get—"

"Two hundred and fifty dollars," says Archie. "Yee-hee. I told you the Italians love high-quality chestnuts."

Ollie pats him on the back. "We ought to frame those golden rules of yours, Archie-boy. They truly *are* golden."

"Thanks, Ollie. Now let's close the deal." Archie exits the huddle and says to Luigi, "That will be two hundred and fifty dollars, please."

Luigi pulls out a rolled-up wad of cash from his pocket. Using a professional thumb-flicking action, he counts the money and hands it to Archie, who hands it to Pippa, who hands it to Ollie, who checks the total and puts it in the tin.

Quickly, the friends load fifty chestnut bags into two large cardboard boxes and pass them to the men.

Federico pokes his nose into the box and inhales the fresh aroma. "Ahhhhhhh. Very good nut-a. Just pick-ed tomorrow. Very fresh-a, very fresh-a. Good for me whole-a family." He removes the yellow rose from his pocket and hands it to Pippa. "I pick-ed the nose-a myself. Bella rosa per una bella bambina." (*A beautiful rose for a beautiful little girl.*) "Arrivederci, bambini." (*Goodbye until we meet again, kids.*)

A moment later, over at the regal white Valiant, the nonna inspects the chestnuts and pinches her sons' cheeks in appreciation of their good work.

Gloating with pride, Luigi and Federico place the boxes into the car boot, and one by one, the Valiants depart.

Pippa and Ollie cheer, "Hooray, we're rich!"

"Settle down, you lot. We've still got fifty bags to sell. This is just the beginning." Archie points to three shiny cars turning onto the gravel. "Battle stations, everyone. The tourists are coming!"

Now mid-morning, the tourists are flocking to the hills for Devonshire tea—scones, jam and cream, served with a hot drink, in a cosy cottage, beside a warm fire. But above all, they want to immerse themselves in the hills' culture, to experience some local colour and pizazz.

Soon a crowd of excited tourists gather around the kids' fancy, colourful stall. Bubbling with excitement, Pippa and Archie spring to action, serving the customers in a mad flurry.

When one bag sells, Ollie restocks the table with another. He feels important, successful, productive, and so overflowing with happiness, he bursts into an Italian-inspired song:

We picked the chestnuts from Old Crow,
We nearly lost them and the bag.
We couldn't find Kimba, and we were really sad,
We set up our stall, and we couldn't get a sale.
But then the winds they changed, and I'm here to tell the tale.
Bella, bella, bella, chestnuts in my soup,
Bella, bella, bella, mashed they make a sticky gloop.
Bella, bella, bella, we sell them by the road,
Bella, bella, bella, in the fire they explode!
Leo and Neville, they stole our selling spot,
But by lying and by cheating, they were finally made to stop.
Italians love chestnuts, but cheating they don't like,
And by chasing off the bullies, Archie's gonna get his bike!
Bella, bella, bella, chestnuts in my soup,
Bella, bella, bella, mashed they make a sticky gloop.
Bella, bella, bella, we sell them by the road,
Bella, bella, bella, in the fire they explode—*BANG!*

A few hours later, Ollie tips a cardboard box upside down and taps out a dry leaf. "Down tools, you fools. We've sold out!"

The friends gather around the stall, staring goggle-eyed at Hilda's biscuit tin, busting to see their profits.

As Archie opens the lid, a mound of cash overflows onto the table. They scoop their hands into the tin and scrabble through the money, sprinkling gold and silver coins through their fingers, delighting in the tinkling sounds.

Archie clasps a fistful of the cash, eyes sparkling at the thought of a shiny new BMX bike. "We did it!"

FORTY-SIX

MONEY MAKES ME FUNNY

The following day after school, Archie attacks his money tin with a can opener, struggling to rotate the handle but doing enough to get it half open. He bends up the jagged lid with a butter knife and pours his life savings onto the bed. Next, he empties a little wooden box containing the chestnut takings, creating an even bigger pile of money.

"Awesome," he whispers, proceeding to place the coins into one-dollar stacks and the notes into colour-coded piles, jotting down the running total as he goes.

Finally, after completing the riveting counting task, Archie jumps off the bed and skips around in celebration. "Yippee! Check out my savings, Kimba! Three hundred and twenty-six dollars and fifteen cents! I'm not sure if it's enough for a Supergoose, but I'll get a great BMX for sure!"

"Arrrchieeee! Where are you?" calls Florence.

"In my bedroom," he shouts back.

Florence bursts in, all flustered and excited. "Oh, there you are. I've got great news! The gasman's at the front door. They're digging a gas pipeline up the road. He says if we sign up for an account, we can get a brand-new heater installed for half price!"

"That's great, Mum."

"Yes, it's wonderful. But to get the deal, I have to pay a deposit of three hundred dollars—*today!*"

Archie's shoulders squeeze into rocks. *Oh no, she's gonna ask me for a loan.*

"I'd give him a cheque, but it'll bounce," says Florence. "My pay doesn't go into the bank until next month, and I just paid a fortune getting the leaky roof fixed."

Archie glances at the pile of money on the bed.

Florence glances at the pile of money on the bed.

Kimba *sits* on the pile of money on the bed.

"I promise I'll pay you back after my study trip to Europe, and once the car's fixed, and when I pay off the credit card. Imagine the difference a heater will make in winter. Don't you want a toasty gas heater?"

"Yes, but the money's for my new BMX. I need a decent bike to go riding with Ollie and Pippa. We're planning on racing Puffing Billy to Emerald Lake."

"Please, Archie, it's critical I give the gasman the money today or we'll miss out."

Archie peers at the floorboards, his eyes glazed over and distant. Memories flash through his mind: collecting damp logs from the woodpile on stormy winter nights, dodging huntsman spiders, shivering with Kimba beside a smoky fire, waking in the morning with ice crystals on his nose.

"Pleeeeease," begs Florence with puppy dog eyes, squeezing her palms together.

Archie's heart melts. "Well, all right then. As long as you pay me back." He pushes Kimba to the side and counts out three hundred dollars.

Florence beams. "Oh, Archie, you're such a good boy." She pinches his cheeks, whisks the cash from his hands and rushes back to the gasman.

Archie flops onto the bed, sinking his face into a pillow next to the remnants of his savings—a measly twenty-six dollars and fifteen cents. *How will I get my dream bike now? I'll have to save up all over again.*

FORTY-SEVEN

A PARTY IN THE HILLS

Three weeks later, the hills folk are partying under the stars in a paddock behind Fergus's art studio. They're gathering to farewell Banjo because he's heading home to the Kimberley. Archie and Ollie are sitting by a roaring fire, roasting chestnuts and cooking damper wrapped around long sticks.

"Hey, did you prick ya chestnuts?" says Archie, rotating his damper. "They'll explode if you didn't."

"Yeah, I'm sure I did," says Ollie. Flames whoosh through the air as he withdraws his stick from the hot coals. "Ooooh, looking good."

"Your damper's on fire, you maniac."

Ollie puffs out the flames and inspects the smoking charred surface. "Oh, don't worry about that. Perfectly cooked on the inside, I'd say."

"Mine's ready," says Archie. He slides the golden-brown damper off the stick, tosses it from hand to hand a few times and rips it open. Sweet-smelling steam bursts out in a billowing cloud that flushes his face. "Mmmm, reminds me of Mrs Marpin's scones."

"Mmm, reminds me of hot playdough," says Ollie, breaking his creation in half and poking his thumb into the gooey centre. "Just needs a little butter and honey." *Blob-blob, dribble-dribble.* "There we go." *Crunch-squish.* "Yummy, soooo good."

"Hey, how's your new computer going?" says Archie.

"Pretty good. I'm writing a program to learn the periodic table of the elements. Did you know *Au* is the symbol for gold and *Hg* is the symbol for mercury?"

"Nope."

"That's my point exactly. Nobody knows them. They're nearly impossible to learn. But with my computer program, I'll be able to memorise the symbol and atomic number of every element on the planet. How brilliant will that be? I'll be the talk of the school, maybe even make it into the local paper."

"Awesome," says Archie through a mouthful of damper.

"I've also started my very first computer composition—an opera," says Ollie. "I'm calling it *Il Corvo e la Castagna (The Crow and the Chestnut)*."

"*Hee-hehe,* I like it," chuckles Archie. "I wonder what gave you that idea?"

"Well, I owe it to you, my friend. Better than *The Crow and the Honey Joy,* don't you think?"

"You got that right."

Ollie pokes his roasting chestnuts with a stick and leans back on a hay bale. "Too bad about your new bike. Has your mum said when she'll pay you back?"

"Nah, I haven't heard a thing. She's heading to Europe next week for her study trip, so I expect it'll be a while."

"Never mind, Puffing Billy can wait. So where are you staying while she's away? With your dad?"

"Nah, he's too far away. I'm staying at Pippa's place."

"Speak of the rebel!"

Pippa jumps onto a hay bail. “Hey, guys. You have to come look through the telescope I bought with my chestnut money. Follow me. It’s amazing. The stars are so bright.” As she skips off into the darkness, spinning across the grass, the roasting chestnuts explode. *BANG! BANG! POPFF! POPFF! BANG! POP-POPFF! BANG!*

“Arrrrrgghh!” scream the boys as hot powdery-white pulp sprays all over their hair and clothes. And as more nutty bombs go off, they spring off the hay bales and chase Pippa across the paddock.

“I thought you pricked them?” shouts Archie.

“What? You’re supposed to prick them?” replies Ollie with a naughty giggle.

At the far edge of the field, the boys find Pippa peering through the telescope. “Behold, Earth’s sister, the brightest planet in the night sky, named after the Roman goddess of love and beauty—planet Venus! Take a look.”

“Where do you learn all this stuff from?” says Archie, pressing an eye to the rubber viewfinder.

“Mum’s an expert on astronomy,” says Pippa. “She’s been teaching me all about the stars since I was little.”

A ten-pointed starburst beams through the telescope into Archie’s eye. “Wow, I wonder what’s up there.”

“Aliens, of course,” blurts Ollie, taking a turn.

Pippa shakes her head. “I’m not so sure about that. Venus has a rocky surface like Earth, but the atmosphere is so thick with carbon dioxide, the sun’s heat gets trapped in like an oven. Aliens couldn’t possibly survive. They’d turn to charcoal faster than that damper of yours.”

"What? My damper's not charcoal," says Ollie, chomping into the crisp black crust. "See. Al dente as the Italians say."

"Yoo-de-hoo!" calls Hilda in the distance. "Da bush dansh ish about to shtart. Hurry, kidsh, or you'll mish out."

"Let's go. I love folk dancing," says Pippa, skipping across the field ahead of the boys.

As Archie races after her, he trips on a pot plant pyramid and face-plants in a clover patch.

Ollie darts back and clicks on his koala head torch. "Hope you had a nice trip? Didn't get a postcard though."

"Huh!" gasps Archie.

"What? What is it?"

In the centre of the pyramid, directly in front of Archie's nose, is something amazing. "It's a four-leaf clover. Wait till Pippa sees this. She's gonna go cabanas!"

"And you, my friend, now have the power to see forest fairies. Can you see any? Can you? Can you?"

"Not yet. It might take a few minutes for the power to kick in." Archie reaches for the four-leaf clover, and as he plucks it from the grass, magic zaps into his heart. He tucks the prize safely inside a folded tissue and pops it into his shirt pocket. "Quick, let's catch up to the others."

"Make way through the hay," says Ollie as he and Archie weave through the crowd and hay bales, jostling for a good position near the band.

Illuminated by the fire, Banjo begins the bush dance with a twangy guitar lick, *doo da-de do de do-de do daa*.

Broos toots on his harmonica, *wooo wa-wee wo wee woo wee wooo waaaaaaa*.

Old Bill, wearing a beret, replies on the fiddle, *diddly widdly diddly doddly doodly waa-waa-weeeeee.*

And after a nod from Banjo, the trio play up a storm.

While continuing to toot on his harmonica, Broos takes Hilda by the hand and spins her round and round. "Yo-dee-ho-hee-ho, around we go!" she sings.

Fergus hooks arms with Florence, whizzing her in circles. Then he jumps into the middle of the crowd, squatting in the style of a Cossack dancer, kicking his legs to the side and flicking out his arms as he chants, "Heh! Heh! Heh! Heh!"

Pippa, Archie and Ollie join the boisterous Cossack fun but end up tumbling onto their bottoms in fits of laughter.

Dion grabs Josephine's hand and yanks her off a hay bale. "Check out this move." Tongue waggling, he stomps his feet and galumphs about like a tribal warrior.

"No, no, no," says Josephine, flitting her eyes to the stars, "this is how it's done." And off she twirls, swishing her silk scarf through the air.

"Watch out!" shouts Russell, leaping down from a hay-bale stack. "The pro's in the dojo."

"Go, Russell. Go, Russell," chant Archie and Pippa.

Inspired by the spotlight, Russell dives into a one-handed handstand, rolls onto his belly, worms his way backwards, then windmills around and monkey-flips back to his feet.

"Woohoo," hoots Pippa.

"Cool moves, dojo boy," shouts Archie.

Next, Pippa launches into a front aerial, followed by a leg hold turn and a crazy triple chest roll that ends in the splits.

Everyone cheers.

"Ooh, ooh, check out my Michael Jackson dance," says Ollie, bounding to centre stage. He jolts his arms up and down robot-style and moonwalks backwards, gliding effortlessly across the dirt. Eager to dazzle the audience, he attempts Michael Jackson's signature move, springing onto pointed toes. Unfortunately, his moon boots have puffy tips that collapse under the pressure. Overwhelmed by gravity, the goofy goose careers into a hay bale stack, the collision launching six paper cups into the air and fruit punch all over his frazzled face.

"Hey, you've invented a new move—*the dingbat!*" jokes Pippa, laughing her head off.

The music and dancing continue long into the night until everyone is so exhausted they flop onto the hay bales for a much-needed rest.

"Oh yeah, I almost forgot. Check this out," says Archie, presenting the four-leaf clover.

Pippa gasps. "Oh my gosh! Where did you find it?"

"Yoo-de-hoo!" calls Hilda. She waddles through the crowd, carrying a scrumptious sweet potato chocolate cake covered in strawberries, mint leaves and fizzing sparklers. The flashing orange light illuminates Banjo's happy face as Hilda places the cake on a table next to an array of desserts, including Ollie's premiere apple, rosewater and chestnut strudel.

Broos taps a glass with a spoon to get everyone's attention, *tink-tink-tink-tink.*

The talking fades to a whisper, leaving only the sound of the fire crackling and crickets chirping in the background.

"Ahem," begins Broos. "I would like to acknowledge dat our wonderful gaddering here tonight ish being held on the traditional landsh of the Wurundjeri and Bunurong people. We pay our reshpect to Eldersh, pasht, preshent and future." He unfolds a note. "And now . . . to our dear friend Banjo. We are fery shad you are leaving ush here in da hillsh. You haff giffen ush your kind heart, beautiful mushic and wishdom. And we are all da better for dat. Tankyou, mate, for reminding us to lishen to the land, to the animalsh, and above all to our heartsh. We will mish you fery much, and we wish you a shafe journey back home. And I know I shpeak for efferyone when I shay dat you are alwaysh welcome here, my friend. Da hillsh ish your home too."

The hills folk clap and cheer.

Banjo tilts back his hat and smiles humbly. "Thank you, Broos. You know, I travelled across this big country all my life. I been here, been there, been everywhere. But there's no place like the hills. When I come here, I feel somethin' special. We one people, one mob. We all family here. And this place got strong spirit. This land is our mother. She love us, protect us, feed us. Even give us chestnuts, hey, kids! So, you all look after this place while I'm away. And, Archie . . . Where's that young fella gone to?"

Ollie leaps up, pointing, "Here he is!"

"Oh, there y'are. You come visit my country and I'll teach you about the bush." He glances at Florence. "Make good bushman, that one, *hee-hee*. And all you kids, you all welcome to my country, up in the Kimberley." He takes a deep breath, holding back a tear. "We all visitors here, just passin' through, learnin' what we can. Now it's time to go home. But my spirit will never leave this place. And remember to watch out for that crow. Coz when ya see a friendly one, you know it's me, come to help out!"

Amid a flurry of claps and cheers, Archie rushes up to Banjo. "I wanna give you this." He unfolds the tissue and presents the four-leaf clover. "It'll bring good luck and keep you safe on your travels."

Touched by the gift, Banjo leans closer, smiling with his heart. "Thanks, Archie." He places the leaf in his hatband. "It'll be safe up here. I never go without my hat. Hey, I feel luckier already!"

Pippa taps Archie's arm and whispers, "That's so nice. Did you know you get extra good luck if you give away a four-leaf clover?"

"No, I didn't know that."

Banjo waves his arms. "Gather round, kids. I got something for ya." He reaches into a dilly bag and hands Ollie a small hand-carved wombat. "Got tough head like you. Stay strong like a wombat, and don't let nothin' get in your way."

Ollie shakes his head as he eagerly inspects the treasure.

Eyes glinting, Banjo passes a carving to Pippa. "That's a ringtail possum. She's a loyal friend and a good tree climber. But ya gotta be on her good side, coz she can bite! You keep standin' up for what's right, Pippa."

"Thanks, Banjo. I sure will."

"Now, let's see what else we got in 'ere . . . Ah, yes, this one's for you, Archie—kangaroo. He's a wild one. Likes adventures, jumpin' fences and roaming all over the place. Don't let anybody box ya in, all right?"

"Nah, I won't. Thanks, Banjo. We're gonna miss you so much."

"Yoo-hoo! Yoo-de-hoo!" calls Hilda. "Dere'sh one more ting we have to do-dee-doo." She shines a torch beam on Fergus's art studio.

The door bursts open, revealing Florence and Russell wheeling a gleaming silver BMX bike with metallic red rims.

Archie's jaw drops and his eyes pop. "Huh! Is this for real?"

"Sure is, babe," says Florence, handing over the bike. "We're square now, okay?"

"Yeah. Thanks, Mum, it's incredible! Just what I've always dreamed of. But where'd you get the money?"

"Well, you know the painting you dragged out from under the house? I shoved it under there years ago, after your father and I split up. We got it for a wedding present from an artist friend. I thought it was worthless, but it turns out he's become quite famous. We agreed to sell it for your new bike."

Russell interjects, slapping Archie's shoulder. "It's a Supergoose, like you. And it's the one you wanted, the Mark 2. I helped your mum choose it. Check out the snakebelly tyres for extra grip. And the unbreakable aircraft-quality chrome-moly frame. She's got stainless steel handlebars, so no rust. And what about the seven-inch Takagi cranks, hey? Totally dialled. She's a killer on the track. Built for flyin', tree jumpin' and powerslides."

"Thanks, Russ. I love it. It's amazing. First thing in the morning, I'm gonna—"

BOOM-Shhhhhhhhhhhhh.

"Fireworks!" squeal the kids, gazing to the sky, faces lit up by shimmering green sparkles.

In the middle of the open paddock, Fergus flips down his protective visor, straightens his cricket pads, lights a fuse and runs for his life, shouting, "All clear!"

Whooosshhh-BOOM-crackle-shhhhhh. A giant red rose sparkles in the sky.

Archie points up. "Look, floating down from the fireworks! Little boxes with parachutes!"

"Whoaaa, they're like flying angels," says Pippa, gazing skyward.

"Woohoo, parachutes! I wonder what's in the boxes," shouts Ollie, galloping across the field to catch some. "This is the best night of my life!"

BOOM-crackle-BOOM-shhhhhh.

Purple and green sparkles light up the paddock, followed by more parachutes, each one carrying a silver or gold box.

"I see two!" shouts Pippa. "They're heading for the fire!" She leaps onto a hay bale, jumps into the air and catches a purple parachute in her fingertips. The other one drifts into the bonfire and melts in a fiery flash.

"I see an orange one!" calls Archie, making chase. Gazing skyward, he weaves around a row of pot plant pyramids and leaps across a garden bed, snatching the parachute mid-air before it lands in a prickly blackberry bush. "Yippee!"

Ollie dashes back with slumped shoulders and droopy sad eyes. "I was following a whole bunch, but I lost them in the pine trees."

Another firework booms overhead. Golden balls of light cascade in the sky, and more parachutes float down.

Ollie stands tall and puffs out his chest. "Incoming! There's one heading for the pond. Don't worry, I've got it covered!" With eyes fixed on the grand prize, he streaks across the paddock, past the bonfire and over the wooden bridge. As the yellow parachute and silver box descend to the pond, he belly-flops into the water. *Ka-SPLASH!*

Pippa and Archie race over to find their friend sitting among the lily pads with a parachute flopped over his head.

A long stream of pond water spurts from Ollie's mouth as he clutches the prize. "Got one!"

"Great," says Archie. "Let's see what's in the boxes."

A gas bubble brews in Ollie's tummy, and he releases a lengthy pond-flavoured burp, *buurrrooowwwurrrp!* "Yes, but first we better get dessert before it runs out. I can't wait to taste my chestnut and rosewater strudel. Come on, you pongo-bongos. Last one there's a soggy frog!"

Pippa bolts after him, shouting, "And sweet potato chocolate cake with strawberries!"

Archie slips over on the wet bridge and glances at his golden parachute box. *I wonder what's inside.* A dinosaur groan burbles from his tummy, and he springs to his feet, screaming, "Save some for me, you dongo-zongoes!"

I hope you enjoyed reading The Hills Kids! Please leave an honest review where the book was purchased. Thanks!

Stay tuned for The Hills Kids Book Two . . .

www.garethvanderhope.com

ACKNOWLEDGMENTS

The Hills Kids could not have been written without the love and support of my wife, Kim, and our daughters, Lily and Mia.

Lily's feedback was insightful, precise and always right! A superstar reader and continuity queen, Lily picked up on the smallest of inconsistencies and identified any writing pitfalls. As she said, "Kids don't like puns, Dad." After reviewing the meaning of pun, I agreed—no puns! Lily's empathy for the characters helped shape the book in many positive ways. As an avid reader, she provided valuable insights into details that older kids appreciate. From start to finish, Lily was enthusiastic and confident that *The Hills Kids* was a book worth writing. Thanks, Lily!

Mia's feedback was equally insightful. As the defender of darlings (those story gems that editors seek to kill), Mia's thoughts were unencumbered by writing rules or social conventions. Her views were instinctive and perceptive, targeting details valued by younger readers.

Being a superstar acro dancer, Mia was my key advisor about all things dance. Her thirst for a good story also buoyed my confidence. One night, after reading a bunch of chapters, she said, “Please, Daddy, keep going.” I replied, “But I haven’t written the next chapter.” She said, “Quickly write more so you can read them tomorrow night.” Thanks, Mia!

From day one, Kim was behind *The Hills Kids*. I am grateful for her respect and enthusiasm for the project. Kim was my sounding board, providing feedback anywhere and anytime. Sometimes her gift was to enjoy the story, giving encouragement along the way. At other times, she was the master untangler, helping to straighten out an awkward sentence in seconds. On her many readings of the book, Kim’s feedback was sharp and sensitive. Thanks, Kim, for your support, your talents and believing in me.

Thanks also to John McAndrew for your editing notes, Simon Ashford for being a mentor and giving me the confidence to illustrate the cover, Sascha Frydman for proofreading and feedback, Antonella Mangraviti for advising about the Italian dialogue, and Lotje Boer and Dassi de Wit for advising about the Dutch dialogue.

Thanks to Mum, Dad and Gwendolen De Lacy for your blessings and feedback. Thanks to Marianne for your encour-agement. Thanks to Kym Postma for your support and our unforgettable chestnutting adventure. Thanks to Dean Martin for our chestnutting adventures and Brett Hutson for your blessings. Thanks to Jade Trapp, Aris Prabawa and Naomi Parer for your inspiration and nudging me to illustrate by hand, Django and Loretta Bening for enjoying the story around a campfire, Frank Amato for cultural insights about cars, and Sean Tonnet, Kylie Mowbray-Allen, Mark Seiffert, Glenn Cardwell, Michael Speechley, Colin Dyte, and Bev McAlister OAM for your support. Finally, thanks to all my friends and family for asking, "How's your book going?"

The Hills Kids is inspired by experiences shared with family, friends and the zany community that made the Hills an exciting place to grow up. Thanks for the memories. I hope my story captures some of your story.

ABOUT THE AUTHOR

Gareth Vanderhope is an internationally acclaimed storyteller through sound. A two-time BAFTA winner, his sonic wizardry has reached millions of people worldwide via films including Lorenzo's Oil, Babe 1 & 2, Shine, Baz Luhrmann's Romeo and Juliet, Moulin Rouge and the Quiet American. As a writer, Gareth uses his sound design experience to harness the sonic qualities of words and letters as storytelling devices and to create atmospheric worlds within the imagination.

Also an award-winning health educator, Gareth's writing explores the environmental and cultural influences of kids' food choices, behaviour and development.

Born in Melbourne, Australia, Gareth grew up in the Dandenong Ranges during the 1970s. His free-spirited childhood, coupled with an eclectic, creative community and wild environment, inspire the wacky, fun and exciting themes in *The Hills Kids* book series.

Now living in the Northern Rivers of New South Wales with his wife and two daughters, Gareth writes and illustrates in between teaching, cooking and adventuring with his family.

www.garethvanderhope.com

Lightning Source UK Ltd.
Milton Keynes UK
UKHW011830030122
396573UK00002B/39